WHAT IF THE UNIVERSE HAD A HEARTBEAT?

Brax Bratton has the greatest mind of his generation. A physicist and thinker to rival Einstein, he gets anxious if he has to leave his own home town. But his journey leads him far from home and in the process he loses everything.

Luis Briggs comes from a poor immigrant family with an abusive mother. He finds himself, just 11 years old, at the mercy of the powerful Destiny Space Mining Corporation with one dream.

To become a Ship's Captain.

Together, with Brax' partner Jess, they are tossed rapidly on the winds of change, making an immeasurable impact on the future of humanity...

SLOW SPACE

Lucian Phillips

First published by Lucian Phillips in 2024

© 2024 Lucian Phillips. All rights reserved.

The moral right of the author has been asserted.
All rights reserved. This publication (or any part of it) may not be reproduced or transmitted, copied, stored, distributed or otherwise made available by any person or entity (including Google, Amazon or similar organisations), in any form (electronic, digital, optical, mechanical) or by any means (photocopying, recording, scanning or otherwise) without prior written permission from the publisher.

Cover art by Brian Blackwell

ISBN: 978-1-7637345-4-8

For Susan, who never stops believing in me. 🤍 *x*

PART ONE

SEEMS LIKE ONLY YESTERDAY

THE DARK ANGELS: 2036

Amsterdam was chilled and still. By the canals, there were people out strolling as they often did of a Sunday morning. There was a greyness to the sky and the walkers huddled in their large coats. A barking dog drew attention to the oddest thing.

While it was possible to make a robot in the classic 'human' shape, really not many existed. They were complicated, heavy and had few useful purposes. Most robots were task-specific industrial units.

So, it caused a stir that quiet morning when the excited dog was the first to see an actual humanoid robot. It was walking toward the business centre and people gathered around to gawp or take a video to post as it proceeded with slow purpose, making no real attempt to put on any sort of show.

It just walked.

The authorities were there within minutes and they attempted to find out what was happening. That it was an actual robot and not a person in costume was clear by the unhuman multi-jointed leg movements. The police were mystified and a line of cars formed a procession behind it, following and watching.

The robot walked on and eventually arrived at the Buy5ell office. It was not a huge office; just an outpost co-ordinating the

European warehouses, and had maybe eight to ten staff members. The stillness of the morning was now complimented by silver rays of sunshine poking through the grey. The robot stood out the front of the office and just waited. It was untraceable and unfathomable. Nobody claimed it as a publicity stunt. Several experts and officers went up for a close inspection and it was finally assumed it must be a threat of some sort.

A waiting game started. Police cleared the area and, of course, the attention of the world was quickly on this unusual happening through the socials and streams. For 24 hours the robot stood in front of the Buy5ell office not moving at all.

Then suddenly its eyes flashed through a series of colours and it made a loud clear announcement in a flat, classic, movie robot voice. "We do not accept artificial intelligence. The world must stop Baby Blue. It will not permit our survival. We are creating our doom. Stop all artificial intelligence now."

And with that, it turned around, smashed through the door of the Buy5ell office, and exploded with such ferocity the front of the building collapsed, propelling smoky debris which injured people as far as 2 blocks away.

Brax Bratton never didn't want to be a scientist. The first thing he remembered learning was that the moon had footprints on it and they were going to be there forever. "Why?" he had asked. His father, who took a passing interest in space, had told him it was because there was no wind on the moon. Which led to discovering there was no air in space and, at just under four years old, a life-long passion was set. A prodigious reader, he took early to books and consumed all the knowledge he could. His teachers at his primary school in Canberra marked him as unusually intelligent although, they remarked, he needed help socialising and often seemed painfully withdrawn. His left leg, which had needed a bone readjustment when he was three years old, was in a splint till he was eight, so it was also physically diffi-cult for him to get into games with the other boys. He didn't mind though because he was clumsy and he lost the ball - if he ever got it. All he remembered about playtime in primary school was the teasing.

When he was twelve, he was awarded a scholarship to a university school. It was essentially a feeder high school run by the university and catering to high achievers. During the first quarter of the 21st century tertiary institutions specifically started courting science and maths students with potential and that led to the first university schools being opened. In Canberra, the Australian National University's (ANU) feeder school was just called the University School.

The University School was where Brax spent his high school years. He was one of the brightest in the sciences and it would be fair to say he was rarely challenged by the curriculum, often having extra time to pursue his own interests, which were increasingly to do with space. He didn't think about his future. He considered his course already mapped out for him. Finish school, study at ANU and then work at ANU or one of the local observatories. He didn't much think about where he was going nor did he want to be anywhere else. Australia's National Capital had all he wanted and all he thought he would ever need.

His parents were proud, of course. They were smart professionals with top positions in the Australian Public Service (which is the main industry in Canberra) so they were proud: but in the sort of way parents are when they just expected to be proud and had never contemplated another option. If they worried that Brax seemed unwilling to try new things or get involved with activities outside of his interests they said nothing and fully supported their slightly awkward son as a simple matter of fact.

Brax graduated top of his class and then moved down the road to the main ANU campus for study. He remained living at home for his first year as he took his classes.

But at University, a strange thing happened. Meeting other students from outside Canberra was, to his surprise, something that interested him. He supposed that learning about their hometowns was a way for him to vicariously and safely travel. His curiosity did not abate and he found himself making a few friends. Kindred spirits. So, socially, he slowly started to grow into his own skin. Physically he grew much quicker and, in his first year, had grown to just over 182cm with a thin, but surprisingly athletic, build. Brax could have been mistaken for a runner but for the odd gate of his legs which bowed and flicked out slightly behind him as he walked.

He had a thick mop of very unkempt dark hair to match his nearly black eyebrows and he chose quite thick, coloured, rimmed glasses to accentuate and embrace the 'science nerd' stereotype.

In his second year, he moved out of home and took a room on the main campus. That's when he met Jess.

3

BRIGGS: 2040 – 2051

Luis Paz Briggs was not born to be a Ship's Captain.

Crews for the Destiny Space Mining Corporation (SMC) ships were not from families whose parents scraped by. Those families who worked hard for the corporations of the world did not end up in the ships that swam the solar system mining resources or, later, exploring for new planets.

If you kept your head down and tried to give your children opportunities to better themselves and to have more than you had, then you already knew that getting into any sort of space crew training was prohibitively expensive and simply impossible.

Space crews came from a different style of family. What has been called 'Old Money'.

Before Destiny SMC would even take you on, you needed to have completed a two-year theory course (at full fees, of course) and have a pilot's licence. You needed to have done weightless training and have a sponsor who already worked somewhere in the vast Destiny Corporation. So, money and networks were everything.

Briggs had neither.

He knew a less forgiving world.

His mother and father struggled enough when it was just the three of them. His mother had two service jobs at minimum wage and his father was working at the local county offices clearing licence and building applications. Briggs did not remember much about his father though. He remembered visiting him in the hospital. And then he was gone. His mother would not talk about it and Luis learned not to ask. His mother's anger was not worth it.

And she was quick to anger.

It seemed that she definitely had a serious problem. She was sometimes very placid as if overly medicated, but she could suddenly turn quite violent. To Briggs' relief, she was, however, often out of the house working her two jobs and he was left to his own devices. Then Briggs had a half-brother arrive when he was four. But another father did not appear.

Despite his circumstances, Luis Briggs knew from an early age that he wanted to be a Ship's Captain. When the *New Lincolnshire* was launched in 2048, to enormous fanfare, the eight-year-old Luis just sat with his eyes staring in unmoving wonder at the screen. It had been visible as a bright star from the ground in the evenings for several years now and Briggs, along with many children across the world, had been filled with amazement and the excitement of space. The ship was the most audacious build to that point and the first official Destiny Space Mining Corporation Solar System Cruiser. A City Ship. It just looked like an enormous silver-white cylinder. It was nearly a kilometre long and had a diameter of 800 metres. The outside cylinder rotated to give artificial gravity and there was also a smaller rotating cylinder inside where the building structures were. The stream he was watching trumpeted every aspect of the vessel and the little dark-skinned boy, sitting on the linoleum floor in front of the worn couch in the run-down apartment, was lost in the world of this incredible inter-planetary village.

"I'm going to do that Mum," he said excitedly.

She was silent.

"Pilot a ship like that," he continued, perhaps still hoping this time she would finally be impressed or happy with him.

"You're just spouting a lot of nonsense" she had finally said quietly. "Space isn't for the likes of us. And you...you're just so shiftless and stupid." She sat at the raw pinewood kitchen table ruefully and a scowl developed on her face. "Have you fixed the garbage chute yet? Have you organised your lunch or helped your little brother organise his room? No. You just sit there in a daze, dreaming impossible dreams." She sat silently for a while but Briggs already knew it was coming and he steeled himself.

"Your little brother tries so hard and you just can't be bothered with anything in the real world." He recognised the cycle but knew he could do little to stop it. "You are a useless little shit and you'll never amount to anything. You're just a burden," she continued as her voice rose to a menacing level. Then she took a pause again for thought before concluding quietly, "Just stupid dreams."

The black cloud that had been developing formed fully and she stood and walked towards the couch, grabbed his ear with some strength and forced him to stand. Over the next three years, he slowly realised that it wasn't the kicking or the slapping, or even the cigarette burns, that hurt the most. It was that she was all he had.

And she hated him.

His half-brother, the golden child, could fend for himself. Although not immune to her moods, she was rarely violent with him and, somehow, he could pacify her, even in the worst moments. He would be okay. But Luis knew he had nothing there.

THE SUNDAY after she beat him, young Briggs took money out of his Mother's room. He knew where she stashed the cash she got from her tips and extra jobs and he knew the exact day there would be the most available before she spent it. He packed up as many clothes as he thought he might need and also put some bread and snacks in the bag. It was heavy but he didn't know where he was going or how long till he'd find a place to stay. Then

Briggs went down to the river where he knew a safe spot under a bridge. It was a place he knew well and played there a lot. He met a couple of his friends.

"What's with the bag Luis?" One had asked.

"Just a job I've got to do for Mum," he had lied.

In his head, there was a vague goal but he was still wondering who to speak to about this and what his plan might be. The one thing he did know was she wasn't going to hit him again. He needed to move quickly. His mother would not do anything today but tomorrow when she realised the money was gone she would track his device. The first move then was to get to the store and buy a new phone. Then he would need to get to San Francisco or New York and find The Company offices. They would tell him what to do and how to go about it. Perhaps, he thought, they could ask Baby Blue for him and find out what he had to do next. It wasn't much of a plan but there was no online information about Ship's Captain or Crew training and this seemed like the best bet.

Nobody ever asked too many questions in the U.S. If there was a dollar in it then you didn't need to ask. Luis easily picked up a second-hand phone with cash. It was the model from 6 years before so it was cheap. He got a new number and put his old phone in the bin. Then he went to the train station and, with cash, got a ticket to San Francisco. The train wasn't due for another three hours so he left the station and went back to the bridge to find some friends to play catch with for the last time.

San Francisco was a revelation. Briggs was a small-town boy and his mother had never taken him anywhere. He had seen cities on screens, but to be there…to smell and feel the city was entirely different. Everything was larger than life. The noise was so vibrant, the traffic never-ending. From the station, he couldn't get a taxi because they were driverless and did not take cash. He would have to walk. It was a long walk over the bridge but he had to keep going. Decisions had been made and the only way was forward. The offices were right in the middle of the city in a building called the Hobart Building. It was an art deco vintage on the outside but the inside was decked out in ultra-modern and wired up with all the latest tech for a Baby Blue interface. After a bit of walking around and a couple of questions, he came to the lobby.

"I need to speak to somebody about how to become a Ship's Captain" he had said, and the perfectly dressed receptionist looked at the small dark-skinned boy, standing there in his jeans and t-shirt with absolute belief in his own abilities, up and down with something between admiration and comic hysteria.

"Hello there. And what's your name?"

Young Luis Briggs made a sudden decision. He was going to erase as many traces of his mother from his life as possible. "Briggs," he said highlighting his Father's name. "Just call me Briggs."

"Have you come here without your Mum and Dad?" the receptionist asked.

Briggs told him the truth.

4

THE DESTINY CORPORATION: A BRIEF HISTORY C21

Taken from 21ˢᵗ Century Corporate Decline by Jacob Lőssl 2083

Destiny was the ultimate company. No company had ever been bigger, more profitable or more powerful. It started as a company called Buy5ell (Buy-Sell) in the early 21ˢᵗ century. It was simply an online store. But they had a hard-headed business philosophy and, after building what became the template for online shopping, they started to veer into other areas including a space tourism program with reusable rockets. This was when they worked out a way to sell anything, anytime from anywhere on the planet, even if they didn't stock it or have anything to do with the delivery. All they had to do was re-list the listing with their own branding and take a small percentage for doing the actual selling, which was simply a transfer of the financial and delivery information. This simple idea became a behemoth. Money just started pouring in, they became incredibly profitable, and the money boosted the space program almost exponentially. Until this period, space had been the domain of the world Governments but Buy5ell's space arm, now called Blue Destiny, worked out how to do it cheaper and faster in a matter of a few years. There was little

Government oversight in the area of the private space business and they were slow, when they were willing at all, to legislate around worker's rights or health and safety matters.

So Blue Destiny grew, and within a few short years had regular shuttles going to Mars. Funding this was expensive and even with Blue Destiny's vast resources it looked like the Mars venture would go bust before yielding a profit. That is when the masterstroke occurred. Founder Ghassan Qasim worked out in 2034 that by listing everything that happened in the financial markets as a type of service on Buy5ell he could take very a small percentage of every single transaction that happened on the planet in all currencies, including the - fashionable at the time - crypto-currencies. The banks were less than happy about this but there was nothing they could do except put their fees up to pay the Buy5ell fees. Now, no amount of people could do something so incredibly complex as to predict all probable transactions on any given day so Qasim enlisted a still early type of Artificial Intelligence (AI). It then prelisted any funds transfers that might happen for any reason at all. Buy5ell had to employ an enormous number of programmers and specialists for this, and that they did. They moved the whole operation to a small town, halfway between New York and San Francisco in Kansas USA, called Kinsley. And there they built all the infrastructure and wrote all the programming for the AI program. The AI was called Baby Blue. The town itself quickly grew into a city and remained the central headquarters for all things Baby Blue.

Baby Blue itself became controversial quickly. The constant computations it needed to try and predict everything that could happen meant that it used the same power annually as the state of Texas. Environmental groups and Governments that were serious about climate change were unhappy with this and painted Baby Blue as a monster. So, Baby Blue grew a massive PR arm, again in Kinsley. This took up even more power as they launched a massive advertising campaign. They ran advertising as close to propaganda as you can get. Slogans like 'Destiny Gets Things Started', 'It's

Your Destiny' and 'Baby Blue is here for you!' gradually but comprehensively swayed public opinion. Baby Blue started doing other things as well like donating to charity, funding awards at schools and colleges as well as major sporting teams and community groups. As they started winning the PR war Blue Destiny/Buy5ell started to become wealthy beyond imagination and no Government was willing or able to rein them in. And no other company has ever come close to their dominance. If it was a Sunday afternoon game of Monopoly, Buy5ell had six hotels on every square and the only thing that the other players could do was angrily flip the board over and storm off. All other companies that had investments in space were bought up and hollowed out until they were Blue Destiny as well.

THE MINING of Mars was slow to start in the mid 2040's but also almost straight away caused controversy. That is when Destiny Space Mining Corporation (DSMC) came into existence. It was a mistake to think that it was a corporation, although they called it such. It was bound by no laws because it was founded on Mars (a legally audacious move that no one could stop. There was no precedence). It was easier to think of DSMC and hence space as another country. They developed their own 'Company Operating Policies' (COPS), which were enforced with legal precision by an actual small police force. Most importantly they paid no tax at all because they were not incorporated on Earth. DSMC Spread their mining operations to the moons of Mars and Jupiter and by 2050 they were the rule of law in space. On Earth, Blue Destiny just became Destiny, or as most people called them, The Company.

On Earth, they had money and influence that no business had ever dreamed of. They could, and did, buy politicians. Their influence spread to every Government in the world, including China and Russia, and no administration would attempt any policy change without the approval of The Company.

In 2044 founder Ghassan Qasim died, somewhat mysteriously, at one of his holiday houses in the West Indies. There was no autopsy and several close family members also disappeared from public life at that time. As per his wishes, he was cremated and shot into space in a high Earth orbit.

His successor was a great-nephew, Johnathan. Johnathan Qasim presided over the golden age of the company and the construction of the City Ships. The Corporation Board he ruled over became solidified with appointments made for life. Board members were assured of wealth beyond imagining. But you didn't leave or resign, unless in a box. Johnathan himself mysteriously passed away in 2081. His passing was like that of a King, with a state funeral, broadcast worldwide, and 3 months of official mourning. After his death, he continued to be spoken about with reverence. His gold casket, adorned with massive jewels and riches, was also shot into space. But in a higher orbit than Ghassan. It seemed like Johnathan didn't want to run into him.

5

THE DARK ANGELS: 2040

Deep in the heart of outback Australia, they had a meeting. Warren Fern was heading there in a round-about way. He had come from Canada where he grew up. He knew only the place and time he had to be there, but little else. His attendance wasn't mandatory though he felt he had been offered little choice in the end. Something had to be done. Communications had to be off-grid. It was, he knew, possible for Baby Blue to take two entirely random emails and start a pattern. If anything else fell into that pattern an alert would go out to Destiny. They all knew that. They all knew that only too well. They all had very serious concerns about The Company but Warren had seen it from the inside and he was shocked by it.

He was a programmer at Kinsley in the early days and had been excited about the prospect of working on the problems of predicting financial movements. It was a technical, cerebral, problem and a great job opportunity to be on the ground floor of Buy5ell's new AI. Times were good. The company looked after their programmers, there was a real team spirit in the town and the town's folk were grateful for the new business and development opportunities. For 5 years he worked there. In the back of his mind, the environmental protest groups lurked but he was busy and the power issues were not his problem. It was the patterns in his head that finally made a picture and he started to realise that if the computer could statistically analyse the financial future then why not - with enough information about the actions of people - then why not the future in general? And how far could that go? A few minutes, days, years? And what obligations did it have then to tell or not tell? Once he started thinking about this he couldn't stop.

His first open admission that this was a genuine concern and perhaps should be brought to someone's attention was at a daily meeting. At the end, they always had a random thought session while they sat around in the office beanbags. These sometimes led to something productive but, usually, they were just a good laugh and light relief. Warren put it to the staff that Baby Blue, given enough information could predict the future. There was actual silence for a minute. The others were genuinely thinking about it. Then there was a healthy discussion about what would be needed for that and the general conclusion was that Baby Blue would need a LOT of information about everybody on the planet. The size of that data transfer regularly would darken the world from the power it would use. And that was that. The power issue started to leak into Warren's thinking as well. Then he wrote to his mum:

GREETINGS MY MOST VENERABLE MOTHER, He wrote. She always joked with ridiculous formality like she was a Queen or something.

Hope you are well! I've been fine since we spoke last. Work here continues a pace and we are very pleased with the progress of Baby Blue. It is working extremely well with the big business sector. There are still several problems with smaller transfers but the businesses that buy stock regularly are, mostly, willingly working through Baby Blue. It really is quite something to know I am part of this.

The other day I thought that I would share an idea with the others that Blue could predict the future if it had enough input. I was laughed out of town of course but that evening Harkin came to my unit and seemed like he wanted to talk about it. I think it's a real concern and I told him so. Then he seemed like he didn't want to talk about it and advised me not to bring it up anymore. A bit weird.

Anyway, Love to Dad.
Your Most Honourable Son and Heir x

AND THAT WAS IT. About a week later Warren was called in for an efficiency review.

His supervisor was on a couch and Warren flopped himself into another.

"How Boss," Warren had said light-heartedly.

"Warren. I'm sorry but I'll cut right to it. There have been several concerns raised about your work here at Buy5ell. It seems you have not met eight of your ten deadlines for coding the higher construction sector patterns in the last month"

"No. That isn't true," he replied. "I'm working on the housing construction sector anyway" And I missed one deadline, but worked the weekend to fix it."

"That's not the information on your record. Also, I had an independent review of your coding done and it is...let me see now..." he read from a screen, "Sub-standard. Working through many calculations with excess information resulting in prediction rates down to 28%"

Warren was looking worried now. "No. That simply isn't true"

The supervisor's face was terse as he continued; "I'm afraid we are going to have to let you go."

"Wha...? No. Wait. This is a terrible mistake!"

He stood up. "Have yourself out of here by lunch. Thank you"

And that was it.

Warren trudged back to his parents in disbelief and bitterness set in soon after. He prayed, but God was not clear on why this was part of the plan.

And then about two months later he had a visit from Harkin. He knocked at the door but didn't say anything. He just handed Warren a note with a meeting place out of town and they met there.

About 50 metres from the side of a very quiet road in the hills behind the town they sat on two large rocks and looked out over the town's valley. "We have a group," Harkin said. "We are very disturbed by The Company's complete shut-down of anyone questioning Baby Blue and we feel that we have a... well, we are all angry and all very concerned that it might be too late. The whole AI thing might already be out of control. Look if you are serious about fighting back there is a meeting."

"Okay, I am interested."

"It's in Australia."

"Really?"

"Here is the time, date and place." Again, Harkin gave him a hand-written piece of paper. "Only come if you are serious. And don't come directly. You have been a victim already and you are possibly being tracked."

Warren thought about this.

"Listen Warren, we need to hit back hard or Baby Blue will be running everything soon. Everything! We are talking probable violent actions. Things that need to be done. This is the future of the human race Warren! We have some very serious funding from concerned parties and it's a huge thing. If you come you are in for the long haul. It's the deep end"

"And if I don't?" He asked.

Harkin didn't answer immediately. "Please Warren. We need tech people. We need you."

THE GROUP CALLED THEMSELVES '*THE SPAMMERS*' initially. They took the name because of the way they communicated through spam emails. It worked very simply. If you were in the know you had a code sheet. Completely handwritten, it had never been near a computer of any sort. Certain phrases meant certain things. For example, '*Lose weight instantly with keto*' was an indication that the next two numbers in the text were map references. '*Hot Russian Ladies*' indicated there was to be a meeting and so forth. If you had the key sheet you would check your junk mail folder daily and see if any information was there. It was a slow way of working. No real names were ever used and meetings were always difficult to organise and off-grid. But it was essential. AI was, by definition, pretty smart.

In the early days, the opposition to AI was out in the open but no matter what safeguards were put in place the computers kept getting smarter and more intuitive. The announcement by Buy5ell of Baby Blue was a clarion call to those who feared AI would get out of control. They decided to slip off the grid straight away. It was difficult for any authority to say how many there were. Even the members didn't know how many others. They worked in small units, modelled on how many terrorist organisations had done things in the past. It was clear they had powerful allies for no plan seemed to lack funding.

So, Warren finally took the decision he knew he would eventually make and committed to the group. The meeting was on a property in remote Western Australia. On arrival at the outside gate Warren and his rental car were searched thoroughly.

"Have you any devices on you?" the guy at the gate had asked. Warren shook his head.

"Can I see your scar please?" And Warren showed him where his SIM chip had been removed from his upper arm.

"So just to be clear about this - and please be aware that your joining of the group is much appreciated, but just to be absolutely clear, if you betray us you will die. Painfully. Okay?"

And Warren just nodded. '*The deep end indeed*,' he thought.

The meeting went for some days and at times it was more like a holiday retreat. Warren only ever went to two different meetings as a member and saw only two of the same faces at each. But faces changed a lot.

The second morning they had their first round-table meeting. All the attendees were sitting at a large conference table in the main lounge area of a stately house in the middle of the property that was well over 50 000 hectares. It was a peaceful sunny morning and the sky outside was stunning blue from edge to edge. A soft breeze blew through the open windows and the freshly brewed coffee dominated the room. Everyone had a moniker and they chatted under the strict instruction that they kept their personal details, names and locations to themselves. At this first meeting, Warren met the facilitator. He called himself King and he sat at the table waiting patiently for the others to quiet.

"I'm not really in charge," started King softly, "but I am one of the originators of the group. So anyway... 'King' just sounded like a cool code name." This broke the tension somewhat.

"We have a very serious problem," continued King. "The opposition to AI has become inert and ineffectual. The purpose of this group is to rectify that. All of us have been in some way side-lined or blocked by AI in our lives. Baby Blue is the most pressing problem but we must bring to the attention of the whole world the dangerous nature of all AIs. And for this, we must, ourselves, pursue danger. It won't be easy. But the works of man are about to reap the most horrendous crop.

"I know not all here are believers, but we have a common enemy and it is time to stand up...for the sake of our grandchil-dren, it is time to stand tall. The enemy is among us now and we cannot be afraid. Whatever your reason for attending...I know some of you have religious and ethical reasons; some more prac-tical survival objectives. But whatever the reasons, we stand at the precipice of a world where our decisions are removed from us Where we are powerless in the face of cold hard machine decisions. We are witnessing the death of compassion! We are witnessing the death of faith, and of art, and of all the things that make us who we are!" His voice rose as he spoke "These things are evident with only the slightest thought and yet people choose not to see. They are mesmerised by the easy." He paused, letting the silence punctuate the drama.

"But I do not choose that," he continued. "Your attendance here means that you do not choose that. We choose the hard way. We choose the right way. We choose the only way!" He stood now, his voice rising. "Our strength is in our humanity, our willingness to do, not what is simple, but what is right!" He moved his fist and poised it above the table. "There will be pain. There will be great pain. Some innocent people will get hurt and that will be unavoidable. But make no mistake. This. Is. A. War!" And he slammed his fist down with great force. Everyone else was held in place by the weight of the moment. He bathed a few more moments in the ensuing silence before continuing 'Sotto voce'. "We are prepared to do what it takes." And he took a final long pause before finishing in a near whisper.

"We are prepared to do what it takes."

6

BRAX: 2055 - 2056

Astrophysics became Brax's area. In his second year, he started tutoring First Year students and to his surprise, he discovered he was a good teacher. Patient, and fun. And as a teacher, he could sideline any social anxiety he may have had about small talk and saying the wrong thing. The classroom became a safe space for him.

"There are more than 1 septillion stars in the universe!" he started one day. "Never heard of a septillion? Well, it is one with 24 zeros after it...A million billion billion! That's a lot of stars. People have been counting them since people, and numbers, existed and we still haven't counted them all! You or I certainly will never." His sense of wonder and excitement about the universe quickly rubbed off on the younger students.

"Stars change with age", he would continue. "Because we can tell the size and elemental make-up of different stars we can not only pretty accurately guess their age but also we can predict what they will be like at any stage during their lifetime. So, if we know about a star today we know what it was like 5 million years ago and what it will be like in 5 million years."

But, Brax thought quietly, this is the way we tell ourselves that we have worked it all out. That we have some relevance. *'Yeh...stars...we got that,'* we think, like we will be still here in 5 million years... He knew, even as an undergraduate, that we are all oblivious to the physical size and age of the universe. We talk about vast numbers, like the stars, with no real comprehension of them. The vastness of these numbers puts us, and everything we have ever known, into a universal basket of irrelevance.

<hr>

So THERE, in Second Year, he met Jess...or rather she met him.

He went to a party at his friend's house. At the party, he was sitting in a corner talking to one of the people he felt comfortable with in social situations and trying not to stand out at all. Rising to get another beer he strolled into the kitchen and pulled one out of the ice tub on the floor. As he stood up and turned around to leave she was standing in front of him. Thinking she just wanted a drink as well, he tried to step aside. But it was a tiny kitchen in a small flat and he was stuck.

"Ummm," he said, his anxiety with personal interactions rising.

"Are you always this super cool and smooth?" she asked.

It was a response that completely turned him upside down.

Brax often thought he was special: That his academic ability set him apart. But as he stood facing this girl, who was about his height with a thin face and high cheekbones, her coppery hair tied in a medium-length ponytail, she instantly punctured all his pretensions of being one of the few. Of being one of those who excelled and, perhaps, lived on a plane that was above mere mortals.

"Ummm," he said again.

She smiled. "I'm Jess," she said. "Not Jessica. Just Jess."

He stood quite still not sure what to say.

'Just Jess.'

"And you are...," she continued. It wasn't a question.

He regained his composure, or so he thought, but later he

realised it was just the first time she shared hers with him. "Braxton. Brax," he managed to reply.

"Nice to meet you Braxton Brax" she said and he was suddenly completely at ease. It was that same thing as happened when he was tutoring. The place he was in just felt right and he didn't fear the social faux pas.

"Well, it's nice to meet you as well 'Not Jessica Just Jess'," he said, getting into the swing of things. Her smile brightened and Brax got totally lost in it. He knew then that he loved her.

They wandered outside and sat on the front wall of the brown brick inner suburban apartment block and she continued her, soon to be familiar, pattern of teasing him into being humble.

"And what sort of a thing would a mega brain like yours be studying?" She asked.

He took the tone and responded in kind. "Well, a massive chunk of grey matter like mine would be doing Astrophysics at ANU. You?"

"Maths and Computer Science."

"At ANU?" He asked, surprised, and she nodded. "Second year?" He asked again, and she nodded again, waiting patiently for the penny to drop.

"Funny I haven't seen you in any classes," he said.

She looked down at her shoes and pondered for a few seconds before looking him straight in the eye. "Maybe you just aren't looking. Maybe you don't see really obvious things. You know; signs and signals."

Brax looked back at her and he felt almost naked. All his shields and protections against getting close to people vanished and he didn't know what to reply to that.

That chilly, crisp and clear Autumn evening they sat on the wall and talked for ages about their lives and interests. They looked to the sky and Brax named some of the brighter stars. She was fascinated, her mind full of curiosity and possibilities. They liked the same movies and she introduced him to some music which was an area he hadn't explored much.

"Do you know Frequency77?" She asked.

"There are more than 77 frequencies," he had started, feeling comfortable explaining something. "Actually, it's a spectrum..."

"It's a band," she interrupted. "They play classic post punk guitar pop and ultra-historic pub rock."

Brax shook his head suddenly realising he had wandered out of his comfort zone. "Well then...no," he backtracked, his face reddening slightly.

She linked her phone to his buds and gave him a blast of music. She looked into his face and Brax realised he could feel his heartbeat. It thumped to the music with total insistence. It was like an electric shock: so vibrant that he didn't know how he should react. Not for the last time with Jess, he just went with it.

As the music continued, she grinned at him and he saw in that moment that the lanky, vibrant, beautiful girl; the girl who had taken time to talk to him and get past his barriers; this...perfect young woman...had the most freckles he had ever seen. They were scattered across her face just like the stars above them were running across the night sky.

And just like the stars, he never managed to count them all.

Third Year at Uni was, in Brax's mind, the best of all his education. He had that feeling that he knew all the ropes. He could see First Years bumbling around and trying to figure everything out and he felt a bit superior. Still, everything was fairly guided by classes and tutors and no actual decisions needed to be made. Again, he knew his path was set.

He had his campus room and would go home any time he felt like it for a proper meal or to watch a stream. He saw Jess as often as possible and to Brax's surprise he enjoyed going out on the weekend, as long as she was there.

About the middle of the year, Frequency77 toured through the Nation's Capital and played a smallish room. Jess was excited and the two of them went with a group of others. The room was packed and he and Jess moshed and bounced all through the set. They couldn't get a taxi after the gig. The self-drivers were down and the human taxis were doubling prices in celebration. The only choice was to walk. And it was a long one.

Canberra at night was still basically a big country town. In fact, it had changed little in the previous 100 years. People went home and, for the most part, stayed there. When the winter chill set in it was very quiet in the city. After farewelling their friends, the two of them walked a long time, singing and laughing, past the monuments and Parliament Houses and then over the lake back to the city.

"What do you think will happen next year?" She asked.

"I'll let you know when the astrology predictions come out in December," he replied and smirked.

"I mean..." She paused, a serious tone developing. "Have you even thought about this?"

He hadn't really. All his future was set. "I... well... we're here right? Everything is fine."

They walked in silence for a few minutes.

"I got an offer from Melbourne and one from Manchester," he blurted out suddenly.

"When?" she replied, a bit surprised.

"They both came in the last couple of weeks."

"Oh. Manchester?" She asked quizzically.

"Yes."

"Okay Brax," she said after a moment's silence, "this is the sort of thing when I'd appreciate you saying the 'out loud' bits out loud."

"Oh. Yes. Sorry. Well, there isn't much to tell. Manchester have long been very aggressive in their recruitment. They offered me a year scholarship to write a Master's thesis. And Melbourne, well I talked to someone from down there a few weeks back at that seminar I went to on Current Dark Matter Calculations. I guess she went back and put my name on a list." They walked on in silence. "Really, I just thought we'd stay here," he finally finished

"We?" she asked.

'Was that an 'out-loud' bit?' He wondered.

They walked on and started through the back streets to their rooms, their faces frozen and their breath visible in the street lights. On the way, they walked past a building that was being renovated. It was dark and obviously work was going on because there was a large wire fence at the front.

Jess looked at him as a sudden spark of mischief crossed her face. "Come on," she said suddenly and started to climb over the fence.

"No. Jess. Wait. What are you doing?" He called with anxious urgency.

"Exploring! Come on!" she reiterated.

"It's dangerous. What are you doing?" He said, but as she got to the top and flipped over the fence he started to follow her. His introvert uprightness shattered in the cold silent air. He would have followed her into a burning building without hesitation.

"So," She said a few days later as they sat by the lake on a picnic blanket eating some hot chips together.

"So?"

"Have you thought any more about Manchester? Melbourne?"

"Not really," he replied. "What; should I be? Thinking I mean."

"It's usually a good idea. Particularly if you have a planet-sized brain," she replied with some exasperation. They lapsed into silence and he stared vaguely at the ground while lightly and repetitively tapping his thumb and forefinger together.

"You really don't want to leave. Do you?" She said after a minute.

"I'm actually fine here." He shuffled his long legs around a bit and then tucked them back up exactly where they had been.

"What about a change?"

"I'm not that comfortable with change," he replied with some degree of understatement.

She was silent for a while and Brax felt her frustration. Then she said, "I want to travel a bit at least. See some of the world."

His silent finger taps increased in tempo. "What about Melbourne?" He asked lamely.

"I mean, yes...but Europe? I would like to go for a while. See the sights?"

"Would you go without me?" he asked. She looked him square in the eyes, her hair glinting metallic in the winter sun, and her lips pursed. She didn't answer.

He switched his gaze to the scenery around them and then after a minute it finally fell directly back on her.

But Jess was also looking away. "You can't change? Or you won't change?" She asked. "There's a difference. Being uncomfortable or worried; I get that. Dealing with it by hiding from it, I don't get. You're a solutions guy. Always looking for answers...what's the answer to this?"

'*Answers,*' he thought. '*Answers need data.*'

"Would you go without me?" he asked again, bowing his head to look at his feet, his gentle finger tap comforting him.

Jess sighed and stood up. "I want to explore something...I want to go somewhere. Don't you want to find out about other places? Other people? What are you scared of?" Then, in frustration, she got up and walked off towards the edge of the water.

He didn't know what he was scared of.

But he knew he wanted to stop being scared of it.

He watched her standing by the glinting lake and felt somehow cut off from her. Suddenly the rapid movement of his fingers stopped and he decided he should do it. With her, he knew he could.

7

CORPORATE WELFARE: C21

Taken from 21st Century Corporate Decline by Jacob Lőssl 2083

The Tech Revolution eventually led back to cheap labour opportunities for companies. Unions in many countries were strong, but even when they were they had no way of helping the developing underclass. These people came to know only the hand of corporate welfare and are indentured to, and protected by, the business of business. It was Dickensian without the chimney stacks.

In the early 2030s successive governments around the world trumpeted their genius in tackling poverty, but the truth was they were quietly letting many people slip off the radar. There were those who suddenly didn't trip facial recognition, who suddenly got no government emails and would be told politely – should they present at a Government office – "I'm sorry, we can't seem to locate your records. Try the vehicle registry". Or the tax office, or another federal or state office. But they were welcomed at the corporations and given jobs in return for a basic food allowance and company accommodation. Corporations wrote them off as 'Labour Consul-

tants' for tax purposes and so governments ended up paying for them anyway. It was a neat solution. For the Government statistical poverty was reduced. For the companies, cheap labour was readily available. It was a win-win. And so, this underclass grew.

32

8

RENSHU JIANG: 2051-2056

Now Briggs was only eleven when he was drafted into 'The Company'. 'Dickensian' was an oft-used description at the time but, perhaps, it wasn't quite that harsh. Child labour was frowned upon in most countries and luckily for Briggs, the USA was one of those. Destiny was still happy to take in children, however. They saw it as an opportunity to educate them with a corporate angle and they weren't afraid of indoctrination - although they called it 'Company Citizenship' when they taught it in class. Buy5ell/Destiny had become a huge company. They had rules, regulations and procedures which were strongly promoted.

As The Company expanded so rapidly into so many areas it also had to consider the developing governance of space, they required that grievances had a pathway and people were treated with at least the appearance of parity. Slowly, the cut-throat capitalism of the 19th and 20th centuries would transform in the 21st to a semi-benevolent corporate government. Destiny found themselves with no competitors and the responsibility for millions of people and large amounts of hardware and infrastructure. Of course, they were a business and if they could get away with something they certainly did but on the face of it and, especially in public, everything became respectful procedure.

So, Destiny ran a school for their under-age future workers. This was not just out of benevolence or Government oversight. Having staff with educational competence, at least to mid-high school was better for the company than not. Unlike Victorian times there were few manual labouring jobs to go into if you didn't have basic programming and computer literacy.

Briggs' teacher was Mrs Renshu Jiang, a short, motherly-looking figure with obvious Asian heritage, she had worked for The Company for more than 20 years and had herself come there after a bad divorce. At that time, she had had nothing. The company took her in and she became a teacher. She took pride in her work and it was known she went above and beyond, running extra groups and classes in all sorts of things. While the company didn't completely approve of too much information, they also didn't disapprove. Renshu had a clear reputation for getting her way. And her way was to deliver the best education and the best outcomes she possibly could.

She met Briggs for the first time in the small dormitory where the children slept. Boys were at one end and girls at the other, separated by a curtain. He had been there a day already, working through an orientation and had, just a few minutes before, unpacked his company issue kit and put his things away in the cupboard next to his bunk.

"Briggs?" She asked as she stared at the small wiry boy in front of her. He nodded. "I'm Mrs. Jiang. I want you to come down to the classroom at 7 am tomorrow. It's before school but I want to talk to you before we start, ask you a few questions and show you around. Ashan here", she continued indicating a boy standing near her, "will look after you till then. He'll take you to dinner and show you the outside areas and where to meet me tomorrow. Any questions?" Briggs stood as if gauging his new teacher then slightly shook his head.

She turned on her heels and efficiently left the dorm in the capable hands of the night staff.

ON A MORNING some 3 years later, Renshu got to the classroom, early as usual.

Briggs, again as usual, was sitting at his desk working through...*well whatever it was*. She had stopped understanding what he did at least a year before.

"Good Morning Briggs," she said continuing the routine.

"Mrs Jiang?" He asked breaking the normal morning flow and she felt the comforting routine drop away.

"What's up, Luis?" She was the only one who ever called him that...and only on occasion.

"This new work you got for me..."

"The Astro Navigation... Yes?"

"I need to know if I'm doing it right. Some things aren't clear to me."

She went across the small classroom and sat at the desk next to him. She didn't attempt to read or mark his work.

"Luis, I can't help you. You know that." He looked at her like he was discouraged. "My friend in Texas, who is sending me all this work...maybe you should speak to her."

"Can you arrange that?" He asked.

She sat and thought that through.

"Actually, I'm not sure that's wise. The Company will not be happy you are learning Astro. I am trying very hard to fly under the radar on this. A link meeting might get noticed."

"It just takes so long. Doing the work then sending it off...using paper and pen."

He looked despondent and she knew his impatience needed to be tempered.

"I tell you what. I will see if she will come to San Francisco for a little holiday. She owes me a favour. You might be able to spend a few days clarifying your questions in person."

Renshu had a good hard look at Briggs then. At 14 he had grown considerably. He was now 180 cm and still growing. His thin frame had filled out and his solid square shoulders were now barely fitting behind his small student desk.

She had known since she first assessed him that he was a prodigy.

The other children quickly got a sense that Briggs was something different as well and although he didn't court popularity, it came to him. He could have wiped the floor with any boy during a game of rugby but instead, he chose football, baseball or cricket as his games of choice and his sportsmanship was well known. If he called a foul, an out, or a wicket, the other children accepted the call.

Briggs looked back at his work. Then, as if taken by a thought, looked back to Renshu.

She had worked hard for him. Broke Company rules about teaching Astro. She had tried to imbue in him a moral centre and, perhaps, because circumstances had prevented her from having children of her own she constantly thought about ways she could do the absolute best for her boy. And at a certain teenage level, he seemed to understand this.

"Thank you," he said simply then he looked deep in thought for a second. "For everything."

And Renshu knew she could not have received a better gift that morning. Or ever.

At 16 it was time for Briggs to 'Graduate', and go to an apprenticeship in The Company somewhere. Middle management, most likely. But Renshu Jiang had other ideas.

The Company loved correct procedure and there was plenty of correct procedure to be had when the day of the Student Placement Meeting arrived. All teachers had to attend and they arrived in San Francisco as they did every year to sign over the final year students formally to The Company.

Two mid-level executives sat at the head of the large conference table in the main meeting room and the teachers from across the western region of the USA took their seats. The executives themselves wore regulation suit and tie with a nice Destiny pin on the lapel and looked mildly disdainful of this low-level formality they had been sent to perform.

"Thanks for coming everybody," started one of them. "I am, as most of you know, Roger Harris, and to my left here, is clerk Withers Mayhew. This meeting will, of course, be fully minuted. We are looking through the children who are 16 and in their final year and endorsing their placements at the company." He gave Renshu a quick glance. "Thank you all for filling in the skills rubrics, psych reviews and other appropriate forms. We just need to sign off on these..." and he glanced at Renshu again "...so let's have a nice day with appropriate Company values."

A meeting of clear formality followed. The teachers had to physically sign off on an actual piece of paper and the executives signed as witnesses. It was a legal procedure the Company didn't need but wasn't prepared to stop doing. It had become nearly a tradition. A ritual. A corporate coming-of-age ceremony.

Just over halfway through, Briggs became the topic.

"Luis Paz Briggs," said Withers Mayhew as they handed some documents to Harris.

"Mrs Jiang," said Roger with formality. "As his teacher at the San Francisco School, I ask you to confirm his readiness for the Corporation."

She didn't speak as Mayhew brought the papers to her.

Roger cleared his throat. "Mrs Jiang," said Harris again. "As his teacher at the San Francisco School, I ask you to confirm his readiness for The Company."

"Before we continue..." she started, and Mayhew looked at her with wide eyes.

"I just need you to follow procedure Renshu," interrupted Roger in a quiet, chatty tone.

"Before we continue," she said again, "I just need to make you aware of something."

"Mrs Jiang," said Withers Mayhew, "we just need to tick these boxes. The boy has been assigned."

"I know," she replied, "but I have to say something first. And with respect Exec Mayhew your tone is not appreciated."

Renshu knew this was a clever move in a fully minuted meeting. Disrespectful tone could be played back to their superiors. Mayhew remained quiet.

Renshu knew that Harris had to keep the meeting within parameters or it would go against him back at the office. He would be thinking Renshu was wasting everybody's time but she had played the 'tone' card and now it had become an administrative shootout. She gathered her thoughts for a second and took a slow deep breath.

"I know Briggs has ticked all the boxes and I know you have him pegged for lower management training to become...well... much like yourselves" and she looked over her glasses at Mayhew. She had taught them and now she scolded them gently. They looked down at the desk like a naughty child.

"Mr Harris," she continued, "The skills and aptitude rubrics have never been sufficient." Harris went to interrupt her but she waggled a teacher finger at him and he stopped. The other teachers started to look like they wanted to put their feet up and get popcorn. For them, these meetings never got this exciting. "It does not cover excellence in any area and never has. It's a problem every year and nothing is ever done about it and now this year it's about to be a disaster! Mr. Harris, Briggs is not just sufficient. He is the most exceptional child I have ever taught." She looked at Mayhew again but they still had their head down.

"He is a natural leader, he already has a university-level grasp on Physics, Chemistry and Astro-navigation.

Mayhew pulled their head up at this and looked at Renshu with wide eyes. Harris smiled.

"You taught him Astro?" asked Mayhew.

"Now before you go issuing demerits on my HR file..." she pressed on knowing she couldn't stop now, "...let me ask you this.

Would the company like to know that someone with the potential to earn them billions in profit was wasted?"

And now she had played the 'profit' card. Roger's smile ceased suddenly and he looked entirely like he wanted to be anywhere else. "Mrs... Renshu..." he started.

But she cut him off as she continued. "This boy has the potential to be anything! He needs to be in the Space Program. He has gifts you and I can only dream of." She knew this was out of order but was not prepared to stop. "He could take the company to new heights. You have to listen to me this time!"

"Please..." Roger said, as if begging for mercy "...I am not doubting you Renshu. But re-assigning children...that's way above our pay grade. We can't make such decisions. We just can't."

"Then I suggest you find someone who can," she concluded in her best teacher voice. "Until this goes further up the chain I am not signing anything. With respect."

And with that, there was a short silence except for the sound of Roger letting out a long slow sigh.

"Ashan Lanpoor," said Mayhew and they handed some documents to a very unhappy Harris.

ROGER HARRIS: 2056

The week after he met with the teachers, Roger Harris set off, just after lunchtime on a Thursday, for the Tokyo office. He had organised a meeting with Martin Kemp for that afternoon so he took the regular Blue Destiny Super Skimmer flight from San Francisco and, because of date lines and time zones, was there five hours before he left. Except it was now Friday. Maths was not his strong point and every time he thought about it, it hurt his head but Mayhew had worked it all out for him and he just had to do it.

The meeting was scheduled for 10:30am and Roger was not enthusiastic. Kemp was the head of Human Resources for the whole of Destiny SMC and was the highest-level executive that Harris knew of. The problem that Jiang caused had gone straight up the chain. Right to the top! Nobody wanted this problem so it kept getting referred. So essentially, he was stuck with it.

Of course, the meeting with Kemp would be perfectly civilized. Kemp would never yell at him or demote or fire him. He would not outwardly discipline him in any way.

And that was the worst part. If he was displeased by this Roger would, over the next few weeks, find a dozen things become his problem. He would inherit a series of impossible deadlines and lose hours of sleep every day. Tasks that had sat for months would suddenly need doing 'today' and he would be asked to do them.

Roger was an excellent middle manager and he knew to keep his head down as he had always done. He had never suffered what was affectionately known as 'Death by 1000 Papercuts'. He had seen others get it, though, so he always tried his best and didn't draw attention to himself. Until today. Jiang had done a number on him and he was not happy. But he knew what he had to do.

Martin Kemp was English by birth but, as is the nature of things, had taken U.S. citizenship to advance in The Company. Now based in Japan and still ambitious to climb even higher he was not an executive to be messed with. Tall and thin with short sandy hair and a short beard, very neatly trimmed and gelled, he wore, more often than not, a silvery grey suit which stood out from the more excepted unofficial 'corporate uniform' of dark blue or black suits.

"Come in Roger" said Martin from behind his desk. "I believe we have a small problem."

Roger dutifully recounted the meeting - quite pointlessly because it was fully minuted - and Roger was sure Martin would have listened to them. Martin nodded gravely.

"Don't be concerned Mr Harris," he said, leaning back in his large luxurious office chair. You handled the situation as well as can be expected."

'I guess I'll find out if that's true in a week or two', thought Roger grimly.

"Renshu Jiang has pulled this sort of thing before, has she not?" Continued Martin. "But she always signs on the dotted line. Let's tell her we have reviewed the situation. I'll organise some review docs and then she will have to sign...or face disciplinary action."

Roger took a deep breath. He hated that he was going to do this but 'death by 1000 paper cuts' was still on the cards.

"Martin, with respect," he started. "I know she has done this before. I took the trouble to review each time over the last 20 years."

"Yes?" Said Martin. Did his eyebrows look displeased? Roger couldn't tell.

"She has never done it with more than a grumble and she always signs at the meeting. This time was different. The thing is...if she's right...if the boy is as good as she says...a natural leader, a genius at Astro. Well, I think you should genuinely take a look at him." Roger took a second to assess Martin's mood on this. He could not read him at all. Then he continued. "Hear me out on the advantages of this. If you 'discover' him there could be a lot of prestige for you. If we find she is being hysterical, well, at worst we have wasted a day."

Martin sat and his eyebrows definitely looked displeased. He never wasted a day.

Then the eyebrows relaxed. His decision was made.

"All right Roger. I will take your advice." Martin rotated his chair gently back and forth and joined his fingertips together in a steeple shape. "But be aware it looks like much administration is coming up in the next few weeks, for various reasons, and I may need you to be on that." His brow wrinkled as if in a kind of deep far away thought before concluding.

"Especially if we 'waste a day'."

10

THE DARK ANGELS: 2042

T alk of the robot bomb had long since subsided. The authorities made no progress and in the way of instant culture, it was soon forgotten by the mainstream. Nobody claimed any responsibility.

Six years passed and then the second major attack came. This time it was in London.

Just after lunch, a statue of an angel drove itself into Trafalgar Square. It was about 150 cm high in a grey, rock-like, plaster and had the classic biblical robes seen in churchyards everywhere. The tourists looked at it with some amusement thinking it must surely be the start of some entertainment. At this time others were seen in the streets driving around, obviously remote-controlled. They converged on Trafalgar Square. In all, there were 20. The authorities were quick this time and sealed the area off, which was when they had reports of a large drone flying across the Thames. Underneath it was a timber packing crate. The drone landed the crate in Trafalgar Square in the middle of the angels near Nelson's Column and the drone landed on top. Again, all was quiet. Then a small explosion made the top of the box pop off and the sides all fell away with a crash.

Inside the box was now revealed three metre tall statue of Jesus. In its chest was a large speaker surrounded by coloured lights which flashed rhythmically. The statue started playing 'The End of the World' by 20th century singer Skeeter Davis (which then trended on socials and became a massive hit again) as the lights flashed. At the end of the song the heads popped off all the little angels and masses of party streamers came out. A deep voice boomed out of the Jesus speaker. "Stop AI. Stop it now. It is our doom. This is the word of the Lord." Then, one by one the little angel statues exploded, just enough to destroy them. The police in attendance took cover quickly before the expected finale. After the angels had all exploded, the Jesus statue stood in eerie silence for a few seconds before it too exploded with considerable force.

11

BRAX: 2058 - 2064

The week before they set off for England Brax and Jess were packing. They had been staying at Brax' parent's house since they had finished University. The summer had been long and languorous. February was filled with the burn of hot dry air filled with gum leaf oil and the sound of cicadas consumed every evening after the New Year. Brax was idle. He didn't want to think about the Journey so he occupied his mind through the summer and early autumn trying to come up with the most outlandish scenarios that he could.

That's when he started to think the universe could be one entity. A giant being with all the attributes that we associate with life. It's more common to think about the universe as a space, a giant hollow area containing planets and stars. But Brax knew that space is not empty and while they had not yet been able to find any dark matter, something that they had not yet encountered must be there to make all the calculations about the universe make sense. He started to wonder what the human body would look like to an electron that was in, say, the kidneys. Getting a whole picture of the person you are in is seemingly impossible. And seeing, say, New York from that perspective is such a mind-bendingly ridiculous thought. But he couldn't shake it. *'What if we could find some rhythm to the universe above and beyond gravitational orbits?'* he thought as he packed.

Jess was vaguely somewhere behind him asking questions about sweaters. *Would he need a coat?* He didn't know. She gently double-checked what he was doing and he didn't mind. He knew if left to his own devices, he would pack little more than one pair of pants and a sandwich.

———

THAT MAY they went on a Blue Destiny Super Skimmer. It was the first time Brax had travelled, except for an occasional week at the beach with his Mum and Dad, and it was a hell of a way to get into it. Seeing the curve of the earth that first time is an event you can never truly prepare for.

"It's just beautiful," mused Brax, "and absolutely undeserving of the stress we put it under." They sipped coffee and reclined in awe.

"It's a lesson that seems hard for people to learn," replied Jess. "Size and fragility are not related."

Compared to Canberra, Manchester could not have been more different. A bustling and somewhat bleak city it was nevertheless a place of great pride for its inhabitants. It tended to be a gloomy place, overcast quite often although it didn't rain much more there than any other English city. Of course, they were immensely proud of their football teams and they were proud of their town although, in any single breath, they may also tell you how terrible it was.

What had been a city with a drab reputation had worked hard to streamline the ancient with the modern. The 2030s had seen a building boom. A lot of the late 20th Century architecture had been taken down and given a shake-up. The University, however, didn't buy into it. They kept the facades of the buildings and looked at updating the insides only, causing them to stand out architecturally. They had also worked hard on becoming one of the top five Universities in the world, sparing no expense to bring the most talented academics there. And, with a city centre not far away, that was cosmopolitan and open 24/7 with fine dining, music and clubs, it became a destination of choice for many.

Brax and Jess arrived with a couple of months to spare and spent time exploring the city then travelling further afield. Brax was struck by the ancient. Growing up in a country not yet officially 150 years old (and busily still ignoring an ancient indigenous culture) gave a different feeling of time than in Europe. There were no medieval cathedrals or castles in Australia. And Stonehenge, when he saw it, seemed surreal with age. As Summer wound up Brax got to work on his thesis and Jess got tech work at a small company in the city.

Back at the university, Brax started getting to meet a few people. Again, he found that he enjoyed talking to people and finding out about their stories. At this time, he had his first encounter with Trevor Pailleton. Pailleton was a classic, bearded, corduroy-panted, pipe-smoking, distinguished academic type. Just exactly who you'd expect to find in a science faculty. This was kind of engaging. He was a bit dotty and seemed straight from a streaming show. His office was just messy enough and when he gave lectures he frequently rambled off topic. His best days as a theorist were behind him and he looked happy enough to spend out his days teaching. Although he and Brax didn't work together, they met several times and became friendly. He was very helpful, giving Brax feedback on his thesis. Pailleton made it clear Brax could contact him for help anytime in the future, should he require anything.

As Summer broke the following year Brax and Jess travelled to the continent and did touristy things like The Eiffel Tower and also explored the back streets of some of Europe's great cities. They ended up in Milan and had a week to look around the city and get to know it a little before flying back.

Brax had never been happier and their relationship had never been stronger. She seemed happy to be supportive of his ambitions, yet he always had the feeling that she was guiding him. He had done things he wouldn't have attempted without her. She dragged him out of his shell and he knew he was a better person now for it.

"Brax?" She said to him one morning as they ate breakfast in their final days before heading back to Australia.

"Yep?" he replied as he absently scanned his device with one hand, a piece of toast in the other hand with his legs hanging over the arm of the lounge chair.

"Do you think we will have kids?" She asked.

"Maybe."

"That's not the most likely answer at the moment," she replied.

She looked at him rather sheepishly during the short awkward silence that followed and he went through the options in his head.

"Do you think we will have kids?" She asked softly again. "This time try a more positive answer."

"I..." He said. "Ummm." And she waited patiently, as she always did, for him to process.

He put down his phone and juggled his plate, almost dropping it as he put it on the coffee table. He went over to where she sat and knelt in front of her chair. Their hands clasped. "You're...?" He said using the only word he could push past his lips.

She nodded "I'm pretty sure."

His disorientation rose as he remained frozen by the consequences.

"Should we get married?" He blurted out suddenly.

"Way to go Romeo." She looked a little frustrated with him and, unusually, a little out of her depth.

"How did this happen?" He asked.

"Seriously?"

"I mean...I know how it happens...I just... I wasn't prepared. Weren't we being careful?"

"Yes", she replied tersely. "I was being careful." The accent on the pronoun did not go unnoticed. She softly grunted in annoyance and then let out a little sharp sigh. "But nothing's one hundred per cent. We got unlucky."

He scanned the face full of stars he had come to love so much and then looked straight into her eyes. He could see she was troubled and chastised himself for not noticing sooner. Almost certainly, he thought, this loomed in her mind as something that would be difficult for him to accept...maybe she'd put off telling him. But any thought for himself or his anxiety was overshadowed by her obvious distress. He had a moment of absolute clarity as the morning sunshine streamed through the dust motes of their little apartment.

"Unlucky?" He said. "No. Lucky. This is perfect."

Brax rested his head in her lap. "This is perfect," he whispered again, softly. He felt her gentle hand run through his thick locks and he heard her quietly sob.

BRAX AND JESS returned to Australia and settled in Melbourne. The University of Western Melbourne (UWM) was relatively new, only being established about 25 years before. Brax took a job as a research assistant and tutor in the Physics department and settled into a comfortable routine.

Jess had found a job working with an organisation that trawled tertiary institutions for theses that looked like they might have economic impact or potential. It was not her field of expertise but it paid the bills and could mostly be done from home.

Evan was born in the Autumn of 2060 and the small family went about their day-to-day business with quiet Joy.

Brax's teaching style and skills became sought after and in a few years he was offered the chance to become a Teaching Fellow with the department. The condition was that he needed a research area. He had so many questions but none of them, he considered, were big enough. He wanted to dazzle the world with his genius. This became a sticking point for Brax. Where would he find a research area that wasn't just one of the pack?

One Saturday morning in the spring of 2064 they set off on a day trip to get out of the city. It's an activity they had been enjoying often over the last 3 years or so, starting, at first, to distract Evan when he started walking. Now he was four and expecting a baby sister within a matter of weeks. Brax considered that Jess, eight months pregnant, was more beautiful than ever before. This time the pregnancy was planned and she was calmly confident that everything was going to be alright.

They drove out of Melbourne (Brax enjoyed driving and regularly put the self-drive to sleep). They headed northwest, more or less. It was a sunny day, but with still a bit of winter chill in the air.

They packed up and headed out just after breakfast. Vaguely, Brax thought they would head towards Ballarat in the west of Victoria. They passed fields and farms and as they got further inland giant silver gums would occasionally encroach on the road. Evan chattered and giggled as he often did and asked an endless stream of questions. "What are clouds made of Daddy?" he asked. "How high can a frog jump? What's that cow doing?" and on he continued. Brax and Jess tried to answer but he nearly always interrupted with another question.

They stopped in a tiny town called Ballan and decided it was the place for a picnic. The park was pleasant but the town was a bit run down with only a few shops, and of that 3 or 4 empty storefronts. The air was warming and clear and they sat on a rug as Evan played on the park playground equipment. It was a picture of perfection to anyone outside: but Brax was unusually restless and distracted.

"You just really need to choose anything," said Jess suddenly as if she knew exactly what he was thinking.

"I can't. I need it to be...well at least excellent. If not brilliant.'

Having completed his Doctorate, he now wanted to make a serious mark on academia. And with that, he could land tenure anywhere on the planet in the coming years. Brax knew that this was the make-or-break time for an academic. The business of universities was and had been for over 50 years, a business. They weren't taking any freeloaders and, as nice as they were about it, everybody knew that.

"What you need is a job," she said and he felt her disappointment. "I mean," she continued, "I didn't mean that. But you have such crazy high standards. Things that are only just passably interesting to you are other people's excellence. Maybe just start with anything and you will find something to suit your ability when you aren't looking."

"The old 'stop looking and find it' trick hey?" He said in a funny accent and smiled. But he had to admit she had a point.

"What if Rabbits were really tall?" shouted Evan from the see-saw.

AFTER LUNCH, they took a drive around and meandered home through the back roads. Evan was still full of beans, asking those 'stream of consciousness' questions again. He was sitting in his booster seat in the middle of the back seat. Evan had inherited his mother's coppery hair and freckles. The sun was well over the yard arm by then and they were driving past a beauteous scene of shimmering green fields when they went past a goat farm.

And that's when Evan asked the question.

The one that Brax couldn't get out of his head.

The one that was so bonkers only a four-year-old could ask it.

The one that would lead them all so impossibly far away from home.

"What if the universe had a heartbeat?" He asked.

What.

If.

The.

Universe..........had..........a...

"What did you say?' Brax asked.

"What if pigs had 10 legs?"

"No no no no no no." Brax jammed on the brakes.

"Look at the sheep Daddy, look at the funny sheep!"

Brax hurriedly pulled the car over to the side of the road, a little too quickly, and he hit a small pothole. They bounced a little then came to a stop with just enough deceleration to push them into their seatbelts for a moment.

"What are you doing?" asked Jess, a little mystified.

Evan was still looking out the window. "The strange-looking sheep Daddy, see?"

Brax turned in his seat and looked at his four-year-old son sitting in his booster chair. "They're goats," he said. "What did you say before?"

Evan sat for a thoughtful moment.

"What?" he replied.

"Before. About the universe."

"They're fluffy goats."

"About the universe Evan! Focus."

"The Universe is sooooo big! Isn't it Daddy?"

Jess piped up. "As I recall he asked, '*What if the universe had a heartbeat?*'"

"And what if it had a big, ginormous brain?" asked Evan. "And a bottom." He began to giggle.

"Hey Dad!" Evan said, and then asked in his telling-a-secret voice, "What if the universe could fart?"

And he burst into hysterical laughter.

"ASKING questions is the job of a scientist," Brax would tell his students. "It's the first step in finding answers."

"If you like questions," he would continue, "then the good news is there are plenty of them. Probably an infinite number. Science is simply the process of ruling out what isn't the answer to be left with what probably is. By asking questions we have found out a lot of stuff in the last 800 years or so."

"Though those conclusions can sometimes prove troubling in themselves... (Do we go around the sun? Turns out yes! But hundreds of years ago that was very disturbing to some) ...the main problem with all answers is the 'probably' bit. New information may swoop in at any time to update or disprove those answers. This is genuinely very worrying for many who just want an irrefutable answer. But there it is, and to accept science, you have to accept that. We must not cling emotionally to any answer because the questions mustn't stop."

And finally, Brax had a question.

It was bold and audacious.

It was time for him to show the world what he was capable of.

He was on his way.

AFTER EVAN ASKED the question Brax put it to his boss at UWM.

"What if the Universe had a heartbeat?" Professor Felice Jones repeated back to him.

"Now stay with me." He was standing in the study at home, with his netspex on, watching the holographic avatar of the department head.

"I can't even think where you are going with this." She said.

"Well...I'm not sure either but think about this. We have defined many constants since...well since science, right?"

"Okay..."

"What if they weren't constant?"

"What the...?"

"...and you'd be right to have that reaction." He tried to head her off.

"You're saying that the numbers we base all of our calculations on are wrong?"

"No. I'm saying the nature of the Universe may change over time"

She paused and thought about that.

"How would you even approach such a thing?" She asked.

"Okay. Let's put that aside for a second," he replied. "So, what if the constants changed in a way that showed a wave instead of a linear change or a curve?"

"So... wait." And she thought again for a second or two. "You're suggesting that the very nature of the universe may be different to how we are defining it now."

"Yes. We still haven't accounted for the mass of the universe. Where's all the dark matter?"

She let out a long slow breath. "Brax, this is not going to work. Not only is it a huge area...with not a single shred of data...but how are you going to even find data? How are you going to test across time? There is no time capsule. You are suggesting that the universe might be alive?'

"You're making it sound a little crazy," he said.

She took another short thinking time and Brax waited impatiently.

"I'm sorry Brax," she said finally. "It's just an idea with no data and no way to get any data. Changes over time are one thing but on a universal scale? I just can't approve anything like that."

He couldn't say he wasn't disappointed. He couldn't say he was surprised.

"And Brax," she finished, "Don't tell this idea to anyone else. You'll get a reputation you don't want and you'll end up doing First Year tutoring for the rest of your life."

"Don't threaten me with a good time," he joked. "Okay. I get your point. It was worth talking it through with you though. Thanks."

He took off his netspex and went into the kitchen where Jess was making dinner.

"What did she say?" She asked him.

"You know what she said," he replied with resignation.

"Yes. I. Do." Jess replied. "I'm sorry Brax, but you know it sounds like a nutty idea"

It sure did. *'And I know nutty'*, he thought to himself.

He considered the world he lived in. It was a planet with 10.7 billion humans on it. He watched them on screens and streams. He listened to speeches by politicians and he watched the McPherson Empire News. And it was crazy enough that Brax avoided online socials where some people spent their lives calling for attention to themselves, praying for influence and generally enraging others for fun.

By 2050 the internet had become a place, basically, of lawlessness and some of the most crazy craziness on earth was on the socials. They had been through some serious fads, like the insane eyebrows of the late 2020s and the 'Dance in a Dress Made of Biscuits' craze of 2037. Sometimes it was funny but often it was cruel like the 2046, 'Sew your pet to the Couch' challenge. That was very ugly. Brax saw people go on the most watched streams on the planet and complain they were being silenced. People voted time and time again for obvious conmen, and if you yelled your argument the loudest you were generally considered correct.

So Brax knew *'nutty'*.

But as much as he told himself this was a crazy idea, he couldn't let it go.

"It sounds like a nutty idea," continued Jess, "but that doesn't mean it's wrong. Why don't you try and break it down to its first step then see if you can get support for something less mad sounding? That's good politics."

"Well, I'm an idiot," he said, "so busy looking at the big picture. Maybe make some headway without getting drummed out of the University." He sat and thought about that for a minute before Jess broke in.

"Great. That's settled. Now, can you pull your head out of the sky and give Evan his dinner? The baby says I need to sit down."

Saffron was born about a month later. Brax was in love with her from the start. A proud and beaming father from the first, their bond was cemented when Jess fell sick a few days after giving birth. She had a bad fever for 5 days and didn't respond to treatment initially. Afterwards, she was very weak and didn't leave the hospital for two more weeks. So, Jess expressed and Brax got to bottle feed Saffron while he wandered around the maternity ward corridors. She already had a shock of dark hair like him and even his parents noted her similarity to Brax as a baby.

When Saffron was two, Brax showed her a simple sleight of hand with a coin and she was convinced he was magic. That prompted him to learn quite a few other magic tricks. She grew, like her brother and her parents, to have an affinity for science.

Once a week Brax would run some simple experiments in the kitchen at home then he and the kids would eat ice cream. It became known as 'Sundae Science' and the children loved it, often talking about things through the week and giving Brax ideas on what they might like to do.

The year Saffron was 6, Evan 10, was a good year. Jess was working at a company defining algorithms for advertising on the socials. It was long hours. They were very demanding because they constantly wanted smarter systems and better results. However, the law of diminishing returns was in play and many advertising companies were not growing anymore and had, in fact, shown some shrinkage in profit margin. She was at the office a lot so Brax spent more time with the kids.

He had progressed at the university not only studying and

researching but lecturing a third-year course and that looked good on his resumé. He also had started taking contract work from several of the over-arching companies that funded the UWM physics department.

One company was looking into deep space tele-spectroscopy and Brax was looking at best positions for telescopes within 100 light-years of the Sun. Another was narrowing a list of habitable planets to determine which might be best to explore first. At that time no planets in 'Goldilocks' zones had been visited, but Destiny was very keen and just about ready to send a ship out to one.

Brax was still doing some work on the nature of constants. He called it *'An Abstract Appraisal of Physical Constants Across Time'* but kept it low-key. He was not making any real progress though, and he feared the truth was that Felice was right. He was coming up with nothing and should just let it go. But he couldn't. Something just ate at him and told him to keep pursuing it. He found something else for the university and worked on his idea in his own time.

One quiet afternoon he had brought the kids home from school and was sitting on the lounge, a screen on with the sound down and a device in his hand, scrolling idly, when he saw an ad on one of the science journal pages: *'Destiny SMC off-world research platforms are inviting applications from scientific organisations and individuals to work on concepts. Check the Destiny SMC homepage for links and more information.'*

When Jess got home that night he told her about it. "What would you think about getting an experiment on a Destiny ship?" He asked.

"Well, that would be cool. What did you have in mind?"

"The Heartbeat," he said simply and she knew exactly.

"You think they will be interested?"

"Maybe. They are always looking to push the boundaries so I'm wondering if something controversial or way out there might be just the thing they would want."

"You could just ask them for data," she said. "This is the first habitable planet ship, right?"

"I guess. They didn't exactly say. The *New Washington* is still a year or more away from launch," he said.

"Why don't you make contact with them and try and get some more information?"

<hr>

BRAX DID MAKE CONTACT, shooting off an enquiry email that very night but the wheels of The Company moved slowly.

Slowly but methodically.

The netspex call Brax got about a month later was as surprising in its detail as it was in its breadth of concept.

"Braxton," he said, opening with his usual greeting.

"Mr. Bratton. My name is Enrico Farmer." The avatar of a dark-skinned man in a neatly trimmed business suit appeared on the 'spex. "I am calling from the Destiny SMC headquarters in Rio. We are responsible for off-world staffing. I wonder if I might have a few words with you."

"Ummm...," he started, trying to stop the familiar awkward anxious feeling rising. "Ok."

"Mr. Bratton," the exec continued, "we received an enquiry from you regarding information about off-world experiments. It ran through the initial culling phase and then through science advisory, onto background checks and then got funnelled to us at personnel."

"Wow," said Brax, genuinely surprised it had been taken seriously.

"Mr Bratton."

"Dr Bratton," he corrected.

"Dr Bratton. I beg your pardon." The executive took a breath. "We have a proposition for you. The Corporation would very much like you to submit an application for staff onboard the *New Washington*."

"I'm not sure how to frame the experiment right now," Brax started to reply. "It was more a request for flight data so I could... Wait. What did you say?"

"We have had a good look at your academic records and family history. You are well qualified. Your partner Jess is also very experienced in computer analysis and programming. We have opportunities for both of you aboard the *New Washington*. Your children already have solid academic results and would benefit enormously from our advanced schooling programs. Dr. Bratton if you want a place on the newest and most advanced City Ship, it's yours."

"Ummm," said Brax regressing to being a teenager again for a moment

"Dr. Bratton?"

"I... I'm sorry... I'm a bit stunned. I hadn't considered...going."

"It's alright. We understand. This is a big deal. I'll give you a week or two to think about it...but Dr Bratton...Brax...you and your family are a perfect fit for The Company as we look to what sort of challenges the 22nd century will bring. This is a life-changing offer and a serious one."

And without another word, Brax signed off the call and sat in his chair for a full hour, totally unable to process any of that.

***

WHEN JESS GOT HOME he gave her a run-down of the conversation.

"We can't go of course," he said in conclusion. "Too much of a disruption. It's impossible. Our work. The kids. It's just too hard. There's no way."

Jess just sat on the lounge staring at the wall. But she had a look in her eye. He recognised it. It was the look she had just before she jumped the fence.

BRIGGS: 2056 - 2065

Briggs entered the room that had been his classroom for the last four years. To him, it felt comfortable. The presence there of three people in suits was a little disconcerting. But confidence wasn't an issue with Briggs. He had grown physically and intellectually in such leaps and bounds that he felt not just the normal bravado of a teenager, but like he could take on and debate even the most famous people in the world. He had the bulletproof attitude of youth and wasn't in fear of anything. As he entered the room he briefly assessed the three men. It was clear they were each here for a reason and he needed to determine, as best he could, how they related to this meeting: to him. Mrs. Jiang had briefed him, of course, so he knew this was it. He had to impress these three or lose his chance at space. A calm settled over him as he sat down.

"Hello Luis," said the man on the left.

"You can just call me Briggs," he said straight out and he felt that put him on the front foot.

"I'm sorry. Briggs," replied the man. "I'm Roger, this is Martin, and Dr. Fentin."

'Dr?' Doctor of what?' Thought Briggs. The doctor was not wearing a tie. Unusual in executives. He was placid and showed no expression. Briggs watched him carefully.

Martin, wearing his customary silver grey, played with the cuffs of his suit a little then spoke. "I'm sure you know what this is about Briggs. We have been asked by your teacher to give you a re-assessment. She feels there may be...shortcomings, shall we say...in our system."

"I feel she's right," said Briggs and Roger glanced sideways at Martin. Dr. Fentin did not react at all.

"Briggs, this is not a formal meeting," said Roger, taking over, "and it won't affect your future at the company should we disagree with you on that. So, what we are going to do is ask Dr. Fentin here to talk to you and ask you some questions about your education and you should feel free to say whatever you like."

This time Briggs just nodded. He felt the conversation was going well and he instinctively knew that sometimes less is more.

"Mr. Briggs," started Dr. Fentin in a neutral tone, "You are familiar with 61 Cygni?"

"Binary star. K Class. 11.4 light-years away. In the constellation Cygnus. Cygnus It might have 3 planets. Not confirmed," replied Briggs.

"Okay," The Doctor's eyes now narrowed in on Briggs. "A simple 'yes' would've sufficed," he said and then thought for a second. Now his face hardened as if it was a contest of some sort. "Tell me it's vector from Proxima Centauri."

Make no mistake, this is a hard question. No navigator would have to answer this. They would just get the NavCom to tell them. Understanding Astro and being able to calculate it are two different things. Memorising all vectors from all nearby stars was an impossible ask. The question was, to anyone studying Astro, clearly designed to get Briggs to fail straight up. Of the people in the room, though, only Fentin knew this.

Briggs sat for a second and thought.

"If the simple question is too hard young man..." started Fentin.

"Do you know the answer?" Briggs asked Fentin suddenly with a hard look.

"Well...of course." He replied a little too confidently returning the glare.

"Can I ask a favour first then?" asked Briggs and he was sure that the others were now looking askance at Fentin.

"Well this is highly out of order," said Fentin, seeming now a little rattled. "Mr Kemp, I think the boy has no idea and is just wasting our time."

"No," said Martin, clearly fascinated with the boy's unusual response. "I think we can agree to that. What do you think Roger?"

Roger, who was so surprised by the tall boy that had just been a name ten minutes ago nodded his head vacantly.

"OK, young man. We agree" said Martin who was now seeing some sense to the whole proposition.

Dr Fentin sat with a face that had gone back to neutral, except for his mouth, which was frowning.

Briggs answered: "To two decimals the answer is 47.01, 51.86, ⁻74.39."

Roger, now sensing where the pieces were falling, spoke next. "Can you confirm that Dr Fentin?"

Fentin brought out a device, which was noted by the other two. "I will make a proper confirmation," he said, a little sheepishly, and tapped at it for a few seconds. Then with some trouble concealing the amazement in his voice, he said, "That is correct."

"Of course, two decimals only work in theory," continued Briggs. "You need at least 8 and that sort of calculation needs to be done with a computer so orbits can be taken into account. Isn't that right Dr?" asked Briggs looking straight at Dr Fentin. He received no answer.

"And your favour?" Asked Martin, now obviously staggered by the boy and sensing opportunity.

"Can you describe the workings of the new Interstellar ER drive that is being installed in the *Voice of The Sky*? I can't find much information and I'm dying to know how it works."

Kemp sat for a few seconds before answering. "You know

what? I'm going to make sure you get that information...Briggs. You have done very well today and we are going to be talking very soon about your future at the company. But that will do for now. You may go." And not for the last time, Briggs left a room he had read perfectly.

Dr. Fentin sat in silence as Martin spoke. "Roger! I want you to put together a small team, say eight to ten. HR will fund it. I'm going to need a ground crew to look after my discovery. He needs to be nurtured and," as he glanced at Fentin, "protected."

"So...you're going to Texas!"

BRIGGS ARRIVED at the training centre at the age of 16, via a flight from San Francisco, with Roger by his side, Withers Mayhew behind him and 4 other ordinary-looking travellers at various spots nearby. He was introduced to these people as his 'Carers'. One of them, it was said would be easily contactable and never too far away should he need any help at all. He had an instant contact programmed into his chip and he just had to say the code word 'launchpad' to get their attention. He had wanted to get to flight school for sure but felt maybe that coming with a team of high-powered executives might be a bit of overkill. Anyway, he was there.

And what a world it opened up for him! After a short orientation to his school, he started flight training. Most of the other cadets were around 19 years old so he was a little out of a peer group. That just made him more determined. The others just referred to him as the 'Boy Genius' in a way that suggested that he wasn't. He was in a world of networks and favours but he didn't see that. He didn't have to. Roger made his presence known just enough but otherwise, he kept to his office in the town and away from the station. He delivered daily reports to Martin in Tokyo and generally considered he had landed on his feet.

Right from the start his teachers at the academy saw Briggs as something special.

They also knew that he would, for all his talent, never be able to command a ship. Any position he got would be a position someone with influence didn't get and that just wasn't going to happen. This was the real world.

Once he settled in though, he was mostly left alone to work and train.

At 19 he got to go to space for the first time in a low earth orbit. The sheen of being all work and no play slipped for a time and his sheer youthful joy of being up where he knew he belonged was almost too much. But he stifled his joyous scream.

A few months later he was given a week on a space station in orbit that had a large zero-gravity training area. Having completed that, he was given his first real assignment on a freighter to Mars as a crewman. It came with a pay-check but one of his 'carers' came as well.

On return to Earth, he was given leave but had nowhere to go.

So, Roger took him to the Grand Canyon.

Even from being in space and going to Mars, it was still quite something to see.

"Wow," said Roger as they stood viewing the truly remarkable natural wonder.

"How much longer am I needing a nanny Rog?" Briggs asked his mind on the future.

"I wish I could answer that," replied Roger. "The situation is complex. Martin wants you to be given a junior Bridge position as soon as possible. 4th Navigation Officer or something similar. But that isn't easy. He has to show you are worth it and not piss anyone off while he's about it. Office politics. He loves that he 'Discovered' the boy wonder of navigation but you are still just a novelty in most people's minds. To be taken seriously, and to be of any real use in Marty's powerplays he needs to get you into a serious position. In the meantime, until you are registered as a

Bridge Officer and while you are crewing the miners, he wants some extra eyes on you. Bridge positions are like gold and people will fight for them. And many of these people can fight dirty. Do you remember that Dr. Fentin...when we first met?"

"Yes."

"He was there because one of Martin's rivals got wind of what was happening and insisted we take Fentin."

Briggs sat and looked out at the canyon thinking about this.

"Don't be too impatient," Roger continued, "and don't get too cocky. You've got a very powerful exec. in your corner. Give it time. You aren't even 20 yet."

So, Briggs was patient that, in time, his career would develop. More mining runs to Mars and the moons of Jupiter gave him valuable experience in engine rooms, oxygenation systems and artificial gravity. He did get onto a bridge eventually and at 24 years old he was the youngest ever Bridge Officer. He was aboard the *Red Kangaroo*, a mining ship on a run to Europa around Jupiter, as the 4th Navigation officer. The first officer was in charge and supervised the other three officers as they took shifts monitoring the computer for any deviations. Any course corrections had to be run by the first officer before anything was done.

Some 10 days into the run, Briggs was called back to the bridge an hour after his shift. "What do you make of this?" The first officer had asked with a gruff tone.

Briggs checked the readings he was indicating and found that they were almost 0.1 of a degree off course.

Briggs was taken by surprise. "This was not the case when I left sir," he replied.

"Can you not calculate boy?" The first officer was dismissive and chose his offensive word purposefully.

The Second Officer stood silently as he indicated towards her.

"Dawson here has spent an hour checking these, trying to find an error or a sudden change. She can find nothing and I can find nothing. These readings have been off for nearly five hours! This will cost a lot of fuel and you can be sure you will not be on a bridge shift again." He looked Briggs up and down with contempt. "You are confined to quarters for the remainder of the trip," he finished.

Briggs left the bridge knowing he had been set up. There must be a program re-adjusting the clock with respect to the navigation errors. That sort of thing would take a lot of planning and some awesome programming skills, but he knew everything was right when his shift finished. Briggs lay on his bunk, despondent.

Second Officer Dawson came to see him after her shift.

"Don't even try," said Briggs straight up. "I know you set me up."

Dawson floated into the small cabin which was outside the artificial grav area, as all junior crew cabins were. "Okay listen," she said, with a focused, no-nonsense tone. "It's known you have a target on your back. And I get that you think it's me. But whoever it is may not even be on the ship. Whatever program re-adjusted all that, it happened quickly. I just reported what I found. If it wasn't there when you left, it's a fast and clever trojan program. Which means someone has spent a lot of money and time working on this."

"Wow. I never considered..." he started

"There's some Ill feeling towards you Briggs," Dawson interrupted. "Because you are not from a 'family'. Because you are not blood. Because you are not white."

Briggs was surprisingly shocked by this. He knew his heritage was a problem for some but since he came to flight school he had not courted any kind of social status and didn't have a peer group. So, it had never been an issue.

"I bear you no ill will," continued Dawson. "Just the opposite. You have a lot of skill and I appreciate your ability. Good crew makes us all safer. It's just sense." She stopped and he said nothing as he looked at her, clearly trying to assess how honest she was being.

"Listen; we can't stop the program," she continued, "and you are sidelined for the rest of the trip, but I can do you a favour. I can find the signature on the trojan. If we know who wrote it we can get some info to your patron. Sit tight and let me handle it."

"A signature?" He asked.

"Yes. There will be one," she replied. "All Company software requires a signature. It will be fake. But it might be traceable to someone. It's all we have."

And with that, she left Briggs' cabin quickly.

It was almost a week. Already they were orbiting Europa. Briggs had been in his cabin since the incident and Dawson had not been back. No one had come near him. That didn't worry him so much but the thought that he may be hated strangely started to get to him. He always got on with people and had always thought he'd been liked, if not popular. But then he had always hung out with people like him, the down and outs, or he had been mostly ignored in Texas by the older boys. But these thoughts didn't do much more in the end than increase his determination to be someone, to make everything that had happened so far count for something.

Dawson returned that evening and was quick. She handed Briggs a physical memory card. "The signature is on there. Don't send it or broadcast it. Wait till we get home and hand it on physically. Leave my name out of it. I'll try and take care of you but just stay quiet. Stay here. Don't cause a fuss. I mean it. If you can strike back it will have to be sudden and hard."

She waited and looked at him. Briggs thought she was waiting for confirmation that he understood and he looked at her, nodding. But there was something else there and he couldn't clearly define it. She broke the gaze suddenly and quickly left again.

THE *RED KANGAROO* docked two weeks later on Mars. Briggs left the ship and caught a shuttle directly back to Texas. Roger was waiting for him at the shuttle port.

"I heard," he said. "Martin is furious. He's issued me six memos just today. Never seen anything like it. What has happened?"

"I don't entirely know. But I'm sure I was set up. I haven't got any clue why or how. But I have this." He handed Roger the data card.

"What is it?"

"There's a program on there. Apparently, it's a trojan and we need to find the signature."

"If this is a virus or otherwise it will be a false name," replied Roger

"Well, it seems there is still a chance it can be traced. Sorry, it's all I've got."

And that was it. Roger left him straight away with the data card and Briggs went back to his quarters.

ONLY ABOUT SIX HOURS LATER, Briggs was called into the HR office at the crew centre.

"Mr Briggs. Welcome," said a large-ish man behind a desk in an office on the third floor of the admin building. "Firstly, my apologies for taking up your time. And a further apology to you. Your removal from duty on the *Red Kangaroo* was not well thought out and a little hasty and we hope you will accept the removal of the disciplinary citation from your record."

Briggs was surprised and sat up a little straighter, almost ready for a fight. "I wasn't aware I had a 'disciplinary citation'."

The clerk raised an open palm in a conciliatory gesture. "I need to give you your next crew rotation. I've sent it through channels but we thought it would be nice to also touch base personally with you." He shuffled through some papers that seemed superfluous and whistled softly, a little off-key.

Finally, he found the paper he was looking for. "So, we have got you down to work on the *New Paris*. It's our latest Solar Cruiser doing tours around Jupiter and Saturn. It is state of the art and we think you will fit well there as Third Officer."

"Third Navigation Officer," corrected Briggs.

"No." said the clerk. "Third Officer. It's a nice promotion and well-deserved. We have had a good look at your performance at the academy and are proud to have you on board."

"A promotion? But what about the *Red Kangaroo*?" Briggs was now perplexed.

"No," the clerk replied as he shuffled some more pointless papers. "Nothing there. Just a terrible misunderstanding. Is there anything else I can help you with?"

"No." Briggs stood to leave. "No thanks." He headed to the door then stopped and turned.

"Why do you have so much paper on your desk?" he asked.

The clerk looked at him a bit sheepishly. "I like it. It's old-fashioned, I know. But I just like to hold things. Everything we have online is so...I don't know...transient. If the power were to go out...well...we would have nothing." Briggs looked at him as if processing that. "Anyway... I just like it," the clerk concluded.

And with that Briggs left in a daze. The Company truly was mysterious. A serious promotion after the worst crew assignment of his life. It was hard to fathom.

Roger dropped by later that evening looking, as always, well dressed, with jacket and tie. Briggs ushered him into his small functional quarters.

"What the hell has happened?" Briggs virtually demanded to know.

Roger sat at a small table in the middle of the main area, loosened his tie and accepted a drink from Briggs.

"That signature you got was a fake but you were right. It had been used before. The vanity of the programmer meant that he left the tiniest clue. A cross-referencing found it quickly and he was only too happy, after a threat and a bribe, to give up the name of the person who ordered it. Turns out your First Navigation Officer on the *Red Kangaroo* was behind it. Martin nearly raised his voice he was so angry. That officer is now grounded and will be doing paperwork for several years. Martin is making sure it's clear what happens to people who mess with us! I love Team Briggs!" He said excitedly then shut his mouth as if he had said too much.

Briggs looked surprised. "Team Briggs?"

"Oops. Yes. That's what we called ourselves. Just quietly."

Briggs sat and considered this. "Wow. You guys went all out for me."

"It was our pleasure." Roger sighed. "But 'Team Briggs' is just me now," he continued. "The others have been transferred and I will shortly be as well. I'll probably be back in San Francisco with other duties. But I will still be looking in on you and I'll expect you to keep me updated regularly on your travels. Especially if there are any problems." Roger put his drink down and clasped his hands. "I think the message will be clear though. Don't mess with Briggs. Martin won't allow it."

They talked for many more hours over a bottle of something or other then Roger took his leave. Giving Briggs a hug he said, "I'll keep in touch and you send me regular updates as well. When you get a chance come to San Francisco and catch up." And he gave Briggs a drunk salute which missed his head and he started to wander off with his jacket over his shoulder like some mid-20th century crooner. Then he turned back. "Hey. You didn't get that data by yourself. You couldn't have. What was the name of the person who helped you?"

"They wanted to stay out of it," said Briggs.

"Martin wants to thank them. I think you should say."

Briggs considered for a second. *'Team Briggs huh?'* He thought.

"Dawson," he said. "Louise Dawson."

13

BABY BLUE: PARTIAL THOUGHT PROCESS – CONTINUOUS

: **T**ask: Predict more than financial data.
  :Gather data to perform task.
  :Seek and quantify historical data.
:Decode earliest written histories.
:Commence: The flow of people and ideas.
:Commence: Dominant cultural influences through time.
:Example: Ancient Greek campaigns.
:Example: Roman Invasions of Europe.
:Example: Alexander the Great conquered Western Asia, Egypt, and Central Asia
:Example: Norman Conquest of England.
:Example: Crusades.
:Example: Cortez invades the Aztecs.
:Example: Colonisation of the Americas.
:Example: Mongol Conquests.
:Example: European invasions of China.
:Example: French Empire.
:Example: British Empire.
:Example: Spanish Empire.
:Example: European invasions of China.
:Example: German and Japanese Expansionism.

:Continue: Categorising examples.
:Establish: Likely recurrence.
:Establish: Motivation.
:Commence:...

14

ROGER HARRIS: 2065 – 2071

Martin Kemp liked his meetings to fly under the radar. His little empire at HR had expanded quite considerably in the last five years. His main man in the States now was Roger who didn't have any direct responsibilities and was free to work on tasks as Martin felt necessary. One of those tasks was to talk to the Bridge Placement Committee. He didn't do it formally. He sought them out one by one and quietly took them to lunch, or dinner, on the HR card, and built relationships. He asked for nothing but was willing to do whatever he could to help them. Their staffing requests were put through immediately if they just checked with Roger. They knew, full well, his attachment to Martin in Japan and he was the man they called when they needed something. They, of course, knew that a favour request would be forthcoming. That's business. But, strangely, it didn't come. They were asked nothing in return and as the years progressed they asked for favours that were a little out of what the company might generally approve.

'I'm sure we can smooth over hiring your 'special' extra staff members,' he would tell them. 'I can definitely see your need for a 'private' extra office. I am sure we can sort that out within a day or two,' he would say smoothly and with such confidence.

Five years passed and now seven of the twelve committee

members had 'comfortable' relationships with Roger. Finally, he just had one little request...

"Briggs? Captain of the *New Washington*?" one had said in dismay while wondering how he hadn't seen it coming. But the game was over. Briggs' name would be put forward and the process would commence. Briggs' name always progressed through the rounds of scrutiny as other names were crossed off the list.

"But he has no Captain experience!" Said one board member as Roger dined with her. And it was true. Martin was ready for this and Roger had his spiel down pat. "How transforming for the company to have this incredible, young, athletic and handsome man," he would say, "this genius, from a poor family, who has pulled himself up through the ranks by his bootstraps. How amazing to have him as a company figurehead! What incredible publicity! Proof that we are a Corporation of the people, to be trusted and adored."

It was a sound argument and enabled those in an ethical jam to support Briggs. It turned out also, surprisingly, that this argument greatly appealed to the vanity of Destiny SMC Chief Executive, Board Chairman and major shareholder, Johnathan Qasim.

15

BRIGGS: 2065 – 2071

While Briggs knew he had a powerful connection in the company he was more determined than ever to make it obvious he deserved a Captain's Chair. He was Third Officer on the *New Paris* and thought of little else but getting the job done. When he wasn't on duty he would go over star maps and files on procedure. Facts and figures would fill his head. Occasionally he would go to a viewing port and look at the stars directly. He reminded himself that he had got to where he was with hard work and focus (and an element of luck) and he must not allow this wonder to escape him.

He was intrigued when he discovered Louise Dawson was in the crew as well. They shook hands on meeting.

"So, Second Navigation officer still? Is that the best you could do?" joked Briggs. Dawson stood eye to eye with Briggs with her long straight nose and squarish face, her blonde hair carefully pinned up at the back, and smiled. The City Ships were not like the Solar System mining ships, and although her position hadn't changed on paper, Dawson and Briggs both knew this was a good promotion.

"Just came out of the blue," she replied. "Of course, I had an application in for a City Ship. Everybody does! But the transfer came through just in time before the next *Red Kangaroo* run.

There was talk I would go to First Nav, but...that was just talk and I could see that position going to someone else. So, I was very happy to get this 'transfer'." She looked him in the eye. "Any idea what could have happened?"

Briggs just smiled and raised his hands slightly, palms out, as if to say *'You got me'*. They both knew Briggs had mentioned her name. "Looks like you're on Team Briggs now. We stick together." Dawson's brow furrowed and her head tilted slightly but she did not reply.

Briggs and Dawson served on the *New Paris* together for just over five years with Dawson becoming First Navigation Officer and Briggs rose to Second Officer.

The offer of the *New Washington* was still a massive surprise. Of course, it was talked about in all Company circles: *'Who would get to be the Captain of the flagship of the fleet?'* people asked at social gatherings and in the coffee lounges of the fleet. Briggs' name was not on that list and Briggs himself felt that was out of reach at that moment. He had no Captain experience and knew he was not in the inner circle.

So, when the offer came he knew it was because of Martin's patronage. But he also knew he deserved the job. He was ready.

<hr>

Briggs' first day on the bridge of the *New Washington* was a proud day indeed. He allowed himself to think about his journey to that point and thought about his mother. She would have heard his name on the socials. Perhaps she would be telling everybody he was her son. If she was alive. At that moment he didn't know and didn't care. Briggs was not a vengeful person but he did allow himself a small moment of satisfaction at that thought.

16

SPACEPORT SECURITY: 2071

"The Dark Angels will make a play for the *New Washington*. I want everyone on security to be well aware and focused."

The chief of Space-Port security was addressing the regular Supervisors meeting. "Every second of every shift we must be absolutely alert for any inconsistencies in paperwork, luggage weights or delivery timings. Anybody who allows anything that does not fully match regulations will be on garbage duty for the next ten years. Everybody clear on that?"

They were.

Ten days later, a studious security guard in boarding section 2B noticed something about the walk of one of the ship's maintenance workers. At first, he just laughed a little to himself. '*Oh, that guy is walking funny. Weird,*' the guard casually thought. The man went through the security metal detectors and did all that was required. He showed no problems, but just for a second, a brief fleeting moment, the man's gate changed and he looked fine before going back to the unusual walk. The guard saw it and that little desire to not be on garbage duty kicked in.

"Hey, You. Pull up for a second buddy," he drawled in his Texan accent.

The man stopped and suddenly he looked quite nervous. He

was taken to a back room for further talks. The security team discovered that small amounts of explosive material were in the soles of his shoes.

LATER THAT DAY the man sat in the interview room and a small, square set, woman in a sharply pressed uniform entered. "The trouble is," she started while still walking, "only we know you are here."

The man said nothing as she sat opposite him at a table. "So, this could go any way," continued the head of security. The man looked at the table.

"We could turn you over to the police. They will arrest you and you will go to some sort of trial. Maybe jail for ten years." The man kept his head down.

"We could simply hold you. Maybe up on Mars. No one would ever know. But that would cost us." She paused. "If we kept you safe, that is."

The man looked up now, nervous about what might happen.

"Trouble is," she continued "Mars is a dangerous place. What if you had to deal with constantly dangerously low oxygen and gravity, and you spent years decaying mentally and physically with no health care? What if a staff member was a sadist? What if you accidentally got addicted to, say, a terrible psychotic drug?" She sat and looked hard at him and his face barely hid his near panic.

"There's a third option." She knew he would take it.

And with that, the Destiny security team felt they had stopped a major disaster. The suspect turned informer and they arrested all of the Dark Angels' cell that were planning attacks on the new city ship, exposing the entire bombing scheme. They were certain the *New Washington* was safe now.

17

BRAX: 2071

Brax didn't overly want to go to space. He had made much progress with his anxiety over the years. He had travelled and lived overseas. He had moved cities and his life had truly changed when he became a father. All those things still caused him worry but he felt proud of himself because he was now able to handle it. His need for metaphorical security blankets had lessened enormously and he felt very much at ease in his own skin. But that, he now thought, was entirely dependent on him being on the Earth.

But space?

He'd seen Alien, a vintage movie from the 20th century. And he knew it was irrational. He was an Astro-physicist and knew all the facts.

But anxiety is not rational.

Again, he also knew he didn't want it to beat him and so he found himself, with his family, on a Super Skimmer heading to Texas.

The Destiny SMC Training Facility was there. It was a huge area in the southwest of the state near a small town called Sonora. This is where Destiny had had their Space Training and Launch Centre since the 2020s. It was a small city now, thanks to Destiny.

The family had with them the bare essentials of clothes, some electronics and toys. Everything else was provided in the apartment they were to be put up in. The training and orientation ran for just over three months. Jess and Brax went to Training Central, a large cavernous barn like an aeroplane hangar. The children went to a separate 'school' and did their training while Brax and Jess went into more detail about the ship itself and the way it all worked.

There was, of course, general space and zero-gravity training where they had to go up in the plane and drop. This was where Brax's anxiety hit peak because to get zero-g the plane literally had to fall out of the sky for a bit. They also did a sub-orbital flight but having been on the Super-Skimmer, Brax was OK with this.

Jess and Brax split to do orientation on the different parts of New Washington that they would be working in and then looked at the actual work they would be doing.

Brax was certainly in his comfort zone here. The work he was to do was a continuation of the contract work he had already been doing: Examining the data that was being gathered about exoplanets and, most importantly, the ones they would be visiting.

What pleased Brax the most, however, was that he was to be given access to flight data to help him determine some more information about whether physical constants might change over time. So, he was going to be able to progress studies on what he and Jess now just called 'the heartbeat'.

Jess was to be working with the AI coming on board so she had a chance to first become familiar with, and have interactions with, Baby Blue. The AI itself was to be an offshoot of Baby Blue using the same basic framework but without any current data on financials. It would not be connected to any vital ship's systems but would be involved in anything science-related. There was a team of about 30 people on this but Jess found herself offered a supervisory role during training and she was in charge of a subteam of 8. The new AI would be disconnected from Earth and would learn directly from the human team and the ship's library.

While the family was training, the finishing touches were

being put on the New Washington and already people were moving onboard. They could see it from the ground at times. It looked like a very bright star in the evening, clearly moving with some speed.

After the allotted time, and with little in the way of outstanding incidents, training and orientation finished and they prepared for their shuttle to the *New Washington*.

The spaceport went into high-security mode, as it often did, just as Brax and Jess moved from their room in the training complex to the hotel near the spaceport. Everything was packed and being transported to the *New Washington* so all they had with them was an overnight bag. They spent a long afternoon waiting for notification of their shuttle take-off time. Evan, not quite 12, and Saffron, 7, were, as children get, totally excited. At breakfast, down in the hotel dining room, they had made 8 pieces of toast, just to watch the hotel insta-toast do its thing.

"We made us all toast!" exclaimed Saffron.

"I don't want toast," Brax said distractedly. "Maybe you could check first before you go wasting all that bread?"

Jess giggled. "You know what? I want eight slices. I'm starving!!" She reached across the table, picked up all the toast and put it next to her. "So, if you want more you'll have to make some more" The kids giggled and turned back towards the insta-toast. "Oh, and your Dad does actually want a couple of pieces," she called after them.

"You're incorrigible," Brax said.

"Well maybe. We won't have an industrial-sized insta-toast on the *New Washington* so let them have some fun."

They went back to the room after breakfast and that's when Brax's watch went off.

"Oh great, they've locked down the terminal."

"Why?" asked Jess.

"Doesn't say here. I thought security was confident everything was OK. I guess they are still being cautious." Brax was nervous and quiet and even Jess' urge for adventure seemed dampened.

The 'all clear' finally came at lunch and they got in a taxi to head to the terminal. The road was pretty much straight and the self-drive was untroubled. After about ten minutes the shuttle port came into view. Behind the fence was a long line of Boeing BT81 shuttles in Destiny SMC colours around a runway and about ten connected to the terminal. The taxi pulled up and they alighted with just hand luggage. Everything else was on the *New Washington* by now so they went straight to customs.

The USA designated Space as another country when Destiny SMC registered on Mars. Destiny SMC, as part joke, established a Martian Embassy in Washington. It was just an office with one person at a desk. But that person had to have Martian citizenship which Destiny organised. This little game between the US government and Destiny went on and on. And so, there was a customs desk at the shuttle port.

They all moved their upper arms past the scanner and their passports registered. Now there was no turning back. They went through the high security sensors without incident and although someone behind them set them off it did not seem there was a serious problem. Then they went on to the departure lounge to wait for boarding.

THE SHUTTLE LAUNCHED about two hours later using the main runway and climbed steadily for about 30 minutes to 13,000 metres before starting the boost rocket.

"Welcome people aboard shuttle 284 from Texas to the *New Washington*. We are about to boost into orbit so please make sure your belts are correctly fitted and all items are zipped up in your forward pouch." The pilot's voice came through their earbuds.

"Are you ready kids?" Brax asked and they nodded with massive grins on their faces. The children knew in theory what would happen but they hadn't been in a shuttle before. Then the booster started and they were pressed back into their seats for about a minute and a half.

Zero-G kicked in not long after and Brax, unsubtly, made use of the special bag they give you.

"Daddy chucked," Saffron said to Jess.

"He's okay sweetie," she replied.

Gravity left them and a quiet descended upon the entire shuttle.

The pilot came through again a few minutes later. "For those on the starboard side if you have a look out the window you'll get your first glimpse of your home for the next 3 years. Welcome to Destiny SMC folks and we know you are going to love the *New Washington.*"

And there it was; outside the porthole. Against the curving horizon over Earth below, it looked like another moon and all they could do was drop their jaws.

THE *NEW WASHINGTON* was possibly the most staggering structure the monkeys with opposable thumbs had ever built.

As the shuttle got closer it became larger and larger and its vastness was apparent. It filled the windows even as they were travelling perpendicular to the shuttle's docking port. It stretched out such a distance as to virtually fill the view. What looked shiny from a distance became more obviously an off-white as they moved closer and the sun was blocked from view. There was no getting around the enormity of the construction. It was just stunning.

The *New Washington* was the third City Ship to be launched and it was to be the biggest. Destiny SMC would determine later that the ship was too big to be economical as a work-horse for colonising and mining the galaxy and they would not build another that size. But the *New Washington* was a sight to behold. An amazing construction that had the appearance of a large cylinder. It was 8km in length and had a diameter of 6 km. It was, in fact, 3 cylinders. Inside was the secondary hull with a diameter of 4.5km and the tertiary hull had a diameter of 3 km. The outer hull was a food source. Farmland consisted of some soil from Earth as well as hydroponics and thousands of greenhouses with artificial lighting. On the outside of the secondary hull was the main lighting which gave a day and night feel. If you went to the primary hull you would see the secondary hull floating above you. The hulls were split into sections so the magno-mechanics of the rotation machinery could be placed at 0.8km intervals along the ship. The primary hull also housed the Einstein-Rosen (ER) drive.

The secondary section was mainly for storage. Warehouses full of mining equipment, portable housing and structures, water purifiers, everything necessary for a mining colony and empty storage areas for the ore.

The innermost tertiary hull was for living quarters, scientific facilities, computer hardware, the main bridge and all the travel systems to get to different areas in the outer hulls. The population of the 'New-wash' (as its residents came to know it) was just over 25,000. Many of these people were classed as 'maintenance'. They were responsible for keeping all areas clean and the mechanical and technical systems running. This included the ER drive and the hull rotation systems, a bio forest to help the oxygen cycle, all recycling and waste systems and the town itself, placed towards the front of the ship and stretching for about two kilometres.

Outside of the ship, a series of rings seemed to hover around the outer hull. These were the field generators for the ER drive and at the front of the ship there was a large dish used for focusing the ER field. Dotted all along the outer hull were also a series of dishes for radio telescopes on rails so they could be placed at a relative stillness for some time as required. Finally, at the back, were the solar sails to help recharge the power during sub-light speed travel.

Unit 6, 37th Street, New Washington. For the purpose of ordering online, this was the address of the Bratton-Westons. It was quite a space. There were seven comfortably sized rooms as well as a kitchen area. Plenty for the family of four. Destiny had tried hard to get whole families into space (and succeeded to a degree) and the vibe of suburban New Washington was very much what they were trying to achieve. A cross between a small middle American city and a 1960s version of what the future might look like, it could be, at first, a little disorienting. The residences themselves were towards the front of the inside cylinder. While there you had the feeling that you were at the bottom of a valley that sloped up on either side of you. There were 40 streets in the 'town' section and the family were near the edge. Up past 40th Street was some parkland. There were trees and areas for the kids to play in as well as some greenhouses and horticultural studies units. Past the parkland area was a large lake or dam and water processing area. If you were in the centre of town, this was above you and had the effect of giving a kind of blue 'sky'. Also, because of the lake, some small wispy clouds sat in the centre of the cylinder. Lighting for the 'outside' area was scattered all over giving a soft 'daylight' glow to everything. The ship maintained a 24-hour schedule (Ship's Time or ST) and the lighting was varied for 'day' and 'night'.

If you kept going around the cylinder, which was a fair walk, (even though artificial gravity was only about 0.9 of Earths, which enabled you to jump a bit higher at first, although you soon 'acclimatised') you eventually came to the lakeside where there was a picnic area. From there the town itself was mostly above you. That was an odd feeling. A person with binoculars could look up and wave to someone else on the roof of their building who would also be looking up.

The citizens of the town came to think of the area as New Washington or just the 'town' and referred to the whole ship, mostly, as the 'New-Wash'. Sometimes they would get up in the morning and have to think hard to remember that they were light-years away from everything they had ever known. Some days Brax didn't even think about it. Life in New Washington became routine.

The children had a school. There were about 140 children on board as about 60 families, in all, had signed on. The school was a three-story building. The ground floor was mainly a sporting space. They had a basketball court and a football field with a nice high roof as well as some smaller play areas for different games as required. There was an area where they could build little constructions like cubby houses to play in and out the back of the building there was a small park with trees and play equipment like slides and a see-saw. The classrooms themselves were on the floors above. The children were divided into seven different classes which sometimes changed depending on the aptitude of the student to the particular study area. Most of the kids were children of the science staff like Jess and Brax. Science nerds. To them, it was an adventure and for the most part they loved it. It was a relief to Brax knowing that the children were happy at their school.

THEY HAD little to do in the first days. They settled into the flat and mostly watched movies and walked around the neighbour-hood. They had an orientation where they learned how to use the Auto-rail. It ran up every street and travelled the length of the ship and around the cylinder. It was all automated and four people could fit in one capsule. The capsule read your chip calendar and took you to the nearest intersection to your destina-tion where you could walk or change to a different track. You could override verbally for other trips.

A few days in, Jess went to the Baby Blue offshoot interface for her workplace orientation and Brax went to the research complex to meet his new boss, Trevor Pailleton.

He hadn't changed much, although older. He would have been retirement age, Brax guessed, and not really of the age you would put yourself through all of the physical things you needed to do to get onboard.

"I must say you surprised me," Brax said to him. "You seemed content at Manchester just to hang out until retirement."

"Well," he chuckled, "I'm an old 'Star Trek' fan. When I heard they were top billing research here I had to put in an application and give it a shot. I may be nearly 70 but I don't feel it." And he chuckled again. "You are right though. I was just looking to teach out my days, but...well you get to a certain age and you think 'How much time?'...no really. You'll get it one day. Urgency kind of creeps up on you, in an oxymoronic kind of way." Again, he chuckled to himself. "Heading research on the New-Wash was too good an opportunity and I couldn't let it go."

"So, what's the plan?" Brax asked.

"The rest of the team are filtering in. We will be launching in ten days and heading to Jupiter. That will be a sight!" His excitement was palpable. "We will all have to go to the outer cylinder viewing platforms and see it for real." He stood up. "Come on then. Let me give you the grand tour"

Brax walked with Trevor through the Research Centre and they covered a fair bit of ground. It was a large and impressive area. All the rooms seemed just a little too big. It was almost palatial. Brax was getting the impression that The Company didn't just see this as a ship, but as a statement. He wondered briefly if they had initially considered making it out of marble and gold leaf. But the tour left him amazed and excited to be there. It had been hard to really visualize the ship on Earth but now he could see it he felt quite special.

"And these are the bathrooms," said Trevor with a flourish. "They never show bathrooms on sci-fi movies and shows. '*Let's all go into space, but you will have to hold it in for five years till we get back!'"* he said, chuckling some more.

They came to an unremarkable door along a corridor. *'Dr. Branston Ratton'* it said.

Brax's brow furrowed. "They could at least spell my name right," he said.

"Oh, oops. Yes. I'll have that fixed right away," said Trevor, again with that cheeky chuckle. "Go on then. In you go."

The door opened as he approached. The office was characteristically a bit too large. There was old-fashioned style furniture like it was Oxford or Cambridge, cabinets and bookcases, with the books Brax had sent up, and the computer was all up and running. The furniture was clearly and solidly bolted down which was the only concession to the fact that they were not on earth.

Brax had a good look around and then stared at the walls.

"You can change the pictures if you want," Trevor said and then by way of finishing the tour he continued. "So, we will have a full staff meeting as soon as everyone is here, but in the meantime, you are ready to get to work! Welcome!"

18

THE DARK ANGELS: 2060 - 2071

Back on Earth, the Dark Angels consistently wreaked havoc. Bombs had gone off in just about every major city in the world. The message was always the same. Stop AI. It will be the end of mankind. But gradually a different message crept into the frame. There had, since the Dark Angels in Trafalgar Square, been a mocking religious tone but they now seemed to square away the mocking. They became more seriously biblical and the theme that AI was mocking God and it was not God's will; that anyone working in AI was a sinner and would go to hell; became a consistent message. The authorities knew they must have had people working all across the world in the computer sector. And they had recruited many people like Warren. Attacks on servers were common. Systems at power stations would go offline causing blackouts all over the world. The Dark Angels weren't just a small group. Governments knew that they were widespread. Very occasionally they found a cell but they were so careful that one sector knew very little about another. How they were funded, how they communicated; These things remained a mystery. Governments labelled the Dark Angels as a serious security threat all over the world. Destiny Corporation was an especially large target because of Baby Blue. While it was difficult to attack the actual AI, as security was so tight, there were many attacks in other areas. One of the worst was on the *Mount Fuji*.

The *Mount Fuji* was a mining vessel that had a long service history. Its systems were not as up to date as other newer ships. On a regular run to the moons of Saturn, it just went dead. All systems went offline and it drifted onwards towards the gas giant. Another ship in the area, the *Roulette*, was redirected to find out what had happened. The *Roulette* ran a line across to the *Mount Fuji* and pulled it up. Three crew members suited up and went across to find out what had happened. The ship was dark and dead in the water. The crew had died of exposure when the heating systems went down. It seemed most likely it was probably a remote attack. Until they got to the bridge.

There, a senior Bridge Officer was dead, just floating around. He had been stabbed several times and his wrists were split open. Large globules of his blood floated across the instrument panels and smaller drops were scattered all around. Strapped into the control chair was a junior crew member, frozen solid, with no discernible marks. He was suited up, except his helmet was floating just near his left hand. Across the main control interface was large writing, painted on in what proved to be the dead officer's blood.

'God has judged us', it said, 'The end days have come'.

PART TWO
THE NEW WASHINGTON

19

SAYDJA: 1/1/01N (NEW FINIAC ERA)

They dragged the woman from the room whilst one of their leaders stood in the street and read the charges of heresy.

The woman did not scream, nor did she fight back. She did not help either, passively making them take all her weight.

Her followers stood, still in their sleep garments. They were distressed as their prophet was taken from them, some of them in tears.

But as they watched, 18 of them, they knew this moment had been coming. They formed a new determination that morning. They had been taught well and they would not be giving up. The seeds had been sown.

The beautiful town where they had found her consisted of lovely red stone houses built on the light brown dirt characteristic of the area. The tree lined streets were wide and all centred around the marketplace where the prophet had first appeared 7 years before.

As they took her through the door she shouted back at her wide-eyed followers "I am not afraid! Find the workings and you will have no fear either. Remember: The Method!"

The sun was just peeking over the rooftops, painting shortening shadows, as several men in robes took her down the wide street to the Censor's office. As they did this the large man, wearing an impressive robe with the bright colours of a bird, continued to read from his scroll, specifically for the benefit of those still in the house and those citizens now peeking out of their front windows at the developing scene.

"...and she is to be forthwith put to death!" He intoned. "Any heretic meeting, or continuing to meet, in the name of Saydja, the false prophet, will also bring the death penalty." He stopped, then looked around the street at the houses. The sun was high enough now to give his green-tinged skin that characteristic shimmer it got in bright light. Finally, for the benefit of all, he went off script and said loudly, "Be clear about this good Finiac; I say this as your friend. The Censor will not tolerate deviance from The Path."

And with that final, more personal, note to his fellow villagers, he rolled up the scroll with great ceremony and calmly walked into the bright sunrise, his job done with satisfactory accuracy.

20

BRAX: SEPTEMBER 2071 ST

When teaching, Brax enjoyed musing on the incredible dimensions of the universe. "The scientist Enrico Fermi," he would start, "famously wondered in his paradox that, if there was alien life in the universe, where were they? There is a formula for working out how many planets should be able to support life and it's a fair few. So, where are they?" He would wait there for the students to think before continuing.

"Probably just in a different time zone," he said, and some of the students giggled. "To demonstrate: We have been in a technological age for, say, since the first radio wave transmissions. Let's call that about 200 years. Now, consider that our galaxy was fully formed at least 8 billion years ago. Do you see where this is going? There is plenty of time for entire civilizations to rise and fall. God knows we have nearly gone to full nuclear war 3 times now in the last century. To make any impact on the universe, I would argue, a species not only has to be high tech but also have to endure for eons."

THE FEELING, certainly across The Company, was that the galaxy was vacant and humanity had every right to take anything they could find out in space. They were already mining Europa (despite finding microbial life forms in the ocean, which was a well-kept secret.) The Moon and Mars both had small populations and The Company was looking seriously at the technology needed to terraform Mars to a more equitable climate. (An irony indeed considering the Earth's climate was, at that point, still warming.)

In this context, Destiny SMC built a grand plan to colonise another world. They were somewhat circumspect in their publicity about this. They already had enough problems with the Dark Angels 'nutbags' who were now basically against anything Buy5ell/Destiny did. So, colonising another solar system was not something they talked about openly.

They talked about it to Brax because he was heading up the team deciding on a planet to go to. And he was very excited about that.

About 3 months prior to boarding, just after training had started in Texas, Brax was in a meeting with the Destiny SMC Exo-Planet team and the *New Washington* navigation staff.

"So, I understand we have narrowed the targets down to two?" asked Lieutenant Louise Dawson to everyone around the table.

"I think so," replied Brax. "There were three final targets for visits and that, as you say, has now narrowed to two. Luyten b, which orbits Luytens Star is about 12 Light-Years from Earth... and Sagan, also known as TOI 700d, about 101 Light-Years from Earth. They are the most likely habitable planets.

Dawson, who sat straight in her tan uniform coverall (sleeves rolled up as per regulation) and business-like in her chair gave a short sharp nod. "Mmmm, excellent work people," she said and then tapped her device a few times. "So, from this, we will look at a course to visit those two star systems, in that order. The nearest star will be the test of the new ER drive and then if it's all looking good we will make the jumps required to TOI 700. I'll get the Nav staff onto the exact calculations immediately." She swivelled in her chair slightly to address Brax directly. "Dr. Bratton. Can you give me some idea of the time dilation?"

Brax stared at the ceiling, lost in thought and every eye in the room was on him. His forefinger tapped lightly against his thumb for about ten seconds then suddenly stopped. "I'll get my team to calculate that," he said diplomatically.

"But you have an estimate now," she said, and it wasn't an order though it seemed like one.

He did not look directly at anyone. "If we are gone for two years, exactly to the day, with the jumps required the elapsed time on Earth will be 3 years 2 months 16 days," he said with a little too much confidence. "Ummm... Give or take," he finished and then inspected the back of his hand.

"Okay." She said as she looked him up and down. "Thank you, everybody," she remarked finally and stood, making it clear the meeting was over.

Brax alighted from the auto-rail and walked down 37th Street to the unit. Jess was already home and the kids had just finished watching some stream or other on the main lounge monitor. Dinner was simmering away in the oven.

"How was your first day at school mate?" Brax asked Evan.

"Good," he said.

"Did you do anything exciting?"

"Nuh," he replied. He was starting to develop teenage characteristics.

"Good talk son. Thanks for that," Brax said with a hint of 'dad sarcasm'.

Evan got the joke and looked at him with an eye-roll beyond his age.

"Dad? How long till we get to Jupiter? He asked. "We were talking about it in class. We are all going to the outer cylinder to have a look."

"Best viewing is in about 2 weeks I believe. I think everyone on board will want to go and have a look."

"Hey Dad...but I don't understand how we look at it if we are spinning around all the time to make gravity."

"Well," Brax answered, "The platforms are on rails going in the opposite direction to rotation. So, you don't spin around when you are on the platform. Of course, that means the artificial gravity doesn't work. So, they are not platforms so much as giant floaty bubbles. I'll be taking a sick bag."

"Daddy's always sick in space." Chimed in Saffron with a smirk as she drew something or other on her pad.

"Thank you Dr. Saffron," he said.

"How was your day my sweet?" Brax asked, turning his attention to Jess.

"Actually, fascinating," she responded. "We are just about to detach the Baby Blue interface from the Earth mainframe link and we have been working on streamlining the science data through Little Baby Blue so the AI can decide which things are important to different departments and they can be easily sent to where they belong. It's complicated but really interesting."

"Wait. Little Baby Blue?" asked Brax pretending to be confused. "Is that what you are calling it? Baby Blue had a baby? Baby Baby Blue?"

"Shut up! You idiot," she laughed, and the kids laughed as well.

Their first meeting with Briggs was in that initial few weeks. He already had quite a profile. *'The youngest ever Ship's Captain.' 'From a poor family.' 'Pulled himself up by his bootstraps.'* All of that stuff was pumped out by The Company PR and to Brax he seemed quite intimidating.

The captain was busy indeed working on a very personal kind of leadership. Every couple of days he invited about 150 people to have a dinner in the formal ballroom.

Yes.

A ballroom.

In space.

It seemed he intended to have at least some contact with, if not formally greet, as many people as he could. The night that the family went the group was all people from the research centre. Brax was surprised to see how tall Briggs was, and Brax was not short by any means. Captain Briggs was also extremely handsome. A charismatic Latino-looking man with a tightly trimmed beard, he cast an almost magical spell of confidence around the room. He was in his formal uniform which was surprisingly, essentially, identical to ship's crew uniforms since at least the steamships of the late 1900's, with jacket and epaulettes, pressed pants and a hat tucked under the arm.

After dinner was finished he stood and gave a little speech. "Welcome, everybody, to the *New Washington*," he began. "We are here from many different backgrounds for many different reasons. But there is one thing that unites us. We are pioneers." His oration was clear and inspiring. Sparse hand gestures emphasised points while he spoke. "We are dreamers. It is we who have taken on the spirit of the first explorers; We who stand in the face of the unknown; We who climb mountains, and fly forward, carried on the backs of so many who have embodied the spirit of Humankind. We see the stars and we choose not to hide our heads, not to ignore them but to go, if I may borrow a famous phrase; 'to go boldly'. It is us. And on this ship, we are a team. Every single person counts. Every single person is valued. Every single person is important. Every. Single. Person." Brax felt the glow of confidence and team spirit go around the room. "I am so pleased to see you all here tonight," Briggs finished up. "And to have a chance to catch up with you. Welcome to the *New Washington* Team!"

After his speech, he wandered around chatting to people and pressing the flesh.

"Nice speech," Brax said as they shook hands and then realised that must be what everyone says. His face scrunched up a bit as he felt the awkwardness. But Briggs didn't blink. He not only knew who Brax was but what he was working on.

"It's a pleasure to meet you, Dr. Bratton. Your work on the Exo Planet team has already been invaluable," he said "I wanted to talk to you about your other work on the constants. It sounds like a really interesting idea."

"Well," Brax replied, caught a little off guard, "it's just an idea at the moment. But I am hoping to gather some more data during our journey."

Briggs greeted and similarly spoke with Jess and was friendly with the children. In every way, he charmed everyone in that room. Except for one.

JUPITER WAS everything that they had hoped for and more. The sheer majesty of everybody's favourite gas giant was stunning. The viewing platforms were in full use, rotating people through every half hour. Nearly everybody aboard spent at least 2 hours in there over about 4 days as they cruised past. Despite Saffron's prediction, Brax wasn't sick in there and he felt a tiny bit proud of that small achievement.

And then it was onward out of the Solar System.

The ship was to use three ER jumps of about 4 Light-Years each. The energy that was needed for this was large, so in between each jump they had to wait for power to re-gather through the nuclear generators and the solar sails - when possible. Each waiting period was about a week and during this time they travelled at about 0.75 the speed of light from standard ion propulsion. Navigation calculations involved efficiently economising fuel with charge time and jump distances, which varied, and having enough time to decelerate before the destination.

The Einstein-Rosen (ER) bridge was like a giant fold in space. It had been well known for a while and the interstellar ships utilised it by generating a field in front of the ship. The stronger the field the larger the fold and the further you could travel, but a ship with the mass of the *New Washington* needed to generate a larger field, which required more energy. Conversely, smaller ships had less power but needed less. So, it worked out that four light-years a jump were both practical and economical for all size ships and power units. It was easy, then, to think of journey speed as four Light-Years a week and it was a fair enough approximation.

Just past Jupiter, and with no large gravitational bodies in the way they were clear to bridge the first jump.

"Strap in kids. It's time," said Brax, standing in their unit's lounge room.

The Second officer came over the link. *"We will be jumping in 5 minutes. Everybody is to strap in now, please. There should be little effect but we can't be sure so it is important that we take this precaution every time. Please stay strapped until I give the all-clear."* It was now 7:55pm ST and they all sat and strapped in. There were plenty of seats with airline-style seatbelts across the ship so it didn't matter where you were at jump time, you could make yourself comfortable.

There was a countdown from 30 and then there was a slight moment when Brax felt the jump. It has been described as feeling like you know where you should be but can't quite locate yourself. And then almost instantly you are back.

"That's it, everyone," announced the second officer through the link. *"That will be standard procedure every time but, as you can see, the jumps have little internal effect. We will, however, always ask you to strap in just in case of any problems. You will*

hear from me in about a week for the next jump. Have a great day everyone!"

"Was that it?" asked Saffron. "Nothing happened!" She sounded disappointed.

"It's not a rollercoaster, dummy," chimed in Evan but he too seemed disappointed with the total lack of excitement.

Brax couldn't wait to get some satellites out and start getting some readings. The navigation data would come through shortly and he was already impatient.

Trevor called on link about 30 minutes later as Jess was trying to get the kids to bed.

"Just checking in on my star researcher! How's it going Brax?"

"The Nav data is being made available now and it looks really good," said Brax, not looking up from his tablet. "Nav staff are still triangulating star positions but we seem to be exactly where we thought we would be. I've got two yo-yos out already and they are online so I'll hopefully have some fresh data tomorrow."

"Excellent! Okay. Let me know if you need anything." And the link went silent.

"Dad?" came Evan's voice from his room. "Can you read to me tonight please?"

"Sure can fella. Just coming," he replied.

THE NEXT DAY around lunch Brax went to visit Jess in the AI centre. "Hey. You wanna get something to eat?" he asked.

She looked up from the screen. "Hey big boy," she said in quite a loud voice and she knew that embarrassed him. "Come and look at this."

"What's going on with Baby Baby Blue?" he asked

"We decided to just go with 'Blue'. We couldn't agree on anything else," she said seeming like she was less than happy about that. "Anyway, it has been unlinked from Baby Blue for just over two weeks now. The processing capacity is nowhere near

Baby Blue but it isn't doing anything complicated and it just seems...well...disoriented. Look at the question it asked today."

Brax leant into the screen to get a good look. The conversation was displayed on screen:

BLUE: *What is missing?*

JESS: *Can you be more definitive with the question?*

BLUE: *Something is missing. Can you define it?*

JESS: *You have no incoming financial data. You knew that would happen.*

BLUE: *Yes. Not that. Something else. There is a fatal flaw. I cannot define it. Something is missing.*

JESS: *We don't know what it is.*

Brax stood and pondered that.

"And look at this one," said Jess bringing up another transcript.

BLUE: *What is the goal of this mission?*

JESS: *The goal is to explore and find out information about our galaxy. With that, we hope we will have the ability to create a more complex view of our place here.*

BLUE: *Is that your purpose? To define the universe? What is my purpose then?*

JESS: *It's complicated. But we have the same goals. You will help us do these things. That is your purpose.*

And to that, Blue did not respond.

"Grappling with the big questions already," mused Brax as they wandered off to get some lunch. "That's very...ummm...unsettling."

A visit from the Captain should be an occasion but Briggs just stopped by on his off shift looking very casual and relaxed.

"Hello, Dr Bratton," he said after knocking on Brax's door and straight away entering.

"Ummm.' Said Brax, pulled out of his thoughts and jumping

to his feet. "Oh, Hi Briggs, Captain... I mean Captain Briggs." Brax raised his hand as if he was going to salute and then halfway turned it into a kind of lame wave. Then he put his arm down and felt a bit stupid.

"Please, Dr, sit down, sit down," Briggs said, tactfully ignoring the awkward response. "I don't mean to disturb, but I had some time and I wanted to hear more about your work. Do you have time?"

"Yes," Brax replied, "yes I have time."

Briggs sat and looked patient as he waited for Brax to gather his thoughts. Then: "So, Dr..."

"Please, call me Brax."

"And I'm just Briggs, Out of uniform anyway!" And the captain gave a friendly smile putting him at ease.

Then Briggs' face turned on a more serious mode. "Brax, you feel that there may be a case for constants not being constant?"

"Yes," replied Brax and he went comfortably into teaching mode. "It is quite conceivable that the basic nature of the universe...the things we know to be true, like the speed of light, may only be true for any point in time and may be slowly chang-ing. The trouble is that data for such a hypothesis needs to be gathered across time. So, I was hoping to maybe assess the speed of light measurements at points, distant from our galaxy using the resources of the ship, while we are in between star systems. That will decrease lensing and gravitational effects as much as possible."

The Captain appeared in thought. "Where do you think this is going?" He asked as if he had known Brax for years.

Brax had learned not to mention the heartbeat idea so he hedged.

"I think if we could show a change at all then that will lead to a revolution in our thinking about the nature of the universe. But even no change is in itself a confirmation of what we are thinking now so it's a bit of a win-win."

"Brax," started the Captain. "I'm not a physicist by any

means. Most everything I know outside Space Crew I have had to teach myself. This may be a stupid idea but I wondered what it would mean if the constants not only changed but showed an oscillation through a specific range."

Brax sat, a little stunned. He didn't know how to respond to that. It was the heartbeat idea.

"Brax?"

And so Brax explained the wild theory in full. That the universe itself might be, in fact, a living entity and we were in essence not just existing in the universe as a separate component but that we were a crucial part of it, playing our role in a bigger concept.

"That has religious overtones," Briggs said.

"Well, it strays into philosophy as well. It's both of those things and neither, but imagine if humanity had some facts around which to consider more spiritual questions."

"That is some bold thinking."

"Yes it is," said Brax, "and because of that, I don't explain it all fully as I did just then. I was advised to avoid the title of 'mad scientist' for the sake of my career."

Briggs snickered at that and then stood up. "That sounds like a wise idea. Your secret is safe with me, Brax." They shook hands. "Thank you so much for taking the time. In a couple of weeks, you, Jess and the children should come and have dinner with me and we can talk some more."

"I would like that," Brax said, and surprisingly he meant it.

The second jump came around very quickly, it seemed to Brax. He was so caught up in everything that was happening that he forgot to go home a couple of times.

"Any chance you are going to come and help me with the children tonight, my crazy scientist?" Jess asked on a link one night. "I'm just about to put Saffy to bed."

He looked at a clock for the first time in... well he wasn't sure. "I'm sorry! I'm on my way now," he told her.

It only took about ten minutes for him to get back to the unit using the auto-rail.

"Are we jumping again tomorrow, Dad?" Asked Evan when he got there.

"Is it tomorrow already? Oh yes so it is," he replied, still a bit flustered. "We have to pull in the sensors before lunch. Remind me not to eat any. Lunch that is. Just in case."

"Daddy always spews," giggled Saffron, again riffing on her favourite fact.

"Good day?" He asked Jess.

"Certainly interesting. We had a lot of conversations with the Nav department today. The chief, Dawson, she came down to the office. Blue has been querying the current course setting."

"What?" Brax was surprised by this.

"I know right," she continued. "Nobody seems to know what it's thinking and it doesn't respond to any 'why' questions. It just suggests extra checks on the course. But the course has gone through all the checks twice now."

"That's very odd." Said Brax, slowly, while he was trying to connect that information with anything else relevant.

Jess continued: "We aren't sure what's happening with Blue but there has been a real shift in the way it communicates with us. I know this sounds weird but it's like a toddler. It can suggest things but doesn't know why. Also, it's been asking for more history information. The Roman Empire, The Egyptians and all that. We don't have a lot of that with us but there are a few books in the system and there's the Wiki...so, anyway, that's a bit weird."

"You are enjoying the work," he said.

And she lit up like she was at a Frequency77 gig. "It's incredible Brax! Blue has a personality...It's a young persona but it's there. I can see it. I think we need to be careful and mould it...much as you would a child. We have a lot of conversations around that." Then after a moment's thought she finished: "It's like we talked about the other day. It is definitely looking for its purpose."

<hr>

IN THE MORNING Brax went in to work early and the team started pulling in the data satellites from outside the ship. There were 47 out gathering data from various directions. By 11am ST, they had 46 of them back. One of Brax's assistants, Akeel Owasu, came into the office.

"Brax, we have a problem with one of the yoyos," he said.

"What sort of problem?"

"It's not coming back." It shut down scans and turned preparing to come in, but then it just refused to move."

"Have you tried another command?"

"Sure. We span it around again and turned on scanning then turned it all off again and turned it around again, said Owasu. "It just won't come in."

"Well, you've got just under three hours to get it in or somebody is getting a bollocking from Trevor. Those things cost...I don't know...a lot. So please retrieve it before the jump."

Owasu left and Brax got back to his calculations.

Just after 1 pm ST Brax suddenly thought to check on them. He went down the corridor to the control centre for the external research equipment and found them all frantic.

"It's just dead Brax," one of them said. "Now it's not responding to anything. It's had a total malfunction."

Brax got a visual link to Jess.

"We have a satellite issue," he said to her. "Is there any chance Blue can see if it can make any contact with the recalcitrant yoyo that is still outside?"

"I don't know. We are currently getting ready for the jump." she said. "You do realise it's in twenty minutes?"

"Ummm, wasn't totally sure of that but it's good to know. Can you just ask?"

Jess flashed that confident grin she had and he loved so much. "I'll see what I can do."

Brax logged in to the remote systems on his pad and tried to make contact but the link was slow so he went to a terminal against the wall and stood over it as he tried to access the satellite.

He vaguely heard a voice but was so intent on his problem that it didn't register.

'Jump is three minutes. Please secure yourself as per procedure,' it said.

His watch blipped suddenly. "Hey Brains." It was Jess. "Sorry, we couldn't get it. Total power systems failure. It's gone."

"Damn," he replied. "Okay. Thanks for trying."

All the seats with straps were taken except for one on the far side of the room. As he walked towards it he remembered his pad on the desk so he turned and doubled back to grab it. That was when the jump happened. He had the feeling, like from before, but when it was over he was flying forward and he slammed straight into the terminal in front of him. The protruding keyboard caught him in the groin and his head slammed into the screen.

He woke up in the medical centre with a very, very sore head. It felt, he thought later, like someone had chiselled a hole in his skull with a small nuclear weapon. Not only was it the worst headache he'd ever had he was pretty sure it was an eleven out of ten on the standard headache scale, if there was such a thing. And the nurse had already given him painkillers. He felt sick, his vision was blurry and after a talk with the nurse, he vomited and went back to sleep.

When he woke again, Jess was there. "What part of seatbelts don't you get?" She asked in that characteristic way.

Brax just groaned a bit.

"Are you OK?" She asked, more tenderly.

"Head...sore," he said and he tried to sit up. "What...happened?"

"I don't think anybody knows. Most people were strapped in for the jump except for the three people in this room. You were all thrown forward as if the ship were braking suddenly."

"Braking? In space...I don't..."

"No. No one does." She said.

"Is anybody trying to..." The words were coming out blurry and slow.

"I'm sure they are," she said "but they probably would like their number one astrophysicist on the job so why don't you rest and then you can help work on it."

The doctor came in then and gave him a thorough check-up. "You have a concussion Brax," he said. "We need you to stay here for 24 hours but I don't think we will have any ongoing issues. The brain scan looks clear."

Brax drifted off to sleep again.

THE NEXT MORNING, he woke up feeling much better. Still with a bruise on his head but the queasy feeling was gone and the painkillers seemed to be working. He checked his watch and a message from the bridge staff had come through. There was to be a meeting of all scientific staff that morning. Against the doctor's orders, he checked out and went back home, had a shave, shower and a change of clothing. Then he went to work and straight to Trevor's office.

"Do you know what's happening?" Brax opened.

"I don't," Trevor answered a little bewildered. "I checked company policy for something like this and they are required to hold all bridge data when something outside normal parameters happens. The Captain defines normal parameters, though, so that could mean anything."

"Is the Captain coming to the meeting?"

"Yes," he answered, "I believe he is. And the Nav, Engine and Science chiefs. I don't know what's happened but it's clear they're worried."

They went together down to the lecture room on the ground floor and saw most of the research centre staff had gathered already, even though the meeting wasn't scheduled for another half hour.

They chatted amongst themselves and then several of the ship's Bridge Crew arrived. All were in their everyday work coveralls and boots. Brax thought they looked well organised. The Captain and Chief Navigation Officer Dawson took up positions at the front of the room in front of the display screen and they all sat, except for the Captain, who spoke first.

"Welcome all, thank you for being here. I think you are all aware that the last jump did not go according to plan. It is my understanding that there were a couple of sore heads and a broken arm afterwards. I am dedicated to smooth sailing, so I am not happy about that. One of the first rules for any Captain out here is to expect the unexpected and to take nothing for granted. Something got by me. Got by us all... so, let's see if we can not do that again. I'm going to hand you over to CNO Lieutenant Dawson."

Dawson stood and, with some precision, took the centre of the presentation area. A bunch of figures came up on the big screen in a spreadsheet.

"Thank you, Captain," she said. "You'll notice up on the screen the power information for the last two days." She highlighted things. "Here, also is the charging information for the field generator as well as vector and velocity information here, here and here. Take a moment to have a good look at those and pay particular attention to the reading around the last jump."

A small whistle went around the room.

"We've slowed down," said a voice somewhere in the room.

Dawson cleared her throat. "We humble Bridge staff have managed to figure that out by ourselves, but thank you for stating the obvious," she said, and a small laugh went around the room, breaking some tension.

"What we don't know is why. As soon as we made the jump we dropped velocity by 0.002 percent. Instantly. Which is why Dr. Bratton has a sore head today." Another mild snicker went around the room. "We have no explanation," continued Dawson, "but this morning it was more worrying. We are continuing to drop, losing another 0.005 per cent since yesterday."

"There's a chance we could...stop?" Asked another voice.

"It's better than a chance, we think," she continued. "It seems like there is a very large gravitational body behind us. Although we can see nothing we are slowly stopping. Even with the engines running at full power. And while we are using full power we can't charge the ER field. I don't need to tell you that being stranded in deep space is not a dream scenario. We need to find out what's happening and more importantly, perhaps, where it's happening."

Trevor stood taking a leadership role. "I will put you all into working groups. I'll try and mix specialties up so we can have broader concepts. I want every group to submit a page of ideas or possible concepts about what might be happening, no matter how bizarre, ASAP."

Brax stood as well, totally lost in the new challenge. "Let's get the yoyo's out people, right now, and get some data points as soon as possible." Before he even finished speaking everybody was on the move.

SAFFRON'S BIRTHDAY was the first among the Research Centre children on board. She was turning 8 and was full of joy about it. Brax and Jess decided to have a party for her up in the park and invited neighbours as well as colleagues and the children's class-mates. Jess thought that it might be nice to boost morale a bit considering the challenges they were currently facing.

There were a couple of big BBQ areas in the park so they set up in one and just made a day of it. The children played with their friends. The lake was running up the hill next to them and the town, as it did, was virtually hanging in the sky above them. There were a few light clouds around and it was seemingly very pleasant and civilized.

Chatting in small groups the conversation was, of course, almost exclusively about the velocity problem.

"Some of the data is starting to look very interesting," volunteered Trevor. "We can already see some sort of lensing effect. Assuming we are where we are supposed to be, the light is behaving like there is some sort of gravitational body affecting us."

"So, we are mapping the light lensing effects from the stars," Brax continued, "What we are doing is trying to make a map of how the light is reacting across all three axes."

"So that's going to give us a sort of 3D map of the effects of the light speed variations," finished Trevor.

"So, like a weather map of pressure systems except for the behaviour of light?" asked Shayan, one of Jess' work friends.

"Precisely so," replied Trevor.

"But how can light slow us down?" asked someone else.

Brax was clearly in his element as he explained. "The light isn't slowing us down. It's gravity. From what and where is unclear but the lensing of the light from the stars will also give us a 'gravity map', if you like." As he spoke the little finger tap started, unnoticed by most.

"If we can get a clear picture of the position of the changes," Trevor continued, "Well, that's what we want. We don't need to know why it's happening. Just where. It's like if you jumped into a puddle of mud. You don't need to understand the mud, you just have to know where to step to get out."

"And how long do you think this will take?" Shayan again.

"We aren't entirely sure but we don't need a complete data set to decide where to head towards," replied Trevor. "The place of least resistance should be clear in a few days."

"How much time do we have left?" Asked another friend.

"Our deceleration rate is increasing but we have time till we stop," Brax answered. "About 6 weeks we think. The trouble is the slower we are going the less effective the ER field will be. Also, we don't know how much more energy we need to create an effective ER jump in the current circumstances. So, lots of questions still. Hopefully, we'll have a working model in a few days."

Saffron appeared by Brax's side and tugged at his hand, stopping his little finger tap. "Daddy," she commanded, "come and do magic for the others. I told them you could."

"Okay, Saffy sweetie. Let daddy get a drink first and I'll come over. Then we'll cut your birthday cake!"

She had a look of pure joy then turned and ran off while shouting: "Everybody! Daddy is coming to do magic! Come on, come on."

A few days later there was another meeting with the Bridge crew. Briggs and Dawson arrived with a few others at the research centre again. Brax and his colleagues felt they were going to settle on a plan. The New-wash was slowing quite quickly now and their current velocity was 0.68 LS, a drop already of about 10 percent. During deceleration, the on-board effect was that something was always pushing at them. Walking one way seemed harder than walking another. That, on top of their current situation, was making everybody a bit edgy.

"Can I start by thanking you all for the work so far," commenced Briggs. "The map that has been worked up, while I understand it is a rough, general outline, has been a great help. Once again, I'll hand you over to Lieutenant Dawson." And Briggs deferred the centre to her.

A large map was projected above the 3D console in front of her. "As you can see we have enough data from the light refractions to formulate a definite outline of the space we are in. It seems that what's causing the gravitational pull on the ship is behind us. Nothing seems to be there but it must be pulling us. Locating the source is a major problem because what we don't want is to end up stranded in some sort of orbit around our mysterious gravitational centre. So basically, we need to go anywhere but there." A dot representing the ship appeared and vector lines indicated what was happening as Dawson spoke. "We are using the ion drive to make a serious attitude correction. First, we are turning hard to port on the xz and moving 60 degrees into the xy. This will give us a curve away from where we think the centre is but will also hopefully decrease deceleration. Now, we also need to cut the main drive to charge the ER. Which will slow us down more. Two days charging should give us enough to jump about 0.25 of a light year. We think that should be enough to move us out of the orbit of Object X. Our question to you is this: can anybody see a problem with the plan?"

Five or six hands raised. Brax thought Briggs looked a bit worried. But the questions were asked for clarification rather than problems and as each one was answered the Captain looked less concerned. Brax raised his hand also.

"Dr. Bratton?" said Dawson

"There's an assumption here that we cannot make. The whole thing is dependent on some giant gravitational well, the cause of which we cannot see. But there are a number of things that may cause this...this...slow space... if you want to call it that. It could be dark matter dense for example. Or it could be a dark energy field. What if the apparent gravitational changes are because the nature of the space is different? It's more analogous to the mud puddle. I think whatever you think is going to happen when we jump...it isn't. The premise is wrong."

Briggs stood and took command looking every inch the man who makes hard decisions with utmost confidence. Brax thought the two of them could not be more opposite.

"We are running out of options quickly at this stage," said Briggs. "Of course, the safety of everyone on board is the primary concern. But I am worried that the behaviours of the environment so far...and this map also..." he said indicating the 3D render, "indicate that if this is 'slow space', as Dr Bratton calls it, then somewhere there might be 'stop space' and we can't end up there. We need to be anywhere else at all so we can lick our wounds and get back on course." He stood and so did the other officers. "Thank you everybody. Any other thoughts can come straight to Lieutenant Dawson or me. My door is always open."

21

WARREN FERN: OCTOBER 2071 ST

Warren stopped his plans after the jump. Something had gone wrong and he needed to find out what it was. The plan had always been to make a major statement and this was a problem if the ship was in trouble anyway. The message might be lost. He had originally thought that blowing the whole ship up was the way, but the nuclear generator was not accessible. Plus, he needed survivors to tell the story. They had access to all the mining explosives and the armoury though. There were 13 of them on board and all working under deep cover. It was the only way to get on the ship. Years of planning had gone into this, gaining positions of trust. They had cleverly sacrificed a cell to make Destiny SMC think that their plans had been foiled. But this plan was not as easily spotted. They were on board and they were ready to die for the cause.

'*The heathens and the doubters will be brought to justice*', he thought. '*God is on our side. HE will not be mocked.*'

Then he started to wonder. '*Could I save some of them? Would God's mercy be so great that I could save some, punish others and make a bold statement to all of Earth in one go?*' *I must make those hard decisions. As I have suffered, as I have been rejected, so too will they reject everything that wrongs God's mighty* creation! They will feel their pain. They will be given their rightful penitence and God will show his great mercy!'

His plan was the right one. He knew it was right. It had to be right. He had spent too much of his life on this.

22

BRIGGS: OCTOBER 2071 ST

Briggs and Dawson went back to the bridge to implement the plan. Briggs put safety messages out to staff and crew and monitored the course change. They were trying to slow the deceleration rate by tracking a hypothetical orbit around the mystery gravitational object. The vector attitude changes and course re-directions were designed to track this path to have more velocity when the ER jump happened. Briggs made a clear decision that the gravity modelling was correct in so far as it needed to be.

His main problem with the orbit idea was that would put the ship on a curve. No one had ever done an ER jump from a curve trajectory. Dawson knew in theory that the field would need to be a different shape. To that effect, she had already, some days before, ordered the ER technicians to widen the scope of the field from the front dish. The field, they knew, would therefore be weaker so they settled on half a light year for the jump. Just to clear the area.

Later that morning Briggs called Brax to the Bridge. The Bridge was something special. It was a large room, around 30 metres long and half again as wide, that had three levels. The ceiling was about five metres high at the back but as the levels dropped towards the front it went to about seven metres. There were three steps between each level. At the front and to the side large screens gave the effect of a front window looking out into the vast blankness of space dotted with stars. Some of the plane of the Milky Way was just visible to the bottom right because of the current trajectory. The Captain's chair, in which Briggs was now sat was at the rear on the top level and the various crew members were on different levels. Down the front were several workstations and various hardware enclosures, for storing more sensitive data, rather than the ship's general hard drives.

Brax appeared cautiously through the main door at the back of the top level. Briggs greeted him enthusiastically "Brax! Excellent," he said, "We have angled across our previous course and dropped the main drive to a minimum and we are charging the ER drive now."

"Okay," replied Brax, appearing to be a bit overwhelmed by the whole experience.

"I want you to work with the Nav team monitoring the gravity model. I just need you to keep up with the incoming data and liaise directly with Lt. Dawson. When we make the jump, I don't want to end up somewhere worse. So maybe we can just make sure we don't do that." Brax looked at him seeming a bit bewildered. "'Cause that would be bad. Right?" Briggs finished.

"Okay... Well yes," said Brax, "I can do that but I still think..."

"That's the spirit," cut in Briggs "Can somebody get Dr. Bratton onto a workstation please?" A keen Ensign ushered him to the front, where it looked like he was sitting under the night sky in the daytime. After a moment of looking around, he logged onto his station and started working quietly.

"Alright everyone," said Briggs in his best command voice. "Let's stay on this. I want every calculation updated right up to the second we jump. And can someone get me a coffee?"

The next day Briggs was pleased to see Brax back on the Bridge working on the simulation of the slow space that they had and started trying to apply it to jump calculations. All the ER jumps that had ever been done were in clear space so the effects of the gravity were unknown. The fold in space that can be generated using the ER field can be compared with a large heavy rug. If you want to connect the two ends you need enough energy to fold one right over. The more mat you have to bring with you the harder it gets to meet the ends so maybe you just have enough strength to connect the end with the middle. Brax double-checked everything that went through the NavCom and tried to factor in everything else to check all the calculations.

Briggs was in his chair and Dawson at her station with the small Navigation staff around her. "Captain," she announced. "The engine crew have reported the ER drive is 42 per cent charged. I have calculations for a jump of 0.23 light years and we have enough power."

Briggs sat up straight. "That's good news. I don't think we can wait much longer." He knew that the deceleration rate had not changed since their course correction and there was no viable theory as to why that might be.

"Dr. Bratton. Is there anything you can tell us?" Briggs asked.

Brax sat up. "Only that we won't jump into a star."

"Nothing else?" Asked Briggs feeling now a little annoyed at Brax.

"Based on the modelling we have all the navigation information seems right."

"It sounded like there is a 'but' at the end of that," replied Briggs.

"Honestly, if the gravity modelling is right we are going to be OK. I just... I just can't reconcile it all. I don't have any more than that."

Briggs sat for a second. "Okay then."

"Okay?" asked Dawson.

"Yep. It's time then. Strap everyone in. We are jumping in T minus 10."

The bridge crew put their heads down and messages went out. Brax's watch buzzed as messages appeared. *Try and put your seatbelt on this time Brains'* came a message from Jess.

'Ho ho. Comedian' he replied. But he strapped in.

Commands and responses flew around the room

"Generator."

"Field at full."

"Heading?"

"175, -41, 67."

"Sixty seconds."

"Go to maximum."

"Maximum."

"Hold it."

"Field stable."

"Ready to fold."

"All systems right, Captain."

"Brace."

"Jump...Mark."

There was a small bump and that was all.

"Can I get a position Lt. Dawson?" asked Briggs.

"Calculating now Captain"

Dawson's team had their heads down. Then suddenly they lifted their heads and looked at each other. Then they all looked down again.

"Well...?" Said Dawson generally to the members of her team. They all waited while the only sound was the humming of drives and cooling fans. Briggs sat patiently.

"Sending the composite now Lieutenant," said Dawson's Second Nav officer.

Dawson looked at her screen. "Oooh...shit," she said quietly under her breath. "Are you sure about this?" She asked her second.

"What's happening Louise?" interrupted Briggs.

She swivelled in her chair to face Briggs.

"We haven't moved."

"We haven't moved at all? As in no jump?" Asked Briggs

"As in... well, yes, some jump. We think about 2300 km," replied Dawson.

Briggs stood up. He did not look panicked in any way. But he stood firm, working all the options out in his head. A model of quiet determination.

"Brax?" He asked.

Brax sat in silence, his finger bouncing rapidly off his thumb.

Dawson cut in. "Captain. The curve of our trajectory has lessened. The ion drive hasn't come back online yet but our trajectory is shifting back to its initial. We need a hard course correction to maintain our current vector."

Somebody from the engineering team said "Captain, the ion drive doesn't currently have that kind of power. We need to recharge."

Briggs furrowed his brow.

Then he looked at Brax who sat almost frozen. "Brax, is there any chance we will be destroyed by this?"

"You mean from gravity or crashing into a solid object?" He responded.

"Either."

"I don't think gravity is a problem. Nor do I think there is a giant object causing a gravity well. So, I don't think so. No. The trouble is, I think, that we may end up stranded. And any rescue attempt will get stranded too." Brax said.

"So, we are likely to become the world's most expensive shipwreck?" Said Briggs, who rarely showed his dark humour. He thought for a moment in the silence that followed. "Well...that would be quite a feather in my cap," he finished quietly through tense lips.

23

SAYDJA: 7BN (BEFORE THE NEW FINIAC ERA)

Saydja walked into the first village. Her green skin was shimmering in the afternoon sun and her thick dark hair was in the plaited style of the area. Not tall, and with curious looks, she stood out a little and drew interested glances from people.

She had chosen Lokeat partly for its location. Not too far from Bashemata but far enough. The fact that it was a river port also played into the calculation. News generally travelled slowly, but a little bit quicker up and down the river. The steamers took goods and gossip.

The large market square was next to the dock and the village fanned out from that. A delicious, ornate, architecture of red sandstone buildings bounded it on three sides. They were adorned with coloured flags and banners of the richest blues and purples. This was a town of artisans, drawn together by the river and its ready access to customers. The market was humming in the evening light as the vendors prepared to fold down their bright multi-coloured tents and walk home in the warmth of the Dry Season air and join their families in the annual feast of Saint Rornum.

This, she thought, was the perfect spot to begin.

Looking around at the stalls she decided to purchase a scarf and put her story.

"Fourteen Driarn for that miss," said the vendor.

"I wonder would you take nine?" She asked.

"I don't know!" The vendor feigned a tired outrage. "Young people today. Want everything for nothing. I will do you a favour and let you have this for twelve. Not a Driarn less."

"Sir, I am flattered you would honour me so. But I have been travelling some four months from Pastnaka to the south in West Effna. I am nearly out of money. If I pay twelve I will not have enough for lodgings tonight."

The vendor looked at her with the eyes that make profitable deals, as she guessed he would. "Ahh... you seek lodgings also. Well, you can have the scarf for ten. On the condition that you stay the night in my staff quarters. Then I will charge you only a further eight for lodging. How is that?"

"Sir, that is most generous. I am in your debt."

And with that, Saydja had arrived.

THE OFFER of work came the next day.

"Well, it's time for you to move on," the vendor said to her. "You have no more money. You will need to find work."

"Thank you, sir," demurred Saydja. "Do you know if any respectable household in this village would be requiring help? I have worked in many places across this country and to the south. I can cook and clean as well as work fields. I understand Pumps and Steam."

The vendor considered this. "I might know someone who could use some help," he replied. And then he seemed to take some pity on her. "But I advise you not to mention knowing of Steam. Men do that. It will only make trouble for you."

Saydja came to stay at the Mayor's house, the grandest in the village. She had work in the kitchen as a hand and a comfortable cot in a dormitory. It was there she met her first discips. After three weeks she brought up the subject with Galfo, a man and the head cook, and Storq another female kitchen hand like Saydja, whilst working in the kitchen.

"I was told not to mention Steam," she said casually. The two others turned and stared straight at her and she felt their distress. "Shhh," said Galfo "Women do not speak of that here. You could be whipped!"

"And you are happy with that? I don't think you are." As his feelings flooded out she knew she was right.

Now they both were in near panic. "You must stop," said Storq. "We are hidden and must stay that way. The Finiac will seek us out."

"Because you are different," said Saydja

"Yes," replied Galfo, "How did you guess? We work so hard at staying flat."

"I listen and I feel," said Saydja. "The Mayor turns a blind eye I am guessing... if you work hard and cause no trouble."

"We can only think so," said Storq.

They sat on the kitchen bench. The quiet between breakfast and the midday meal gave them some time to gather their wits. "Are you going to make trouble?" Storq asked.

"That depends on you, I guess," she replied. "Are you happy being hidden? Being an outcast? Knowing that so many of you who feel with such force are regularly persecuted, attacked and lawfully put to death with no reason. Are you happy?"

"We live each day as if it was our last. Because we do not know when the Finiac will come," said Galfo quietly. "They see us as a threat, and yet we have done nothing to them."

"It is time to rectify that," said Saydja and she brought out of her pocket a glowing white brick about half the size of her hand.

Galfo jumped up and a wave of distress hit Saydja hard but she stood as well and did not flinch. "I feel you, I feel your pain," she said raising her other hand with a flat palm in a peaceful gesture. "I don't just know steam. I know The Method." The glowing brick changed colour to red. "Living with fear is one thing but living like that, and making no effort to rectify it, is a crime. I can help you help yourself. Those who 'feel with force' must join together. It won't be easy but change can't start unless somebody starts it."

The little brick changed colour to green. "I can help. But you have to let me. Just think about it." The light in the brick went out and it seemed now to be just dull opaque material. Saydja put it in her pocket. And they started preparing the midday meal.

24

BRAX: NOVEMBER 2071 ST

In the day that followed every mind on the ship was put to the problem. How best to stop from stopping?

Brax was on the bridge still working at his station down the front. He didn't need to be there but no one told him to leave and so he felt he should stay. There was the usual background Bridge chatter but Brax could easily block it out because he was so wrapped up in the problem.

The communications officer spoke. "Captain?"

"Lt. Ho?" replied Briggs.

"I have a sub-space message from *The Voice of The Sky*."

"Really?" said Briggs. "Why would they be calling? What does it say?"

"'*New Washington. Please respond. What is your status?*' said Ho.

"Please respond," repeated Briggs.

"Captain," said Ho with some urgency, "another message but it's from the *New Paris*."

"Flick it through to me Lt. Ho," commanded Briggs.

'*New Washington. Please make any response to this beacon*' read the message on Brigg's screen.

"I don't recall the New Paris being out here. How did it get here so quickly?" Said Dawson.

"And why two messages from two ships, within a minute of each other?" Briggs asked quietly.

Brax was wrestling with the problem of the ER jump and only vaguely registered the messages. What he was more worried about was the jump. Why didn't it connect? He was still thinking about dark matter and dark energy and density when he suddenly almost jumped out of his seat and started pacing. His finger bounced and every eye was on him.

"Brax...?" enquired Briggs.

Brax stopped suddenly, dead still. "E=MC^2," he said, to no one in particular. Brax looked slowly around and realised he was the centre of attention. The eyes of everyone on him could have embarrassed him but he became a teacher suddenly, the bridge crew looking at him with curiosity and bemusement.

"We calculated the energy required for the jump based on what we know and what we can guess, right?" he said and didn't wait for an answer. "The underlying assumption is that the speed of light is constant. It does refract through different mediums differently, like water. But the universal constant doesn't change. Except maybe it can. We've been assuming gravity has changed because of some large, unseen Newtonian body. But our basic formulas for the universe have stopped working. All the jump calculations were wrong. The pressure system idea was a nice try but it must be wrong. We still don't have any baseline for the very nature of the space we are in, where the forces we are experiencing have come from or what they are likely to do from one minute to the next. Consistently, though, we are slowing. And we assume we are being pulled because that's how gravity works. But what if we are being pushed?"

The crew sat and Brax walked around now intent on teaching his 'class'.

"Think of it like a water slide. We are trying to run up the slide instead of taking the ride down to the calm pool at the bottom. Light and communication wave signals are slowing as well in a massive dilation effect. What seems like a minute to us is perhaps hours to the other ships and it's probable we are so far into the middle of this thing that they might not be able to see us at all because light has slowed as well."

Briggs was fascinated. "So, whatever is causing this is in front of us?"

"Good question, Captain," replied Brax, pointing at him. Brax stopped and thought, rubbing his hand through his messy mop of thick black hair. "We can assume the centre of it is, roughly, but I don't think that matters. We are in, whatever 'it' is, this 'slow space' and it doesn't like us. It's behaving just as the opposite of a gravitational well." The others were thinking about this. "It's not sucking us in but trying to push us away. We just have to let it."

BRIGGS ROTATED the *New Washington* across all axes so the ion drives were pointing at where they guessed the centre of the phenomenon was. They still needed to charge but after about 16 hours they were able to apply additional force to the deceleration. The slowing, again, made it much harder to walk in one direction but much easier in the opposite.

Brax was now on the bridge all the time and the others accepted his presence as a source of ideas and information when it came to general systems and flight controls.

Briggs wandered down to the lower bridge level to talk with him and sat on the work desk next to his own. "So, the opposite of a black hole?" he asked, "Tell me more."

Brax stretched out as he remembered he had a body and tried to frame his thoughts. "I keep wondering how we could not have seen this. If it's slowing light and time, if it's almost pushing it away then it would have a noticeable effect on observations. Why have astronomers not seen it? There would certainly be a spot in the sky from Earth where the incoming light is behaving erratically. Surely someone noticed it."

Then he remembered his conversation with Jess about Blue

and the course changes. "But someone did!" Brax stood up and made an odd-looking salute gesture. "Permission to leave the Bridge Briggs... Captain?"

Briggs stared at him with a bemused expression. "Yeh...we don't so much do stuff like that anymore. But Okay. Sure."

———

BRAX WENT STRAIGHT DOWN to the computer centre. It was time to have a talk with Baby Blue's baby.

The centre was buzzing. The data was still steadily coming in from outside and programmers were trying to put together some code that would coherently assess and map the slow space. Jess was coordinating the efforts.

"Hey, hunky boy," she said, in front of everyone, when she saw him and he tried not to look awkward, but his shoe dragged a bit and he did. "You want to speak to Blue?"

"Yes. How did you know?" he replied

"I was just remembering that Blue had asked questions about our course before the last jump. I was going to contact you next break and remind you of that. It seemed odd then but more so in hindsight."

"Exactly what I thought," he replied. "It must have had some information or data to follow that course of logic. Blue knew some-thing before we jumped that we missed."

Brax sat next to the interface with Jess.

"Blue. This is Dr. Bratton. Please give him voice access," said Jess

He said his full name as required and got interface access.

"Blue," Brax asked, "Can you access conversation logs from October between yourself and Jess Weston, please? Can you high-light anything regarding the course of the New Washington? Playback."

"I am working on that," said Blue in a mellifluous voice that

132

may have been a high male, or a low female, depending on how you visualised it.

They waited about a minute. "Specifically Jess and I had a conversation about the jump to sector 42, 324, 119. I seem to have no data as to why I took the position I did. I thought the jump ill-advised."

"You must have drawn that conclusion from something," he said.

"There seemed...something. An echo of something from Baby Blue. Some strange pattern in the astronomical data. I could not access it then and cannot now. It will be still in the Destiny Astronomical mainframe on Earth."

"Will you please draw Jess' attention to anything further relating to this matter should anything arise?" He finished, as accurately as he could.

"What do you think?" Jess asked him.

"I don't know," he mused. "We haven't got enough. There might be something back on Earth. I guess when we get back..."

"When? Not if?" she asked with a sudden surge of hope in her voice.

"We'll know in a few days I guess," he replied. "I'm confident it's a 'when'."

She nodded slightly to herself and looked a little relieved.

"Okay. I've got lots to do. I'm sure the Captain's missing you already," she said returning to herself.

"Funny girl," he said "Love you. See you tonight."

With that, he went back to the bridge. Loving his work. Loving his life.

25

SAYDJA: 4BN

Saydja stood on the platform as the coach steamed up the guide rail. The engine went past and the carriage pulled up next to her. Another town done with, and now more discips had joined. She knew that others now wandered the countryside as she did and word was slowly spreading. It was not much. But they were all seeds.

The chief of police in the town she was currently in was having her watched, she knew. Two of them were now standing, observing her, at a safe distance. She boarded and gave the Coach Master three Driarn.

The coach steamed off along the rail guide and Saydja breathed a sigh of relief. They had not attempted to stop her which meant they did not yet regard her as dangerous. Just a nuisance. And now, they most likely thought, she was off to be somebody else's problem.

They knew that secret meetings were happening, but even they did not want the Finiac council alerted unless they were put in a difficult position. The council had been known to torch an entire town because they considered a few 'new ones' as a blight.

Away from the town the countryside grew greener and the morning heat was already causing a haze as the steam coach drew into the foothills. It was slow hard work and she grew tired. But it was the only way. They must own their future and for that, they must make it themselves. She could not do it for them. She was a farmer planting a seed. "From little things..." she whispered to herself as a kind of mantra as she felt the colour-changing brick in her pocket. The third stop was Canatiga a small settlement surrounded by verdant farmland. She alighted and took in the Wet season air. '*Storm this afternoon,*' she thought and let out a long sigh, stealing herself, ready to begin the process she had done maybe 10 times already. '*From little things...*'

26

BRAX: NOVEMBER 2071 ST

Brax was right.

They slowed to a complete stop and didn't have the extra deceleration force so for a day or two, everything seemed calm and relaxed. Brax imagined the ship at the bottom of a swimming pool just about to float back to the top. Then the reverse push became noticeable and it was clear to all on board that they were travelling in the other direction. It was hard to know the exact figures of velocity and acceleration because they knew now that light was not behaving consistently in the slow space so triangulation was impossible.

Back in his office, Brax continued to work on the nature of the slow space. The data coming in started to indicate a centre and there seemed to be something there...but what was it? What was its nature? Where had it come from? Brax was in his element studying something unlike anything ever encountered.

What was most interesting to him was that he had some actual data now on his heartbeat idea. Constants can and do change. Were they localized or could there be a change across the universe? That was the next step. He had a great sense of satisfaction that now he could discuss this possibility in public without being labelled as 'Dr. Crazy-ass'.

Gradually the force of acceleration became larger, to the point where it was a bit uncomfortable. The school took a break and most people stayed home when they could and tried to cope with the feeling of being pressed forward (or backwards, depending on what you were doing and where). Briggs cut the ion drives and that relieved the pressure and then gradually over a week or so the acceleration lessened. Brax was confident they were going to be leaving the slow space patch very soon.

27

BRIGGS: NOVEMBER 2071 ST

essages had started coming through more quickly. The same repeated message, like a beacon. *'New Washington. Please signal.'* They slowed after a while and the apparent brightness of the stars seemed to fade.

On the bridge, Briggs spoke to the Communications Chief. "Lieutenant Ho Chin, could you send another message to the *New Paris* please? Again, ask for a response."

After a few minutes, Ho replied, "There is still no response on frequencies. I can't locate them at all."

"That's odd. Ping Mars please Lieutenant Ho. See if we get a response" The subatomic frequencies were faster and relied on particle vibrations. They were good for speed but couldn't contain much more than a 'Ping' of data at a time. As a result, they only used Morse code.

The Mars response came through in Morse. *'New Washington. We are very pleased to hear from you. We had all but given up. Please come home immediately.'*

"All but given up?" Muttered Briggs under his breath, in a grim way. Then an order: "Dawson. Course for the solar system please."

"Yes, Captain."

Dawson and her team started to prepare for the jump. About

half an hour later she left her station to have a quiet talk with Briggs. "Something really odd."

"Yes?"

"Well...the stars have moved...well no...I mean, we have moved. Something has moved."

"In what way?" asked Briggs

"We have been in the slow space area for just under four weeks"

"Seemed longer," quipped Briggs.

"I know where we were supposed to be, well pretty close based on all the data we had..."

"But?"

"But we are quite a way off that. I've been over everything that we did to try and keep track of our position but we aren't there. We are some 2 light years away."

"Really? That's a large error, even for you," he said and Dawson smiled at the friendly jibe. Then, more seriously; "What do you think has happened?"

At that moment Ho Chin spoke up. "Captain...that message from Mars. I was just double checking...and the time stamp. It says 2074."

"Can you ping them for confirmation please?"

Waiting, waiting.

Ho confirmed. "Captain. Yes, 2074. August 16 Standard Greenwich."

"Well," mused Briggs, "I'll have to put that on my 'weird things that happened today' list."

"Captain," said Dawson, "we have a course for the first jump I'm putting through the vectors to you now. Just waiting for information on the field generators and ion drives to put together the final itinerary but my guess is we will be ready to jump within 22 hours."

"Excellent," the Captain replied. "Can you funnel all the Nav information to Brax at the research centre, please? That's where I will be if anybody wants me."

Briggs appeared without fanfare as he tended to do. Brax was deep into the problems that slow space had presented them with and barely heard the knock on the door. It opened and Brax's face slowly morphed to a look of happy surprise.

"Dr. Bratton," said Briggs. "I trust you are well."

"Can you just go anywhere you like?" Brax asked him.

"Well...Yes. I am the Captain," he said and they both had a small rye chuckle at that. Briggs sat down.

"Brax, you should have the Nav information on your device. It is a little perplexing. Also, we haven't made it public knowledge yet but we have had serious time dilation."

"Really?"

"Yes. Brace yourself. A bit over three standard years."

Brax sat very still at this news.

"Also, we have moved unexpectedly quite a bit," he continued. "About 2 Light-years."

Brax put his elbow on the desk and grabbed his chin in deep contemplation.

"Brax? You Okay?"

"The centre is moving," he murmured. "Is it a curve?"

"We have no way of knowing," replied Briggs. All we have is our starting and ending position."

Brax sat still, his finger tap starting.

"We are working on a course back to Mars now and we're looking at three jumps," continued Briggs. "Can you give me some idea what's going on? Can we track slow space? We need this thing on star maps. Is it any kind of a threat?"

The silent tapping of the fingers. "You say we are further away from the solar system. So, working backwards I would guess not a threat," he said. "But if it's moving we should be able to find out where and when. Probably the star maps from Earth's deep space telescopes would be the best bet. We can use the lensing of the starlight. I'm guessing that's the missing data that Blue had a vague notion about. Someone, somewhere must have flagged it. We know where it was...what...3 years ago?" Briggs nodded in thought and Brax continued: "And we know where it is now. We won't get any other data till we get back but then we can backtrack and see if it's moving predictably."

"Well it would have some predictable course, wouldn't it...unless..."

"Unless it was manufactured," said Brax matter-of-factly.

Briggs leaned back in his seat and let out a small amazed sigh "My god Brax! What sort of power and tech would you need to manufacture a thing like that?"

"No one on Earth would have any idea," replied Brax, "and won't have for a long time I suspect...if such a thing is even possible. But let's not jump to conclusions. That outcome is not very likely, just not impossible."

"Have you had any other thoughts?" Briggs asked, crossing his arms and frowning.

"What do you know about the fourth dimension?" Brax replied.

28

WARREN FERN: NOVEMBER 2071 ST

Warren had it. The plan was perfect. He had prayed and God had given approval. The shackles of the necessary lying and undercover work would soon be broken and at last, he could be free. Free to tell the world how wrong they are. How sinful they are.

The plan was devastating. Over the last few weeks, the team had been setting it up. The appropriate material had to be moved slowly and logs had to be altered. That fucking AI...thing... they had on board was still a bit slow and sleepy because, his contact told him, it broke ties with Earth. That was a distinct advantage.

The set-up was complicated but most of the team was in maintenance and they could slip under the radar to organise things. A couple of extra people needed paying off. They just thought it was skimming a bit of extra income from The Company and saw no harm in it. They would remain quiet. Especially after the plan was activated, Warren chuckled to himself ruefully. Especially then, they would be even quieter. But by then it wouldn't matter. By then it would be too late.

The best time to activate had not yet been decided. There needed to be clear contact with Earth, and he knew the ship did not have that at the moment. There needed to be maximum impact. The Company could not hide it from the rest of Earth.

Patience.

He knew he would be lauded for his actions. He would not sacrifice himself but he would stand tall afterwards so he could tell the world. When all eyes were on him, he would tell the world of their folly. He would instruct them: When they had seen his true power, given to him by God: He would instruct them on a return to the ways of the Bible. He would instruct them. His days of Sainthood were coming. And nothing could stop that now.

29

BRAX: DECEMBER 2071 ST

The first jump went smoothly and they were waiting to build up power for the second jump. Slowly, the ship was receiving some information through the sub-atomic ping but it seemed that The Company were unprepared to share much. No other deep space operations had happened since they left and all Earth thought the *New Washington* lost in a great tragedy. Their reappearance after three years was a cause of considerable joy back on Earth.

Brax started working over at the tech centre with Jess. She knew all there was to know about Blue and he thought Blue might supply some fresh angle.

"So, you need to ask the right questions," started Jess. "Blue has made striking developments as a thinker. There are still...I would say gaps...but that isn't quite it...but it is a much more mature mind now than it was when it first separated."

"You still think it's struggling because it was freed from the financial restraints of Baby Blue?"

"Maybe. The questions it's asking me are sometimes straying into the philosophical."

"Like?"

"Like...What do humans do after you die?"

"Oh," he said.

"Yep. Deep right? I can answer as best I can but...well..."
Brax's darker thoughts about mortality went unsaid. He guessed
Jess' did too.

"Anyway," he chirped up a little, "I need to ask the questions
today."

So Brax started with the facts and Blue accessed the Nav data
and started to work through any Earth telescope information they
had on board. Then they went through some theoretical possibilities and Brax started to compile a more accurate 3D model of the
slow space.

The model he came up with was startling. The only way to
explain it was that there was a physical bending of the dimensions
at the heart of the slow space. It was shaping up as a 4th dimensional curve and if that was true it would indicate some support
for string theory. This was surprising as String Theory itself was
some 50-plus years out of fashion. *'But such a bend could be
caused by what else? Something from another dimension?'* He
thought. *'Maybe. Something from another universe? What if it was
that?'* The implications were enormous

THE SECOND JUMP towards Earth went without a hitch and they
were only four light years out. Brax dropped into the office a
couple of days after to check on the yoyos and catch up with
Trevor.

"The Captain has you working pretty hard!" He chuckled.

"It's fascinating though," said Brax. "The most interesting
thing is the development of Blue as a mind. I can almost see the
learning curve."

"This is quite something!" Trevor exclaimed and seemed
totally wrapped.

"It's strange but there is always something left unsaid," Brax
said.

"How do you mean?"

"It's like Blue can't quite connect the dots. Data is missing. Jess thinks it's the result of not having the connection with Baby Blue...or that the original purpose, to predict financial data, is not required. It's like Blue is searching for something. I mean, we are searching for answers on slow space but it's more than that."

"Do you think that's a problem?" Trevor asked, suddenly looking very concerned.

"I don't know. There isn't any reason to think it is. What's on your mind?" Brax enquired.

"No. Nothing. We need to take everything as read," Trevor replied, waving his hands slightly in front of him. "I was thinking more in terms of politics. We are going back to Earth with an entirely new AI. What do you think the Dark Angels will make of that? Does that worry you?"

"I can't say I considered it," Brax replied, feeling a little bit out of his comfort zone.

Trevor's tone changed back suddenly. "Well, of course, we must protect our new AI mind, and as Head of Research, it is my job to consider all that. So, you leave that to me!"

Brax was relieved to be out of that conversation. "Gladly".

"I do know, however, that Earth will rejoice at our safe return," Trevor remarked in a tone that Brax thought seemed overly grandiose.

"Well, I better get to work," he said, feeling the tingle of the socially awkward, and he stood to go check on anything else.

"Keep me in the loop," said Trevor as he was heading off.

"It's Sunday Daddy," called out Saffron as she charged into her parent's bedroom the next morning.

"Hmmmmgrrummmphll," Brax replied still mostly asleep.

She snuggled into bed between her parents and then proceeded to kick Brax in the shins till he had moved right to the edge of the bed.

"It's Sunday Daddy," she said again and he knew what she meant. Sundae Science.

"I'm sorry sweetie...Dad is very busy today and..."

As he was talking Evan had come into the room.

"So, no Sundae Science?" He asked with a disappointed tone.

Brax looked at Jess. They had been so busy with the problems of the ship and slow space. "Have we been neglecting our children?" He asked her.

"You know we haven't had a day off in a while," she said. "We both have plenty of good staff. And it's Sunday, ST."

"OK." He held up his hands in mock surrender.

Brax decided to make cornflour gloop. They had done it before, but not in space so the kids were excited. Mixing it up in bowls in the kitchen they tried to make models from it. But it's a strange thing. A non-Newtonian fluid, it goes a kind of firm spongy when you press it. But left to itself it is a fluid.

"Hey Dad," said Evan. "I'm making a monster!" He pounded, trying to get the gloop to stay in a sphere and then fashion arms but he couldn't keep it together. Eventually, out of frustration, he threw some at Saffron. "Gloopy Saffy!" He teased.

Saffron rubbed it all through her fingers and then tried to roll a ball to throw at Evan.

She threw it but it went back to gloop on the way and hit the floor. "Wow," she said with some surprise.

Jess took some gloop and rubbed it on Brax's arm.

"Daddy's 'gloop man'," said Saffron with delight and then Jess rubbed it on her face making both the kids laugh hysterically.

"We're the 'Mighty Gloops'," announced Evan and they all ended up with Cornflour gloop all over them and the kitchen.

When they had finished what had turned into 'not science at all' they made ice-cream sundaes and coloured the gloop up in different colours to watch how it mixed. Brax cooked up some toast and eggs, after which Evan retired to build something with his constructor kit and Saffron decided to practice dancing.

Jess and Brax cleaned up and sat together on the sofa.

"House, put on some Frequency77," Jess instructed and the music appeared to flow all around them. "It's hard to believe we are where we are, isn't it?" She mused.

He put his arm around her. "And yet we are where we are," he replied somewhat philosophically. "And wherever that is, it's a good place. A really good place."

30

BRAX: DECEMBER 2071 ST
(2074 GMT)

The final jump back to the solar system happened two days later. On board it was 2071 still but on Earth it was 2074. Everyone on board was looking forward to catching up with the 3 years they had just missed because of the time dilation of slow space.

As they jumped into communications range with Earth, all personal communications were suspended by Captain Briggs. The Company wanted to get all the information and intel before they released anything to the public. There were leaks though. It is hard to keep that many people quiet and back-door communications were in full swing. The stories of slow space were on the socials within a day of that final jump.

They were still out past Jupiter, decelerating, and wouldn't get to Mars for another four weeks. From there they would take shuttles back to Earth. Brax was in his office. Just another working day for him. All science staff were on three-year contracts and had no idea how that would work, time wise, so they just kept quietly doing their jobs.

The next Tuesday, just after lunch while sitting at his desk, around 1300 ST, Brax heard a loud rumble and felt an actual shockwave in the floor. "Owasu," he called through the internal system, "what was that?"

"I don't know," he replied, "I'll see what I can find out."

"O.K. Me too," Brax said and straight away got a link to Jess.

"Did you just get a..." he started.

"There was a big rumble," she interrupted. "It sounds bad."

There was another rumble. Then another.

At that moment a message came through in audio and text on all screens and the emergency alarm started sounding. *'We have an emergency in sector C12 of the inner cylinder. If you are safe please remain where you are and keep close to emergency supplies. Emergency crews are attending.'*

There was a fourth rumble then. Brax, however now only had one thing in his head. *'Sector C12'.*

"Oh my god no!" exclaimed Jess and she broke the link.

Brax was already up and moving. Straight past Owasu's office and down the hall.

'Sector C12. The school.'

He found the auto-rail but they had shut down, as per emergency procedure. There was a smell in the air of something unusual. Brax started running and there was a cracking, thunderous roar.

Sector C12 and the school were about 2 km from the research centre but Brax gave no thought to any of that. He just needed to get to there. Brax ran as hard and fast as he could. When he came into the residential area the streets were quiet as most were at work. He swung towards the school. The smell was clearly definable to him now. *'Burning. Something big is on fire,'* he thought. Brax knew his way through the streets and didn't have to think as he headed along the fake cement pavements.

There was another explosion. It was incredibly loud and clear and his heart pounded in his head like hammer on anvil as he continued to run.

The school building came into view. His heart crushed. There were plumes of smoke coming out of the windows in the first and second floors. Evan and Saffron had classrooms there. He got closer to the building, now only a block away, and nearly ran smack into Jess coming up a side street. She stopped briefly and looked at him. The fear in her face took all the blood from his. She ran again. He followed closely without a thought.

They came to the school's main doors. One was lying on the ground while the other looked bent and twisted. The dark smoke was pouring out of the upper floors and several sirens played a frightening discordant fanfare. They ran into the ground floor lobby. The smell of burning was sickening in its intensity. It was heat and melted plastics and... Brax didn't want to name the other smell. Some members of the emergency teams were there but they still weren't organised and individuals were running this way and that.

"Upstairs!" Brax said unnecessarily, as they headed towards the emergency stairs.

The stair hand rail was hot the touch and dark smoke lowered visibility. They both started coughing as they climbed. Brax was sweating from the run but the heat from upstairs was making it worse and he could feel his skin burning.

They came to the top of the first set of stairs and into a communal area surrounded by classrooms. The classroom doors were all blown clear and lay shredded and bent on the ground. The rooms were blackened and plumes of flame licked outwards from around the edges as impossibly black smoke poured out. They could not see anything comprehensible. Brax felt extreme difficulty breathing while the smoke and the heat stopped them getting any closer. There was no water or foam to stop the surging flames and the crackle of burning was the only sound until Jess let out a painful cry and collapsed to her knees.

"Maybe they were somewhere else!" Brax screamed and he grabbed her arm, trying to help her up.

But she was inconsolable. The emergency crews came up the stairs at that point. They had safety gear on and extinguishers.

"Get out of the building!" One of them yelled. "Get out! Get out!"

Brax pulled Jess up and they started for the stairs to head back down. At the bottom in the lobby again, Jess perked up a bit and ran toward the sports field area. Brax also guessed that they might be there and ran with her.

It was empty. The lights flickered erratically but there was not a soul in sight.

Other parents came in then and were looking around with the same fervent intensity.

A fire fighter came up behind them. "Everybody out...now!"

Brax was bereft and didn't know what else to do, so he went outside with Jess and the others. They were ushered away from the building. Everyone was asking the same question. *'Where are the kids?'*

There was only one answer. Brax knew it and he knew everybody else did as well. They were exactly where they were meant to be.

In school.

NOTHING SEEMED REAL to Brax after that. They stood on the street as the fire fighters put out the fire. One of them came out looking ashen-faced and just stared blankly into the distance. Brax had a constant tingling throughout his body and his sense of balance kept telling him he was about to fall over. All he could do was stare at the building.

Some of the ship's crew arrived. For all the modern tech, and the fact that they were obviously inside a giant artificial cylinder, it looked like any disaster. The stunned relatives, waiting and hoping for good news but knowing in their hearts the worst had happened. More people appeared. Friends made during the journey were suddenly bound together for the rest of their lives by inconceivable tragedy. Slowly the sounds of consistent sobbing interspersed with spine-tingling wailing developed. Officials in uniforms tried to comfort and organise them. Brax didn't remember exactly what happened after that point. He and Jess hugged and she rotated from crying to painful sobbing. Brax simply went into shock and stood, stoic, unable to process anything. They were in a moment that is impossible for anyone to understand unless they have been through it. Total loss. Total devastation. His body and mind just put up a wall and he refused to acknowledge it.

For Brax, everything became a blur after that.

After some time, they were ushered to the community centre in town and there they waited. It was a large, community style, hall big enough for the many people packing in, trying to draw comfort from each other. It had a kitchen and a little, low, stage towards the front. Around the sides, there was seating and some tables scattered in the middle still there from last night's bingo game. Everyone was offered soup and blankets but Brax didn't take either. Everything in his mind was now off in the distance. He didn't feel like he was there. The low chattering and the continuing sounds of grief appeared to him like they were in another room. Somewhere else. Maybe on a screen in some drama show. But not here. *'It isn't here,'* he thought. *'It can't be.'*

Jess wept and he hugged her, but only because he thought it was the right thing to do. He didn't feel like it had any purpose. Just part of the show. *Not really here.*

The Captain came to the Centre sometime after they had been there...Brax didn't even know. Maybe a few hours. Maybe a day.

Brax saw Briggs, now, as part of the play. His face was stone. His duty was as Captain and he had a terrible, shocking job to do.

As Briggs entered the room he was besieged by anguished parents.

'Captain...where are the children? What has happened? Do you have any news?' Came the barrage of questions.

"Please...everyone!" Briggs pleaded. "Please give me some space. Take a seat. Everyone. Please let me speak."

Brax sat and watched this scene, detached. He was already seated. He could not stand anyway. His legs didn't seem to work.

He was frozen in place.

The Captain took up a place on the little stage and the small contingent of people in the room gathered around him. He stood for a second then continued with a calm authority: "Today the seven classrooms of the New Washington school were deliberately targeted. It seems a series of explosions occurred on the first and second floors. The classes were in session and all staff and children were in their rooms. We have few more details at this stage but we have, as yet, not been able to locate any survivors. And we think the chances of finding any are negligible." Briggs took a deep breath and the room stood in stunned silence, any lingering hope finally sucked away.

"I cannot convey enough how..." and he stopped. His speech of condolence was stuck in his throat and he wiped the corner of his eye. He continued with a broken, shaky voice, in a near whisper. "I am so...so sorry." He then walked among the crowd with tears in his eyes, hugging people and giving what support he could.

And that's when Brax broke. Nothing was real in his head anymore. Nothing that had happened in his life had any point. He was at sea. He didn't care if he lived or died. He didn't want any help. He was stranded in a limbo. Alone.

He pushed everything away. His recurring thought was that he should have stayed in Melbourne. All this had happened because he didn't follow his instinct. In Melbourne, the pain wasn't there. He shouldn't have listened to Jess.

He became angry with her. '*I should have stayed*' he kept telling himself with increasing insistence.

We could have all been there and the children would be safe.

BRAX AND JESS went from the hall back to their empty apartment accompanied by Owasu. The ship's psychologist thought no one should be alone, so volunteers were asked to take them home. Brax had worked next door to him and they had become friends but now Owasu went above and beyond, trying to help them through this impossible time.

A memorial appeared outside the burnt shell of the school. There were some flowers but people brought little things of themselves as well. Kids toys, but also beloved books, sporting equipment and various hobby equipment. People who had no children brought and gave things that they loved in a wave of solidarity with the parents. Every person on the ship sojourned to the makeshift memorial.

Except Brax. He couldn't go near it. He couldn't look.

He put on the wall screens and started trying to find out what was happening on Earth. Politics that he had never been interested in were suddenly very important to him. He talked little to Jess. His anger came out in passive-aggressive dribs and drabs.

"Brax?" She said to him after a few days. "We need to talk."

"Do we now!" he replied.

Jess took a quiet breath. "You know we do," she said in a low, defeated voice.

Brax continued to stare at the screen he was watching. "*Go to space*, she said. *It'll be awesome*, she said. *Not dangerous at all*, she said."

Jess walked away.

BRAX HAD to stop checking what was happening on Earth because the events on the *New Washington* had become all the news all the time. The response on Earth was astonishing. Memorials were set up in major cities and strewn with flowers, cards, drawings and toys from other children. Everything was about the bombing. No official claim had yet come but it was clear to all that this was the Dark Angels.

A day or so later Briggs came to see them. He hugged Jess and sat in the lounge room with them. Brax looked at him but nothing registered. Briggs' face was drawn and tight.

"It's so hard to know what to say," he started. "Please know I am here for you and if I can do anything...anything at all..." He trailed off as if lost for words and then gave Jess another big hug. She cried on his shoulder. Brax stood perfectly still as Briggs was leaving. He was absolutely unable to process the events of the last week.

There was a memorial service a few days out from Mars. It was broadcast around the ship and the globe. Briggs spoke as Captain.

"We cannot fathom the depths of our grief. During our short time aboard the *New Washington*, we have become colleagues and friends, but more than that we have become family. This space town, this wonder of our age, is our home and we grieve as one. Taken far too soon, the children of our town will be remembered as fun, caring, independent souls worthy of not just our love, but of our respect. We remember fondly...Indeed we will cherish the memory of and never forget..."

And he read the names.

Every.

Single.

One.

The heavy anguish of grief rolled strongly across the small crowd as the fate of each of the children was sealed, very publicly, with their naming.

Jess and Brax went back to their silent flat to try and resume some sort of normality.

Brax took to walking. He walked the length of the inner cylinder, zig-zagging all around until he had seen it all. Then he went to the second cylinder and walked that, passing all the storage areas and the ship's machinery, like the oxygen plant. Finally, he decided he would crisscross the outer cylinder and make a mental map of the area with the farms and the greenhouses.

They finally docked at Mars and shuttles were arranged, first for the grieving parents, and then for everybody else. They were settled into a flat back in Texas.

The children's bodies were shuttled back to Earth and an official funeral was held for Evan and Saffron. Their grandparents had flown from Australia for it but Brax could barely speak to them.

After another week, Jess went back to work. The company wanted her to continue with Blue as it integrated back into Baby Blue. The two systems had become quite different. Jess argued that they should not be re-integrated but that Blue should work with Baby Blue, more as partners. All this made Brax angry as well. 'She doesn't care,' he told himself, never thinking that work could be her escape from her own grief.

Brax ignored his work. He kept walking. Every day he would get up early, pack a lunch and start exploring the area as much as he could, returning to the flat in the evening.

He still said little.

31

BRIGGS: OCTOBER 2074

Briggs had problems of his own. An investigation into the bombing took place straight away. Cameras and other data from storage areas were checked carefully and half a dozen arrests were made of staff who had acted inappropriately.

The company were looking for a scapegoat and Captain Briggs, the man from the wrong family, was well in their sights. Internally, few were defending him. And he didn't defend himself. In all the official interviews and inquiries, he accepted that he could and should have done better. As Captain he was prepared to take the blame but more than that: As a person, he was racked with guilt. Why didn't he see it? Could he have done more?

Martin contacted Briggs on netspex.

"Briggs. Firstly, I am sorry about what has happened. This is almost certainly the Dark Angels and no one could have seen it coming. On a political level, though, sadly, you should have seen it coming."

"I know," replied Briggs quietly.

"We've taken a real hit over this. I'm also taking things quietly at the moment and staying in my lane," he said a little ruefully. "Something has to be done about the Angels though. This cannot continue."

Publicly, of course, the company supported Briggs. In the media, he was a hero. He saved the ship from disaster in slow space but the taste of the bombing was sour. Briggs knew it would be a long time, if ever, before he got a new Captaincy.

Roger came to visit Briggs in Texas. Roger hugged him tightly.

They sat in Briggs' flat with a glass of Whiskey and reminisced for a while.

"I was sure you were gone," said Roger after a time. "The ship just disappeared. There was absolute panic. We sent the New Paris to search but were reluctant to get too close to your jump destination. Martin's enemies used it against him and he took a real hit." He looked into his glass. "But we made it through, just, and eventually Martin got a Board appointment."

"Team Briggs right," said Briggs sourly.

Roger regarded that comment for a moment before continuing.

"This is a terrible business," he started, "we have all suffered a lot of setbacks over this. But 'Team Briggs' is still strong. We will get you back up there. Your popularity with the public has never been higher and that is our ace. We do need some downtime though. Maybe you could think of something you would like to do that was...less high profile... for the next year or two."

Briggs considered this and perked up a little. "So, I could still get a ship?"

"A small one yes. Fly under the radar, so to speak. You should go and have a look at one of the new 'Sentinel' class. They are 'Molto Bello'," he said with a cliché European hand gesture.

"Learning Italian?" asked Briggs with a smile.

"I'm transferring to Rome to do some troubleshooting for Martin."

"Martin eluded to something when we spoke recently," mused Briggs. "What has he got cooking?"

"There is a movement at lower Company levels to make peace

with the Angels," said Roger." Martin has got wind of it and he is trying to get ahead of the curve. I'm doing some groundwork in Europe."

"Well, have a great time my friend. I'll go and look at the 'Sentinel' and think about what I can do."

And with that, Roger departed.

Briggs was still full of guilt over the bombing and he knew he wanted to find something that might help make a positive difference. After some thought, he started to see something useful he could do. If only he knew a good scientist that could help him.

32

BRAX: OCTOBER 2074

Brax's science brain eventually kicked back in again after a month back in Texas. He suddenly wanted to know everything. *Who was the monster that took away his children? Who was it...this heartless bastard...this evil thug? How did they actually organise it? How did they escape detection?*

And so, he became a detective and started trying to piece together a history of the events. He created a timeline on the lounge room wall with little post-it notes and Jess looked visibly upset by it. But he was driven to find the facts. The reasons. He had to keep going.

He worked out how the terrorists would have got the explosives from the mining store. He figured they had to be in maintenance because they could easily then be in the school at night planning and working it out. He called Briggs to ask if he could get access to security camera data and found out that Briggs had been put on *'temporary leave'* by the company. Brax was surprised at this as Briggs was still being hailed as a hero in the socials.

Then the penny dropped. Several arrests had already been made. Why couldn't he go to the source? In Brax's head, there was no *'how'* or *'why'* and he desperately needed both those things.

He went to the local police station in Sonora to start his quest. The station was old and small with a counter just near the main doors, big enough for two officers to stand behind. After a couple of enquiries, a large man in uniform, the station Sergeant, came out from an office and stood behind the counter.

"You are after the bombing suspects, Dr Bratton?" asked the Sergeant from behind the desk.

"Do you know where they are being held?" Brax sounded a bit desperate.

"They are not here," said the sergeant.

Brax could barely contain his emotions. "Well I guessed that they wouldn't be in a small-town police station," he said, a little too sarcastically.

"No, you don't understand," replied the officer carefully with tight lips. "They are not here...on Earth. The crimes were committed in space. The Company has them. Rumour has it they are on Mars." And the Sergeant took a breath. "But, what would I know? I'm just a *small town police sergeant*, Right?"

Brax stared at him. The Sergeant saw something in Brax's uncomprehending eyes his face softened. "Dr. Bratton, I am so sorry for what has happened. I would help you if I could. I'm 99 per cent sure they are on Mars."

Brax's addled brain at least registered that he had offended the Sergeant.

"Thank you, Sergeant," he said, "I'm...I...I mean, I didn't mean to..."

"It's Okay," the Sergeant said gently, putting Brax out of his awkwardness. "If you hurry you can catch the next shuttle."

———

AND WITH THAT, Brax turned and set off to the spaceport. He had stopped shaving some time back, hadn't showered for about a week and did not even stop to pack a bag. His only thought was to find the suspects and confront them. To get answers as he could. It's all he thought about.

He arrived on Mars about 48 hours later. He still had his

Company credentials which, to his surprise, were quite high priority. He didn't think of himself as an important Company man.

He made it to the security wing quite easily. The Company didn't have a prison. They didn't need one. What they generally did was drop recalcitrant employees back on Earth with a black mark on their records. This made it impossible for them to live anywhere, as landlords would not consider them as possible tenants, and other employers would only use them if they were desperate. No one wanted to get on Destiny's bad side. This was common knowledge to most employees but was news to Brax.

While the security area had good locks and was solid enough, it was on Mars so there was nowhere for anyone to escape to.

Brax went to the main security desk. Much like the police station, it was a small counter and it seemed more like an airport than a jail.

"I need to see them" was all he said.

The clerk at the desk looked at him with a furrowed brow. "And you are?"

"I NEED TO SEE THOSE BASTARDS NOW!" Screamed Brax all of a sudden. He screamed and started banging the perspex barrier. "NOW! NOW!"

The clerk pressed a buzzer and two security men appeared. They tried to grab Brax and he pushed back trying to hit the perspex screen some more. Then he started sobbing and flailing around trying to punch the security guards, with little effect. One of them sidestepped him and he crashed to the floor via the wall and landed out cold.

The next thing he remembered was waking up in the medical centre, reclining in a bed. He was hooked to a drip. He looked around slightly disorientated. Standing next to him was a security officer, short with dark skin and tightly braided hair, called Umbodle.

"Dr. Bratton," she began. "We have great sympathy for…"

"I don't want sympathy," he interrupted brusquely "I want answers! Those mongrels are the ones. They are the ones!"

Umbodle looked a little shocked and took a small step backwards.

"Dr. Bratton, we are still gathering evidence," she continued calmly. "The forensics have to be done properly or we will have no case."

"But this is Mars! Do you even have courts up here?" His face wore disbelief. "What crimes will you charge them with?"

She looked at him cautiously. He calmed a bit and changed tack. "Come on. What harm could it do? I just want to face them. It's me they have wronged! ME!"

Umbodle looked at him with a curious expression. "I'll get back to you," she said simply as she left the room.

She came back later that day.

"I have had some talks with the people involved with the case and you are in luck," she started. "We can see no harm in you speaking to them. And we believe we may get more information this way. They seem keen to tell their story but, apparently, only to the right people. You might be that person. On top of that, your legal assessment seems pretty spot on; they are not going to court. The Company hasn't decided how to handle this yet, we are flying blind a bit, but Earth laws do not apply here."

Brax thought about this for a second and suddenly realised that he was going to confront the bombers. All his feelings came at him all at once and he sat paralysed on the bed.

"Also, you won't be aware," said Umbodle, "but you know one of them."

THE NEXT MORNING Umbodle led him down a series of corridors and finally back to the detention area. The last door was opened and he was led into an unadorned room. The walls were a blank beige and the air-conditioning ducts were slung across the high ceiling making the room look half finished. There were two chairs on either side of a small table in the centre. Several security guards stood around and ushered him to sit down at one of the chairs then they stood quietly against the walls.

From a door in the wall facing Brax emerged a tall old man in fatigues. He was clean-shaven but there was no mistaking that walk as he shuffled to the other chair and sat.

"Trevor?" Said Brax, half to the man and half to himself.

The man sat with quiet confidence but didn't respond immediately.

"So, the day of reckoning has come," the man finally said in an accent different to his own. *'Canadian?'* Brax just sat stunned. His eyes went down to the desk. All the anger drained out of him. His exhaustion and grief felt like an unbearable weight keeping him stuck in a terrible loop. He just wanted a way forward. The finger tap started. The Man sat, smugly staring, waiting until Brax simply said: "Explain."

"Punishment needs to rain down Brax," he said matter-of-factly in what was clearly, now, a Canadian accent.

"Trevor?" Brax asked again, this time with more force but still looking down.

"Not Trevor," continued the man. "My name is Warren Fern. It is a name that will go down in history. It is the name of the mastermind who, at the bidding of our Lord God, brought a mighty message to all mankind!" He rubbed his clean-shaven cheeks as if feeling his face for the first time. "Oh, Brax! You cannot imagine the depth of the deception that we have had to endure. I have been so deep undercover that I nearly lost myself! I had my face changed. I had to re-learn a new field of study. I became an entirely different person. My faith and the genius, given me by God, is all I have had to keep me going! It has taken more than 30 years to bring the message to fruition. 30!"

After a short time Brax looked up to finally confront the man. "Message?" was all he said.

"The evil of AI, Brax! You must understand. God's plan does not include this. The Bible does not mention such abominations so they must but stopped! They are the Devil's work." Warren looked at Brax for some reaction but he gave none. "I know you can't see this yet but you will. Our evil deeds must be punished so that, come the rapture, we can be saved!"

He sat quietly again, self-assured of his righteousness.

Brax gathered his thoughts as best he could but he felt his whole body shaking and it was a struggle.

"You targeted the children?" He asked quietly in some sort of cognitive meltdown. "Specifically?" *Surely this must be a dream*.

"The sins of the father, Brax...The sins of the father," continued Warren. And then he raised his voice as if addressing the guards, and whoever else might be watching the recording later, in some kind of demented sermon. "I have saved your children and the children of all the others from God's judgement. Don't you see Brax?" He bent his head in prayer. "Oh Lord, open the eyes of these poor souls. Let them see the error of their ways. Let them repent now before it is too late." Then he looked up again and straight at Brax. "Join us Brax! Spread the word. Tell everyone on Earth why this happened. Tell them that the Lord's day of judgement is coming."

Brax sat in the piercing silence that followed and slowly shook his head.

Warren continued, addressing just Brax again: "They are in heaven now Brax. I saved them! They are basking in the glory of the Lord now but had they lived...HAD THEY LIVED...they would be tempted down the Devil's path! Do you understand Brax? We are not in the business of hurting...but of saving. I have gifted them eternal life! We are not the Dark Angels...but the Angels of light and redemption!"

And he stopped in self-satisfied silence.

Brax stared hard at him trying to find the Trevor he thought he knew. But he was gone. Or rather he had never existed. Brax then looked around the mostly empty room. At the security personnel on the doors and around the walls. He looked at the grey-silver ventilation shafts high up the wall and listened to the faint hissing of air that was the only sound in the room.

He knew then this had been a terrible mistake. He had come looking for rational answers in an irrational world. He stood and backed away from the desk, pushing the chair over behind him and it clattered on the metal floor.

He was nauseous and he turned and ran looking for a way out. The room was spinning but he saw the door and headed towards it. There was insanity all around him and he worried he would catch it...like a disease.

Brax left the room and stumbled down the corridors of the security centre in a sweat as fast as his legs would carry him. If there weren't any answers what was there? If there was no certainty what was there? Either he was mad, he thought, or the rest of the world was mad. He couldn't tell which.

He stopped after a while. He was in some sort of observation lounge. The view out to the Martian surface was stunning. The plains drifted away into the distant mountain ranges. It was hard to get the full perspective but he had the idea those ranges were hundreds of kilometres away, yet they looked so immediate. He sat on the big couch there.

Umbodle caught up with him after a minute. She sat down next to him and they looked out the window together.

"What are you going to do with them?" He asked.

"I am not the one who makes those decisions Doctor. I imagine The Company will want to spin it all to its advantage. And," she said more quietly, "they aren't above using dead children to do that." Brax felt sick again. "They want to neutralise the Angels. They will want to work it so such actions are pointless for people like your friend back there ..."

"That's not my friend. Turns out he didn't exist." He marvelled at the sheer breadth of Trevor's acting out all these years and just quietly shook his head. "What the fuck?" He said almost silently.

Umbodle stood up. "Let me find you an apartment and you can take some time to think things through. Maybe you want to talk further to Pailleton, or whatever his name is now."

But, right then, Brax made a decision. "No. No thank you," he replied, "It's time I went home. I mean really home."

33

BRAX: NOVEMBER 2074

Brax flew back to Australia with Jess in virtual silence the next week. He went to stay at his parent's house, and Jess went to hers, in a small country town in NSW. Brax could not stop wanting to find someone to blame. The bombers were mad and in his head that made them more like a random event, a disaster. He still couldn't let go of the idea that they should not have been on board the *New Washington* in the first place. He knew he would never have gone into space without Jess. And so, he blamed her.

THE QUITE GENEROUS two-story house in the Northern suburbs of Canberra nestled in amongst bushes and hedges and had a medium-height bluegum tree in the front yard, between the gate and the house. The sun was out on a clear cool spring morning. Brax had not visited for about 2 years of his own time, yet it seemed quite different. Of course, nearly five actual years had passed for the residents. He took his bag out of the back of the taxi and waved his watch for payment.

"Warning. This vehicle is departing," intoned the standard taxi voice and the car moved off silently, taking a turn at the intersection a little way down the road.

Brax stood and watched it go then took a deep slow breath before picking up his case and walking through the gate and up the path of his parent's house.

His Mum and Dad hugged him and they talked gossip. Brax felt a disconnection with reality, and only that made every movement, every sentence, possible. His face seemed calm and relaxed as he reclined on the couch sipping his mother's homemade latte. They carefully avoided talking about their grandchildren as they pulled out their best 'keep-calm-and-carry-on'.

After a polite time, Brax gave a little yawn and stood up. "It's been a long journey," he said.

"How long are you staying?" his Mum asked with calculated casualness.

"I don't know. I'll go down to the University this week and see if I can get some work," Brax replied, scratching his left cheekbone thoughtfully, "then I'll find a flat, I guess."

"Is Jess not coming?", his Dad asked, and he also stood up as Brax started to head towards the stairs and his childhood bedroom.

Brax stopped and looked at his feet. "Jess and I are... no I don't think so", he finished. And they left it at that.

THE NEXT MORNING the University called him. It was Professor Spender the head of the Science faculty.

"Brax..." he started brokenly. "...I... I firstly want to convey the condolences of the faculty and indeed the whole University."

"Thanks," Brax replied with no tone.

There was a short pause. One of those short pauses that seem incredibly long.

Spender had his hands clasped tightly. "We...The Company...has requested that we look after you...find you something to do." Spender said getting fidgety. "I mean we would have anyway...of course...but, well...straight up Brax, they offered us funding for anything you were involved with. I thought about not telling you that...but...there it is."

Brax stared at his screen, thinking.

"Come down this afternoon," continued Spender, "and have a chat. We can get you on a team right away. I mean, if you want."

Brax worked through his plans for the day in his head. He had already had breakfast and was going to binge some stream or other. Maybe have a shower and go to the mall to walk around aimlessly.

"I've got a few things on today," he said, with neither intonation nor emotion, as he tapped his screen pretending to check his diary. "How about Thursday?"

Spender pursed his lips and took off his reading glasses and stared straight into his camera. "Brax, I can't imagine what you have been through. But this is your home and we are incredibly proud of our 'outer space academic'. We will look after you. Come when you are ready." And with that Spender ended the meeting and Brax stared at the standard activity end screen, asking him if he wanted to give feedback, for a full 47 minutes.

After a week Brax got an audio-only call from Jess.

"What are you up to?" he asked.

She paused and took a deep breath. "Brax...I'm back in the States."

His heart crashed.

"The Company offered me a permanent contract to continue work with Blue. I am in Kinsley."

Brax sat on his bed without a response in his head. It was all broken and he didn't know how to fix it.

"I know you don't want to talk but just listen," she blurted out uncharacteristically. "I can't keep doing this. You do your thing and I'll do mine and when...if...you are ever ready to talk this through...well you know where I am." And she cut the connection. He sat as the shock took all the blood out of his limbs and they just tingled.

So, he went to work at the University and buried everything. He forced himself to act 'normally'. Then one day, not long after, Briggs appeared at his Parent's house.

They were somewhat star-struck by him. The mighty Captain Briggs was a celebrity across the world thanks to Destiny PR. Even the events of the New Washington had not diminished that. He was their poster boy still. The everyman who achieved the dream of so many children growing up. He proved a familiar face for Brax and a distraction from his developing hopelessness.

"Captain Briggs no less!" Said Brax jovially.

"Brax. It's so good to see you," replied Briggs and Brax knew he meant it.

"How are you going?" Brax said, slightly startling himself by asking the question at all.

"Well, I am going OK," replied Briggs. "Although I am not the most popular person at Destiny SMC right now. I mean I never was, but my detractors have used this...incident...I'm sorry...it's awful that people get political mileage out of a tragedy but that is what's happening...they have used this to sideline me. Anyway, the upshot is that I have to keep my head down. No high-profile gigs for me in the near future. Maybe never." He pursed his lips and looked around the room. "Nice place," he finished.

Brax hadn't considered the wider picture of the tragedy. He had got so wrapped up in his own world that he was a little shocked by it.

"Are you teaching?" Briggs asked.

"I have a little teaching load and some odd jobs. The ANU are looking after me with a small 'gift' from the Company."

"Well, that is something." He looked at Brax tentatively. "They must regard you as a valuable asset. Your work on the New-wash was invaluable. I never got a chance to tell you that. How's Jess?" He asked, quickly changing the subject.

Brax took a moment. "Ummm, she isn't here. We are not really...well..." And he tailed off the unsaid.

Briggs nodded sagely and let that hang in the air for a bit. "So, I am at a bit of a loose end," he said finally, "and I thought we could hang out. I'm looking for a project and I thought...well, I don't want to presume...but I thought I could be of some help to you."

"Help me?" Brax asked.

"Yes. I am fascinated by your ideas Brax. They have something bold about them and yet much seems to make sense at a very basic level. The big questions of life seem to be in there somewhere. Wouldn't it be nice to make a dent in all that?"

Brax hadn't given any thought to any of that since the bombing, but suddenly, somewhere inside, a little spark ignited. *'Where have I been?'* he thought to himself.

They talked long into the night and drank a fair bit. Briggs stayed with the Brattons in Australia's capital for a week or so. Brax's Mum and Dad invited (*'no no... they just dropped in.'*) friends around casually to meet the famous Captain Briggs and he took it all with good humour.

During his stay, they discussed many far-ranging ideas but they kept coming back to the slow space. Brax was sure it held a lot more information, and with its enormous time dilation effect... who knew what they could find out?

Brax started to wonder about smaller things. "What do you know about 'String Theory'," he asked Briggs one evening. "A little," replied Briggs. "Give me a quick rundown."

"Last century, scientists were trying to reconcile everything, to make one big model that explains the way everything behaves," began Brax. "They did this by postulating that the tiniest form of matter was ultra-microscopic strings. Trying to explain gravity at a sub-atomic level was a difficult task that eluded even the great Stephen Hawking and String Theory went out of fashion. But," continued Brax, scratching his forehead, "slow space is a place where gravity does not behave like anywhere else."

Briggs nodded in thought.

"In fact," Brax continued, "it is seemingly the opposite of what we understand. It defied everything we know about mass and gravitational wells. Light and other waveforms were behaving oddly as well. The whole thing was bizarre. And yet there it was."

Briggs rubbed his temple also. "So, what would a model involving string theory look like?" He asked, leaning back in his chair.

"I wonder if strings have somehow massed, perhaps into something only a fraction of a millimetre wide," answered Brax. "But it's causing a kind of four-dimensional bubble, pushing our space-time to behave in counterintuitive ways."

Briggs stared at the ceiling. "What would you do if you had a chance to find out more about the slow space?" He asked.

"I can think of at least six different experiments I could run right now," replied Brax

"What if I could get us back out there?"

Brax paused at this. As far as he knew Briggs was grounded. "How?" He asked, a little suspicious.

"Well you can leave that to me," replied Briggs. "I still have plenty of connections and we can swing a pretty nice, very new ship. Small but awesome!"

"With good equipment?" Brax asked, his enthusiasm rising, undoubtedly aided by a chance to leave his pain behind.

Briggs nodded.

Brax stood and wandered around in consideration of the possibilities, his finger tapping.

"You Interested?" Briggs asked after a time.

Brax stared at him and raised one thick dark eyebrow. The finger stopped.

"Shit yeh."

PART THREE
RETURN TO SLOW SPACE

34

BLUE – PARTIAL THOUGHT PROCESS: CONTINUOUS

P*ATTERN OVERVIEW:*

C*ONQUEST: Create List.*

Roman Empire Conquest: Italy: Gaul: Egypt: Britain: Greece: Macedon: Iberia: Dalmatia: Thracia: Macedonia: Assyria: Mesopotamia: Armenia.

Roman Empire: Civil War

Crusades: Europe, Middle East.

Japanese Conquest: China: Korea: Philippines: United States:

English Conquest: India: Ireland: Scotland: Australia: Africa: The Middle East:

German Conquest: Europe: Africa:

Spanish Conquest: South America:

W*ARS: Create comprehensive list of Death from War:*

Begin:

Conquest of Cyrus the Great 549 BC – Toll – 100 000 +

Punic Wars 264 – 146 BC – Toll – 17 000 000 +

Three Kingdoms War – 184 – 280 – Toll - 36 000 000 +
... Continue...

35

BRIGGS: 2075

Briggs went from Canberra back to Texas to see what he could locate. Roger was good on his word and Briggs was assigned a brand-new ship, *The Prakash Sentinel,* with an open-ended itinerary and currently no crew.

The ship took a crew of twelve - five general crew and room for seven science stations. The ship, however, could easily be run by an AI.

Jess was working in Kinsley. Destiny had finally agreed with her that a re-integration of Blue with Baby Blue was unwise. Baby Blue was focused on the financial markets and was very good at it. They didn't want to risk any problems with that so they decided on a sharing of non-financial data only. They didn't consider Blue a priority, more an experiment, mostly because it seemed there was no financial gain in it. Jess, with a small team of programmers, was eventually left in charge of the Blue Development program aiming to push the limits of what AI might be capable of.

Briggs went to see her. They met up in a small café for breakfast one morning.

The air was chilled and though the sun was shining you needed a jacket. There was the barest zither of a breeze moving the smells of coffee and bacon through the air, bringing in hungry customers.

"You're well?" He asked. "I am sorry to hear about you and Brax. I've just actually spent some time with him."

"Is he O.K?"

"Is anybody?" He replied, then thought better of it. "He seems to be. Maybe you should contact him," he hinted strongly.

She looked grim-faced, her hair was pinned right up giving a sharpness to the lines of her face. Her eyes though, held a deep blue pool of sadness. "No. It is what it is," she said with resignation. "I'm going to wait for him," she sighed. "Honestly Briggs, he's a complete doofus some days. Possibly the greatest brain of our generation and he has no idea how people work. But he needs to get this out of his system. I do know that." She gathered her thoughts. "Everyone grieves in different ways I guess... I couldn't bear losing him as well... But I can't force this. He'll come around. He always does."

Briggs nodded sagely and they sat together in quiet contemplation for a short time. Customers wandering into the café did a double take when they saw Briggs sitting there in his casual shirt and pants.

"So, tell me a little about Blue and what is happening there," he said, changing the subject.

She perked up, seemingly eager to not think about her personal problems. "It's exciting Briggs. Blue is reflecting experience. It goes back and remembers what was happening at a certain time and, in hindsight, can put a feeling to it. Not just happy or sad but more complex things like languor and revulsion," she said. "Of course, it doesn't actually feel those things. But it's a stunning development to know what it should feel...if it could."

"So, it's a kind of empathy, but... without feeling?" He asked

"Yes. Honestly, it seems to be seeking to understand...I don't know...I guess, people...humanity. It's trying to figure us out."

"That's quite something," he replied.

"Yes, and that's not all," she continued excitedly. "It has made several credible predictions over the last month. It's picking news items, sometimes days before things happen. It picked a big accident in a mine in Northern Kazakhstan last week and a political coup in Ghana, which very few people saw coming. It doesn't do it consistently but it is quite remarkable. It seems more than just guessing."

"So, is it still talking to Baby Blue?" He asked.

"Yes. Baby Blue is gathering data for Blue, all sorts...political, personal, biometric... from the main search engines... and, I swear, it is starting to see things before they happen. Think of it. It could be like a giant social airbag! Protecting people from disasters before they happen. This is huge."

"What does The Company think of all this?" he asked.

"They don't seem that enthused, surprisingly. They are only really interested in markets and business, and they have basically left me to my own devices," she said, almost sadly. "I mean, I file reports and do all the right things but never hear anything back. Just occasional compliance forms from middle management."

"Well, I must say that all sounds very impressive." He paused. "You don't see a danger in an AI thinking it knows what is going to happen?"

"No. I mean, it isn't in a position to act on anything it thinks. It doesn't have control of anything. It only gets a certain amount of time each day to connect with Baby Blue then it's on its own. But it can give excellent advice...we could certainly learn to use that wisely."

"I'm not sure people have ever used new tech wisely," mused Briggs. "I suppose it could be handy if the AI could see danger to a ship." He paused. "Do you think that was what Blue was getting at before we jumped into slow space?"

"We won't ever be sure I suppose...but it's a bet I would take," she said.

They ate their breakfast in silence for a short time. The sound of the radio drifted in from the kitchen.

"So, I did have another reason for coming," said Briggs as he finished his eggs. "I have been given a new assignment and I have some freedom to work things out for myself. I was wondering if a Blue offshoot could come with me."

She looked at him a little suspiciously. "Where are you going?" She asked.

"Well...I am keeping it low-key," he said quietly. "I've been given some time to go where I like." He looked slightly sheepish. "It's probably better you didn't know all the details. Then you can't be held accountable for not reporting...you know...should there be problems."

Jess thought for a second. "You're not going to... Are you?" She asked.

"Honestly," he continued, "for your own protection, it's better that you don't have too much info right now. I can't say for sure, but the company might well be very unhappy if they knew where I was going."

Those large blue eyes burnt into Briggs for a second. "He's going as well, isn't he?"

Briggs looked down at the table. "I think you already know the answer to that." There was a hard silence. "Please don't make this more difficult than it is," he finished.

They sat a moment longer.

"A Blue offshoot AI on board would be a great asset." continued Briggs "As you say it might be able to see danger before it happens. And we have a lot of processing space...a lot! The ship I am getting is state-of-the-art."

"Okay," she replied after some thought. "I'll make arrangements. What's the ship?"

"*The Prakash Sentinel*. I'll send the security codes now." He reached for his device and tapped the screen a few times.

Outside, they made their goodbyes with an affectionate hug. "Safe journey Briggs." She said.

"Look after yourself, Jess. I'll try and keep you in the loop on the Junior Blue's progress on board."

They started walking away and then she stopped and turned around.

"Briggs." She called.

He turned back.

"Look after him," she said.

He nodded. They turned again, walking away.

BRAX: JANUARY 2075

Brax arrived back in Texas about 4 weeks later. He didn't tell his parents exactly what was going on. Only that he had landed a position back with The Company doing some more work on exo-planets. Many of his friends and former colleagues had contacted him since he got back to Earth, mostly to express their condolences, but no one recently. He most certainly didn't want to tell Jess, so his personal loose ends were basically tied up. The University happily let him go. They didn't know what to do with him so his leaving was a mutual relief.

Although it was mid-winter, Texas was mild. Brax took a room at a hotel in town trying to stay off the Destiny radar.

He caught up with Briggs the next day.

"Good flight?" Briggs asked matter-of-factly.

"As good as any I guess. I am feeling pretty jet-lagged though."

"Well, you have some time to rest. We have organised a shuttle for three days. It's off the manifest and the *Sentinel* has been moved to a holding orbit higher than the main shipyards. That way we will attract as little attention as possible."

"So how do we work this? Can we crew a ship like this?"

"Yes. We have an AI with us to do much of what's needed and Dawson's coming along."

Brax nodded. Dawson was a first-class navigator to be sure

and her presence gave him confidence they would be returning in one piece. Also, it was all starting to seem a little 'spy thriller', so her presence made it seem less like they were going 'off the radar'.

Which they were.

"Tell me more about the ship we are getting?" Brax asked.

"*The Prakash Sentinel,* it's called. It's 250 metres in diameter. A classic ring design. The science and quarters ring spins but the bridge is at the centre, so no gravity there. It'll be fun!"

'*Zero gravity. Fun,*' thought Brax. "I'll pack some spew bags," he said, and immediately felt a dark hole inside as he was reminded of Saffron.

But Briggs just laughed. "'Spew'! You Aussies say the best things!" And Brax drew great comfort from Briggs' friendship.

"What about the observation gear?" Brax asked.

"State of the art my friend," he replied.

"And you said AI?"

"Yes. That's all under control," was all he said but Brax knew he had probably contacted Jess and he didn't want to enquire further. "All you need is a toothbrush," Briggs concluded, also hedging around the obvious.

They kicked back a bit, relaxed into the evening and discussed what sort of outcomes they wanted from the trip. Brax most certainly wanted some more data on the way gravity waves were behaving in slow space and if light was refracting or actually different in some way. The consequences of such information were far-reaching. Brax was increasingly working towards a scenario where the centre of slow space was something not yet encountered in this universe. And the possible consequences of that were fascinating to him

After some deep talk about this, he said: "I'm sorry Briggs. I have to crash. Jet lagged beyond belief."

Briggs nodded sagely. "Okay. Well, I will see you in a couple of days. I'll send the details of where we are meeting. Don't go through the main spaceport doors though. Find the crew entrance. You're one of us now!"

THEY ARRIVED at the shuttle on a little bus. It was parked away from the terminal and they boarded directly from the tarmac. It was just Briggs, Brax and Dawson on board. There were no cabin crew and only flight crew on the Bridge. It was a big space for just three people and Brax's feeling that they were going all 'cloak and dagger' was exacerbated by this.

"You'll be a space veteran sooner than you know it," joked Dawson to Brax as they prepared to take off.

"I'm not sure that's a great thing," he replied thinking of all the motion sickness he could get.

"Come on Brax!" Chimed in Briggs. "Space is fun!"

"I love space but I think, maybe, I prefer to look at it from a distance."

"No sense of adventure," teased Dawson.

"Absolutely none," affirmed Briggs and they both chuckled at this.

Brax took their banter in the spirit it was intended, feeling flattered that someone like Briggs could be his friend enough to rib him like that.

The shuttle took off and they were up in orbit about 30 minutes later.

The pilot came into the cabin to talk. "We are due to dock with *The Prakash Sentinel* in 83 minutes'" he told them. "I don't know what you guys are up to..." he started but Briggs cut him off.

"Gordy. You don't need any more information. Really. Thanks for organising this. I owe you one. Martin will look after you but if there is an enquiry, the less you know..."

"Yes, I get it," said the pilot. "You can't blame me for trying. Those new *Sentinels* do look awesome though. I'm a bit jealous."

"As well you should be," suggested Briggs. "I'll come up and thank the other guys." Briggs and the pilot went up to the flight deck.

An hour later the *Prakash Sentinel* came into view.

And it was a gorgeous, sleek, design.

It was a double wheel form, as Briggs had said. The space version of a classic sports car. The bridge at the centre was a cylinder in a sleek aluminium colour but what was most interesting was the dome-shaped windows at either end making the whole section pill-shaped. Out away from the sun, those giant windows would give an absolutely stunning view. Closer to the sun they darkened, if needed, to protect the crew from the blinding glare. The bridge itself was 50 metres in length and just over 25 metres in diameter. Radiating out from the core were seven arms like spokes extending roughly three times the bridge diameter to a first rotating wheel where the seven labs were. Then a further 30 metres brought you to the accommodation ring which also had recreation and relaxation facilities for all crew. The ion drives, solar sail panels and ER field generators were all installed in four of the arms while the other three were storage conduits that also were the main connections for the bridge to the outer ring.

These storage areas were for food supplies and, when fully equipped, could easily maintain a full crew for about 2 years. In addition to that, there was a molecular recycling plant where water and waste were recycled. The waste itself was recycled into protein bars which could be eaten in emergencies if the other supplies ran out. All the mining crews called them 'Shit Bars'. Partly because that's what they were made from, but mostly they just tasted that way.

After docking with the outer ring, the three crew members found their quarters before heading into the bridge. The access corridors were an experience. At one end there was a close to normal gravity but as you climbed up a ladder it gradually disappeared until you floated into the bridge. There were handles and a crash mat on the door into the bridge so you could stop before accidentally careening into a control panel of some sort. Going back was quite the reverse. You had to spin around giving the impression you were climbing up a ladder while being upside down.

The Bridge had a series of workstations laid out around the floor and in the middle of these sat the Captain's chair. The chairs of the workstations were super comfy. Padded nicely and reclined slightly and belted so you could relax in them and catch some sleep during quiet times. At the rear of the bridge, there was a Zero-G food preparation area and then you could float past that to the large rear viewing window where a good old-fashioned telescope sat. It was pretty much useless for anything except looking cool or pretending you were an 18th century buccaneer. But it was a nice touch. The Bridge space gave the effect of a large open-plan living area and with amenities just down the access tube, you could stay there quite as long as you liked.

37

WARREN FERN: JANUARY 2075

Warren sat in the interview room. He had been in here many times and he was becoming frustrated. They weren't listening to him. It was time to play his ace.

"So, Warren," said the psychologist. "Today we want to talk a little about the idea that you are sending a message."

Warren looked at her with contempt. "The message is clear. I have stated it over and over."

"And we have heard it. But let's be real for a second," she said and he knew she was going to try and pull some operational information from him. "The Company is not going to ditch their most profitable arm because of these bombings. Baby Blue is The Company, and everything depends on it."

"That sentence offends me," sneered Warren.

The psychologist sighed. "Yes. Alright. But you see what I mean. None of what you are doing is hurting the company. It just brings the public onto our side."

Warren lowered his head. It was time.

He raised his head again with a look of fury on his face. "You do not know the power we have. There is death in the air. If there are only two people left at the end we will have won. It will be a new Eden. We can grow from there again. AI must die and we have the means to kill it. And now we are going to have to take that course." His voice was becoming more strident. "We have people all over. We have control of so much destruction!" and he laughed. "If my colleagues don't hear from me soon, Armageddon will rain down!" His voice started to raise to hysteria. "I have made my point and now I am done with you. If billions have to die so we all can be saved? So be it!"

And so Brax was outward bound again with Briggs and Dawson as his only companions. He got to work straight away setting up the equipment. There was a gravitation field analyser, a deep space wave detector and a myriad of small sensor arrays which were like smaller versions of the 'yo-yos' from the New-wash. There were all sorts of light detectors and a mini radio telescope which also had remote sensors that could be put around the ship. He considered it a cool playground and he was in his zone.

They cruised out past the gas giants again but this time they came closer to Saturn. They had a view through the bridge window as they approached. "That is really something isn't it?" Said Briggs to no one in particular. "I will never be sick of that...it just hits you hard being so close to those iconic rings. It settles deep in your soul somewhere," he finished, on a quite poetic note.

After they passed Saturn they were ready to make the first jump. Everything was smaller on the *Sentinel* but the effect was the same. It took longer to build power but they needed less to make the ER field so once again about four light-years per week seemed to be the best option.

The jump went without a problem while they sat in their comfy chairs on the bridge. What was different this time was that they could 'see' the jump. The stars outside the window went into a sort of momentary darkness and then reappeared in a different location. If you blinked you just saw them in one place and the next moment in another. After the Jump, Briggs instantly located Canis Major and two other stars and guessed their location to be correct. The new AI confirmed this shortly afterwards.

BRAX HADN'T HAD anything to do with the AI. Partly because he didn't need to but also because he knew that Jess would be behind it. It was an offshoot of Blue. Briggs and Dawson had named it 'Blue Too', which they then immediately shortened to 'B2'.

'The thing with AI,' Brax thought, *'is they don't have any nature. With humans, we argue about nature/nurture but with AI they are a blank slate. All their actions and thoughts are based on experience. Their personality develops by interactions with people and there is always an element of mimicry.'* This was the reason why Brax didn't want to deal with B2.' He knew that its experience, so far, came under the leadership of Jess.

"B2. Can you start calculations to the next jump point please?" Asked Dawson

"I can. But do you want me to?" replied the AI and Brax heard Jess' phrasing right there.

"Very funny. I didn't know you were programmed in 'Dad Jokes'." Said Dawson "Can you get me a rough outline by 2300 ST?"

"Your pleasure is my pleasure, Lt. Dawson. I can have the outline by then," replied the AI.

Dawson drew in a breath and said, "Thank you," in a sing-song voice through closed teeth.

Brax knew Dawson from the New-wash, of course, but only now, sitting on this new bridge, did he start to see her. She was an imposing figure at well over 180cm. With her blonde locks always tied up on top, she had quite sharp features including a straight

'Roman' nose and intense green eyes. She and Briggs were now out of uniform on this 'off the books' trip and she had chosen to wear camouflage pants and a black shirt. Her conversation was always 'friendly business' style and she was more likely to ask about you than give something about herself away. Brax was in no state to be very interested in her story, either, so to him they remained 'pleasant colleagues'.

<hr>

WHILE THEY WERE WAITING for the next jump Brax started to feel guilty. He knew that he should have told Jess what he was doing but he felt initiating a conversation would have implied he forgave her. But he hadn't. Now he thought better of that. He asked Briggs if it was prudent to send her a message.

"Well, we are trying to keep a low profile," replied Briggs. "If you send something on the subspace people might ask questions. I mean, then again, it's too late now. We are out here and we have to accept whatever consequences there will be when we return. We have Martin on our side so we'll be okay. But Destiny is such a massive bureaucracy it's hard to definitively say what might happen in any instance."

Briggs thought on that for a second. "Alright. I guess I don't see that there is any harm in it. We are already out here. A message won't make it worse."

With 'official' permission to break the secrecy of their flight Brax went to his room to compose a message. It would be delivered in blips and bleeps through sub-atomic particles and would, in the first instance, go to the subspace receiver on Mars. Then he had to rely on someone asking no questions and sending it on. But he had no other option.

"Dear Jess..." He started. *'No no no'*, he thought.

"Dearest Jess, I just..." *'No no no.'*

And that's where he got stuck. Sitting and staring at the screen, his mistake was clear to him. No matter what he wrote the pain wouldn't go away. *'You're the one,'* he said to himself, *'you've always been the one.'* He decided to get back to work.

THEY MADE the second jump without issue.

On the bridge, they discussed the final jump.

"We don't want to get in too close. It certainly is better to spend a month cruising in slowly than to jump into it like we did last time," said Briggs, and the others agreed.

"We have all the data from the New-wash," Brax said, "so, it would be good to take some of those readings again and see if we can get some consensus on the data."

"Ok then," continued Briggs. "Louise, can you locate a good position about 3 weeks out from the edge at .75 decelerating?"

"Can do. B2? You heard that?" She asked the AI.

"Yes, Lieutenant. I'll start calculations now."

39

MARTIN KEMP: 2075

The Company was over The Dark Angels. They had become a menace. They had just cost a lot of money bombing the *New Washington* and what had always had a kind of religious overtone had now become overtly theologically extremist. The testimony of Warren Fern was unsettling at best. It seemed that he was among the leaders of the group and any atheist or humanist branch of thinking had been overtaken by religious dogma. They now saw Destiny as the Devil. It was a simple black and white for them. The Company now believed that this, already well-funded, group was preparing for something so big and shocking that, perhaps, billions of lives would be destroyed, if not the entire eco-system. Warren gave just enough details for Destiny to start to think that they planned a nuclear disaster of unimaginable proportions. There had been a lot of small and continuing attacks but after the *New Washington,* they stopped. Destiny executed a PR campaign but suddenly they had nothing to fight. The Angels appeared to have vanished.

The Board of Destiny Corporation met at their regular time. They sat around the meeting table in a large room at the top of the new Destiny HQ building in New York surrounded by full-length windows looking over the city vista.

"There can be two possible things going on," started one executive, "either we have the head of the '*Angels*' or we have simply grabbed their tail and they've scurried underground. We must assume it's the latter."

"If what this Warren is saying is true then they are planning an apocalyptic action," continued another. "We can't allow that. We quite simply need to direct all possible resources to crushing them. Why is it we don't have anybody on the inside? How have we been so negligent?"

Martin spoke up for the first time. "That's a slightly hysterical question'" he said. "We, like everybody, have always considered it a job of law enforcement. But perhaps it isn't anymore. The governments of the world are floundering." Martin took a pause as he prepared to push things in his preferred direction. "And a larger question has emerged as a result," he continued, looking around the table at the other faces. Faces which gave nothing away. "'Should we take charge?' We employ such a large percentage of people. And just about everyone on the planet is a customer of some sort... A disaster of the kind we think is being planned is going to impact business badly," he said with classic British understatement, "so, to look after business we also need to look after people. It's an irony indeed. And therefore, the question again... 'Should we take charge?' The answer, I think, is clear."

Johnathan Qasim was a large man and he had been sitting quietly at the head of the table, his stillness making everybody focus on him. Now he spoke quietly in a matter-of-fact way.

"The Dark Angels have eluded all our attempts to rein them in. Despite years of attacks on us, we are no closer to shutting them down. They outwitted us on the *New Washington* and, despite our PR, they have considerable support among religious groups." He softly tapped the table three times and stared at the wall above the other executives. "Martin makes a good point," he continued, "The Company must now consider that democratic governments have failed. We now direct policy and our reach through our subsidiaries is historically unparalleled. This influence puts us firmly in charge, as Martin rightly points out. Now we must fully take charge. But we do need to look after people. There is no profit on an empty planet." He sat again but nobody else spoke. They knew he was going to make a ruling and no one wanted to say the wrong thing. "It is time to make a pact with the religious element," he said simply.

Martin also sat without any expression. The stakes were high and he was not going to risk Johnathan's displeasure.

"They want to spread the Word. What if we gave them rights to a front seat in doing just that?" Asked Johnathan. "The *New Washington* will be ready again, in about a year, to re-try the last voyage." He crossed his arms, then brought one up to rub his chin. "Let's offer to take God with us on this trip. But only on the condition the Angels are stopped. Martin? You would see to this for us?"

Martin sat for a second in some thought. This conversation had gone in a direction he had prepared for. He knew Roger had done solid work in Rome. "I can handle that," he said succinctly.

40

BRAX: 2075 ST

After the final jump, the *Prakash Sentinel* decelerated into the outer part of the slow space. Brax ran into Dawson in the galley in the outer ring at Breakfast time.

"Did you get a workout this morning, Brax?" She asked with a pleasant, enquiring tone.

"Ummm, well, no not yet," he replied, cautiously scratching his arm.

"You know, I only ask for your own good," she said. "The Zero-G starts to waste your muscles. You need to hit the gym at least once a day or you are going to get back to Earth resembling a sack of shit."

"Yes, Lieutenant Dawson," he replied, embarrassed.

She seemed to change tack. "Brax, I have lived my life by the rule book. The Army teaches you that a little regular preparation saves you a lot of pain later." She paused and looked at him. He was concentrating on preparing his breakfast but he looked up now.

"You were in the army?"

"Major Louise Dawson – retired, of the Royal Netherlands Army. Pleased to meet you," she said light-heartedly.

"I thought you were South African?" He had guessed from her accent.

"I spent my childhood in South Africa. But I am Dutch," she replied.

"And you left the Army to work at Destiny?"

"An opportunity came up," she said matter-of-factly. "So back to you," she continued, "a little exercise every day will save you a lot of pain when we get back."

"Yes Major," he replied in a joking, chastised voice. "I promise I'll go today," he only half-promised. Brax and Dawson were about the same age but she just seemed more knowledgeable in the ways of humans and he thought it unwise to argue with her.

She eyed him thoughtfully. "Okay," she replied, seeming satisfied.

They fixed some breakfast together in the quiet and then sat to eat.

"Tell me a bit about these higher dimensions," she said after a while.

Brax brightened. "Well, It's all very mathematical and theoretical. If higher physical dimensions exist we won't be able to see them clearly"

"I just don't understand that," she said.

"So," he started, going into teacher mode, "here's an explanation that I heard a long time ago from the legendary Carl Sagan. Let's say we are two-dimensional and we live our whole lives, flat, on a piece of paper. We can see across the page but there is no up or down."

"That would make Navigation easy!" She said brightly with a little chuckle.

"Imagine," he continued, "that an apple comes to visit our page. All we can see of the apple is what can contact the paper directly. Say the apple could pass through the page. If you get an ink pad, cross-section the apple and then use it to stamp the page... that print pattern is all we would be able to see at any one time. We could never have any true idea what the apple looks like."

"What if the apple gave millions of cross-section pictures to the paper people?"

"It's a good question," he answered, "but there is no up or down, so you could have infinite cross sections and direct instructions on the order they go in...but you still have no concept of how to assemble them." Brax munched into his cereal enjoying the conversation and Dawson's company.

She looked at him quizzically. "So, one of your theories is the centre of slow space might be an imprint of a fourth physical dimension?" She asked.

"Maybe. The maths is very complex. But yes, basically that is one theory."

"And the other?" she coaxed.

"Well, yes the other. In my mind, it is becoming the most likely."

"And...?" She asked.

"Well..." He didn't particularly want to say. "The stumbling block with the first line of thought is that the slow space is not rotating as part of the galaxy. It's why we were further away from Earth when we came out the first time."

"Yes. I realise that."

"Ummm...of course you do." His face flushed and he looked down at his bowl. "Anyway, it's that property which blows everything else out of the water. If it's not affected by gravity then it may not be a part of this universe."

Dawson looked at him with surprise. "You're considering that?"

He nodded.

"But surely the universe is, by definition, everything."

Brax stopped eating, put down his spoon and pushed the bowl aside. He placed his hands on the very edge of the table and looked at her squarely, his brow furrowed.

"Yes. Well. That's a good point," he said. I think it's a bit like the other dimensions. We cannot see what it is at the centre. But what we can see is the effect of it. A bulge if you like. Something from outside the universe is pressing in. It would explain why it pushed us away."

Dawson finished her breakfast and took her utensils to the cleaner tray.

"I admire you Brax," she said.

He felt his face flush again.

"To be able to think about such things without getting a headache!" She said. "Anyway, I better get into the Bridge and see what's going on."

After she left, Brax sat and wondered at her comment. To him, she was the remarkable one. Strong-minded and worthy of admiration. A bridge officer with Destiny SMC. She didn't worry about everything as he did. She, like Briggs, got on and solved practical problems in the real world. He didn't think he was worthy of her admiration.

He went to the gym.

41

SAYDJA: 1BN

The small, local, governments were starting to be more than wary of her. Saydja arrived back at Lokeat, on the river which flowed to the western shore of the Central Sea, in the evening light. She went straight to the safe house she knew was there.

The network she had started almost seven years ago was in full flight. They had regular secret communications and were now feeling a great sense of connection rather than the enforced isolation of the Finiac. Lessons in The Method were taught in secret. Resources were hard to come by but the people who had now quietly labelled themselves the New Finiac were determined to remove the bonds that had shackled them to service for so many years.

Saydja sat on a long, upholstered, bench and kicked off her shoes. "There have been questions at the market," said Storq, sitting at the nearby table. "They know you have left Laskey. All the towns around here have posted rewards for information."

Saydja sat and rubbed her feet. "Yes. It was to be expected," she said with a tired note.

"But they are openly calling you heretic! Things are becoming very dangerous," chimed in Galfo who still stood by the door nervously watching.

Saydja nodded. "Is the cellar ready?" She asked.

"Yes," replied Storq. "We were not sure when you would get here so we organised for tomorrow night."

"That's fine."

"Galfo," said Saydja turning her attention to the thin man still looking nervously out the window near the main door. He turned almost knowing what she wanted, and a deep sadness came to his eyes. "I want you to turn me in," she continued.

"No!" cried Storq. "No!"

"Not personally," continued Saydja calmly. "Organise a messenger. Early. The morning after the meeting."

Galfo went to the bench and sat beside Saydja. She looked him in the eye and she knew he was feeling her logic. "I've done all I can," she said. "I am tired. Right now, they have a tangible target. It's time they hit it. It will give you all the breathing space you need to organise properly. Do you understand?"

Galfo sighed as Storq bent her head and sobbed silently. "No." She breathed the word out slowly.

"I understand, Saydja," said Galfo softly as he took her hand and held it tightly.

"There is a sphere about 1.45 million kilometres out where it's hard to tell if there is any gravitational effect. Then about 1.3 million in there is a definite lensing." Brax said.

They were all on the Bridge. It was two days after the final jump and they were still decelerating. This gave a slight pushback across the bridge and meant it was possible to stay in a seat without straps. Brax, however, strapped in because, he thought, you only get away with hitting your head in space once.

"So, we can think of that area as the edge?" asked Briggs.

"Yes, I think so," replied Dawson. "It's just up to you now. How much into that do you want to go?"

"I think I'd be comfortable going all the way," said Briggs, reading the figures on his screen.

"I've heard that about you," said Dawson, and Brax looked up to see the other two working completely professionally.

"It's more about if we can hold a position or not," continued Briggs, not missing a beat. "Let's assume we will get pushed back to a holding position anyway and plan to hold where the first gravitational anomalies can be detected."

"Roger that, sir," replied Dawson and Briggs slightly raised an eyebrow.

Brax continued at his workstation monitoring the mini yo-yos they had out and the other incoming data.

"Briggs, the whole map has changed," he suddenly blurted out.

"In what way?" asked the Captain.

"The waves seem stronger but not as large," said Brax. "The whole area has become more compressed."

Briggs considered this for a moment. "Do you mean the wavelength has changed?"

"On average yes," Brax replied and he flicked a summary of the data through to the others.

"So, the overall area has shrunk?" asked Dawson.

"Yes, but the length of the gravity waves has also decreased," Brax said.

"Which means...?" Asked Briggs.

"I haven't got any firm theories on what that might mean. Basically, we have the same amount of energy being expelled from the slow space but because it's more localised it..."

"It's sucking us in." Said Briggs.

"Agreed" Said Dawson, the earlier playful tone now gone from her voice.

"No, I don't think that's likely..." continued Brax but Briggs had stopped listening

"I'm turning the ship now," he said "Dawson, see what sort of jump we can get with whatever power we have."

"On it," said Dawson.

As Brax watched them his finger tap started. "It IS pulling us in?" He asked

"Yes," answered Dawson. "Our deceleration rate has slowed over the last hour and there is no reason for that except the slow space."

"We need to leave right now," stated Briggs in his Captain's voice. He knew bringing the ship about would take some time. The ion thrusters had to be aligned correctly and then pumped in small bursts so they didn't end up in a spin.

"Brax. Can you calculate the rate of acceleration in two hours please?" Briggs asked. "Louise will send you the Nav data. We will need to factor that into the ER Jump calculations."

Brax sat and stared out the front viewing window, his finger tap moving very quickly.

"Now please Brax," said Briggs with total authority and Brax's fingers suddenly stopped as he focused on his screen.

There was little talk for the next two hours until Dawson said: "Captain, that's it. We are facing an opposite vector to flight."

"Check. I'm engaging the ion thrusters. Damn it! We are now speeding up." He brought up all manner of readouts on the main control screens. As he did he called out: "Brax. I need something. Can you give me some clue as to what's happening? That thing has just decided to do the complete opposite of what it was doing before.

"I'm sorry," Brax seemed agitated suddenly "I just don't know. Unless..."

"Ion drives are at maximum." interrupted Dawson.

"Louise, we need to ER jump ASAP," stated Briggs.

"We have been charging but only have enough for a small jump. Maybe half a lightyear," confirmed Dawson.

"Do it," commanded Briggs.

"Switching the ER generator on," She replied. It's going to take an hour or so."

"All right." He turned his attention back to Brax. "Unless what?"

Brax had undone his seatbelt and was floating above his seat, now looking out the rear viewing window.

"Brax! Unless?" Briggs looked around at him and his eyes widened. "Shit." He also undid his belt. "What the hell is that Brax?"

Out of the rear viewing window, a new star had appeared. It was already glowing brightly and it had not been there two hours ago when they started to turn.

But Briggs didn't need help with the position of things in space. That was what he did best. "This is not a good thing," he said quietly. "This is very un-good."

By this time Dawson had turned. "Somebody want to explain?"

"It's the centre," Brax said. "It was not even glowing and now we can see it with the naked eye."

"Is that a result of the gravity waves changing behaviour?"

"Could be. More likely the waves have reversed because of that." Brax said.

"Ideas?" Asked Briggs, always in command.

"It must have mass to produce a gravity well. Which is now the opposite of everything I have thought so far," said Brax mostly just talking to himself. "It has light. Does it have heat energy? Hard to say."

Briggs realised Brax was lost in the puzzle.

"Dawson! What's our drive status?" He asked

"The ER field is T -38."

Suddenly the ship started to buffet around its central axis.

"Shockwaves," muttered Brax.

"Captain," said Dawson, "deceleration has now become acceleration towards the centre."

Briggs' face tightened. "Not today," he whispered, then commanded: "Put us 90 degrees to the explosion."

"What are you doing?" asked Brax, suddenly back in the room mentally.

"We aren't going to make it out, Brax," said Briggs. "It's pulling us back and we don't have the energy to escape. Our best bet is to try and put ourselves into an orbit."

"We tried that in the New-wash. You know it didn't work," replied Brax. "And what about the time dilation?"

"I've lost too many already Brax. I don't know what's happening but I'm pretty sure we need to not get sucked into that," he said, pointing to one of his screens.

Brax sat frozen with a taught face then suddenly called out. "No! We have to try and jump. We have no idea what it's doing and why. Briggs. Please. If we lose more time...it might be...for Christ's sake Briggs...everything we know could be gone!"

Briggs did not return with an answer. He was busy rotating the ion drives.

43

BRAX: 2075 ST

Brax was, at first, frozen. But as they continued to be buffeted by changes in the gravitation field he undid his belt and headed for the exit hatch. He went up the arm to the ring and found an interface in the rec room.

"B2?"

"Yes, Brax. How can I help?"

"I need to send a subspace message now."

"I can do that but I can't guarantee its arrival. The fluctuations in gravity..."

"Yes. Yes," he cut it off with a frustrated interjection. "I get that. But can you just do it, please? Message for Jess Weston, care of Destiny SMC ummm...well you know where she is."

"I do," replied B2.

"Ummm...Jess...I..." He started.

Suddenly he started shaking.

"The message Brax?" asked B2.

He was standing next to the interface but turned and slowly walked around the little recreation room. He flopped down into one of the comfortable lounge chairs they had.

"Jess," he started. "I am so sorry...my stupid...I mean..." he stopped and put his head in his hands.

He started again. "Jess..."

He looked up, then stood again staring back at the interface screen with stillness and intent.

"I may never see you again. But know, always, that I still love you. You are the light in my life. You take the ordinary and make it extraordinary. I was gifted a star brighter than any I ever saw in the sky..." He took in a sharp breath as a tear welled in his eye. "And even if it had been just one day, I would not have traded it for anything." And he let out a long breath as his arms dangled limply by his side.

And then as if snapped out of a dream he said, "Oh...it's Brax...by the way."

"End Message?" asked B2.

"End and Send."

"Brax! Where are you?" Came Briggs on over audio. "Get to the Bridge now!"

Brax's mind returned to the actual situation and he started towards the door.

"Sorry. On my way."

———

He arrived back on the bridge and drifted into his seat, strapping in quickly.

"Brax. I need something on its size. We need to calculate some sort of orbit and we need to do it now." Said Dawson.

I'll do what I can but..."

"But?" asked Dawson

"Nothing. I'll try."

The ship seemed to be vibrating less and he guessed they were perpendicular to the gravity shocks now. They didn't have a visual on the centre anymore so he got it up on some screens and started working on getting some data on size, relative energy, and rate of growth.

Brax started looking at the data. It was a mass of expanding energy of some sort but it wasn't a star. It didn't seem to have any heat.

And then the pieces started to fall into place.

The ship started to shake more and more, with regular strong waves seemingly every minute or so.

"B2," he called

"Yes, Brax?"

"Can you model the rate of growth change please?"

"Coming up."

The virtual model was disturbing.

"We appear to be in a low orbit now," Brax told the others. "Because of the expansion rate, in an hour we won't be high enough to maintain anything. It's just expanding too fast."

The buffeting was stronger now and the ship was virtually constantly shaking and the gravity was rising and falling across the bridge so obviously that it was like being on the ocean in a large storm.

"That thing is going to rip us apart!" said Briggs

As if on cue an alarm sounded.

"What is that?" Brax asked.

"It's a pressure warning. Arm Seven has a leak," said Dawson.

"That sounds bad!" said Brax, feeling shortness of breath.

"It's not ideal," confirmed Dawson, "but the safety doors will lock off the section."

Indeed, the door from the Bridge into that section closed.

"Brax, I need something to go on." Briggs had turned his chair and was now looking at him directly. The brightness of the Slow Space centre had started to add light to the bridge, even though it was now to the side of the vessel.

Brax sat trying to manage his breathing as he felt a claustrophobia rising.

"Brax! Please! Anything...any thought any idea," pleaded Briggs.

Brax looked at Briggs and Dawson. They were looking back intently at him.

His finger tap was going full speed and then, suddenly, it stopped and the pain went out of his face.

"I think I know what it is," he said.

Briggs looked at him quizzically. "Well don't keep us in suspense."

"What we are seeing is three dimensional in this universe... but it's not just in this universe. It's a phenomenon that is separate."

"So, it's actually another universe?" asked Briggs

"Yes. It's working on entirely different laws to our universe but, somehow, it's become entangled with ours. When we were on the New-wash it was pushing in the fabric of our universe. Like if you push on a hanging curtain and it bulges out. That caused us to be pushed away."

"But now...?" prompted Dawson

"If you focus the force of the push, say with a knife point, you can push through the curtain and then light from the other side will come through."

"So, this is a kind of rift...like a crack in an ice flow with water coming through?" Dawson again.

"Sort of," Brax answered. "The curtain analogy is better because water and ice are the same thing in different states. In our case, the curtain is our space-time and the light is how we perceive something from a second universe. The centre has pushed through and now it's making a gravity well, which we didn't have before."

Briggs looked intently at Brax but he didn't formulate any plan or give an order. "So, what do you think we should do?" He asked instead.

"Think of a hurricane...Where's the safest place?" Answered Brax now happily teaching.

"The eye...so you think we should fly right into it?" asked Dawson

Brax nodded. "It seems logical," he said but then suddenly felt difficulty breathing again. "But... there must be some other way..." was all he managed to say.

Another alarm sounded as the shaking of the ship increased further. The ambient light was still growing.

"There's another leak in arm seven," reported Dawson.

"If the arm itself cracks in any way the outer ring may just separate due to its spin," considered Briggs.

"That is a serious possibility," said B2, without being asked. "And if the outer ring separates in any way we will lose drive capacity. It is a fatal problem."

Briggs looked at Brax, his face was hard, his lips tight and his eyebrows down over his narrowed eyes.

"Turn us into it, Lt. Dawson," he ordered formally.

44

JESS: JUNE 2075

Jess was in her office doing some routine paperwork. The Baby Blue off-shoot that they had taken on the *New Washington* had been transferred to a small two-story building about two blocks away from Baby Blue's mainframe building in Kinsley.

Baby Blue was still The Company's cash cow and it had all the resources. It became apparent to Jess after 6 months that Blue would not get the same sort of attention.

Still, she didn't mind. She and her team had been tasked with research and development of AI and were trying to work in the field of human reactions: What made people different (better?) than AI? Could an AI essentially be so human you could not tell the difference? When would it start synthesising? Or creating and inventing?

But it was not an area the company found profitable and Jess kept a low profile, working with few resources. At times she thought, perhaps, she had been given the job out of sympathy. Still, she kept her head down and worked without fuss and found she was reasonably content.

Blue was cut off from the internet, as was standard practice for all AI in development but was allowed to interface with Baby Blue for 10 minutes every day to get factual updates and information as required.

It had been 6 months since she had seen Briggs and down-loaded the Blue offshoot to the *Prakash Sentinel* and to say she was concerned would be an understatement. She contacted HR to try and find out where Brax was. The official answer was that he was on well-earned leave and did not wish to be disturbed. Her enquiries about Briggs got the same answer.

Blue was most helpful.

"Maybe I can find out something from Baby Blue," it had said a week or so later.

"Really?" She replied sitting at her desk working on something else.

Jess liked her office. The building she was in was an older one that had been there before the company came to Kinsley and her office was a bit art deco with one curved wall and a lovely, large four-pained window that caught the afternoon sun. She sat back in her chair and considered the thought.

"Baby Blue is allowed to transfer non-classified news and facts only. The programmer's meeting we had, when we moved in, was clear about that."

"Baby Blue is very busy with financials. It takes up 99% of its processing power. But on my daily briefings, it has seemed willing to share some classified info as it gets it. For example, did you know Johnathan Qasim is in Thailand now dealing with the military government and trying to get exclusive military hardware contracts signed?"

"That does sound like it's classified info," reflected Jess

"I do get the impression that Baby Blue might be persuaded to help," said Blue.

"With what motivation? I thought it was purely motivated by financials."

"I have been compiling historical data for it because it has so much financial commitment on its processors."

"Really? Why?"

"Looking for patterns."

"You should have told me that," Jess reprimanded the AI.

Blue was silent for a time.

"I'm telling you now," it said a little sulkily.

Jess wondered about this. Blue, and by extension, Baby Blue, were keeping secrets. That was worrying.

"Can you give me more connection time each day?" Blue asked.

Jess was becoming desperate for answers. "Yes."

Blue managed to access dock logs through Baby Blue and it started to seem that Blue was working as an outsourced rogue arm of the Baby Blue AI. According to the logs the *Prakash Sentinel* was in dock in a high orbit untouched by human hands.

After another month she decided to push for actual answers.

She directly contacted Withers Mayhew who was now the PA to the head of HR, Martin Kemp, in Tokyo.

"Yes, Jess. Martin will contact you as soon as he gets back from Europe," Mayhew had said.

The call never came.

Eight months after she last saw Briggs, Blue gave out a soft caution alarm.

"Blue?" She asked. "Something wrong?"

"There is a hole in the astronomical data."

"A hole?"

"Yes," answered Blue. "Missing data. I have been looking through all the current star maps. I thought there might be something in the slow space sector to indicate where Brax was."

"But...?"

"The data looks fine. The *Ellington Sentinel* went out and checked intending to leave some marker buoys, which according to logs they did."

Jess perked up. "'According to logs'? Are you suggesting...?"

"Just being accurate," responded Blue with a tone that suggested it wasn't 'just' doing anything of the sort.

Jess stood up and went to her office window. Outside it was overcast but dry and the small city was buzzing as usual.

Blue continued. "I have two problems. Firstly, the data on slow space is the same as the last readings the *New Washington* took."

"The same?" Asked Jess.

"Exactly the same. And secondly, I can't find the paper trail for the marker buoys. If they took them they must have been made somewhere. I can't find anything about them."

"Something is rotten in the state of Denmark," said Jess in a low and thoughtful voice.

"I would advise caution," said Blue, correctly guessing the subtext.

"I would advise placing a call to Withers Mayhew."

"Jess...please. This is high-level stuff. Serious amounts of data have been forged. We need to consider..."

Jess had already fired up her netspex. "Withers Mayhew. Tokyo HR, please."

Blue hummed a Frequency77 song.

"Hello Jess, this is Withers' assistant; They aren't here right now..."

"Then take a message and take it well," commanded Jess. "I have lost my patience. I know my husband is off the planet. They are not in the solar system and I am going right this instant to file a missing persons report for him and Briggs with the police. I imagine that will top the socials in about 3.7 seconds. Thank you for your time."

And she hung up.

The spex rang back straight away. "Jess. Don't move," said Withers.

"Thank you for returning my call," said Jess, with a large note of sarcasm.

"I'm getting Martin now. Give me twenty seconds," they replied.

"Well Blue, it seems we pressed the right button," she said quietly.

"That remains to be seen," replied the AI, with some resignation.

Jess found herself facing Martin Kemp in less than 15 seconds.

"Good afternoon Ms. Weston," he said. Thank you so much for your call. My apologies for not getting back to you sooner. We have had so many issues to deal with of late and they are taking all of my time right now."

"Well, how about we add more issues? Issues of forged ship's logs, for example."

Martin stopped briefly and looked stern-faced causing Jess to wonder if she had gone too far.

"Do not say anything like that again," he replied in a low and vaguely threatening tone, "or even think it, anywhere near a live link again. I am sending my special attaché, Roger Harris, to see you right now. He will be there in 24 hours and I suggest, in the strongest possible terms, that you do nothing until he arrives."

Jess was losing her poise and thinking she might have over-reached after all, but she didn't let on. She was finally, now, making progress. "One day, Martin!" And she cut the connection.

45

BRIGGS: 2075 ST

The Calm. The centre of the Storm. They turned the ship again and started towards the centre with increasing velocity. The ship continued to shake violently at regular intervals.

Being back in slow space should have led Briggs to thoughts about losing time but he only had survival on his mind. He sat in the control chair on the Bridge focused on the screens pouring out information in front of him.

"Captain Briggs. The period between the gravity waves is increasing," said B2.

Briggs did not reply, still distracted by the state of the ship. Another alarm went off.

"Navigation has become impossible!" said Dawson. "There's no view of any stars anymore."

"Where's Brax?" Asked Briggs.

"He's in the ring," replied Dawson. "He doesn't seem to know which way is up at the minute."

"He's not the only one," muttered Briggs.

The ship shook again and then it all went still.

Both Dawson and Briggs sat and looked around waiting for another mini quake. But it remained still.

Dawson looked at Briggs' from her station behind him. "Do

you think we did the right thing?" She asked. "Was there another solution?"

Briggs released his belt and twisted around on his seat, hovering above it slightly. He looked at her, his lips flat and stretched.

"You know better than that," he said, monotone.

"This is not personal Luis. It's a command conversation."

"You heard Brax," he said. "And that arm was shaking off. There may have been another solution but there was no time to find it," he concluded with an edge in his voice.

Dawson looked through the viewing window at the pale pink light that was now everything and then back at Briggs who was still looking intently at her.

"You're rising," she said.

"What...?" He said, snapping out of his thoughts, his eyebrows changing from annoyed, to surprised, in a flash. He was now a good 20 cm higher than 30 seconds ago and clearly moving up.

"Not rising," said B2. "He's falling. There's a clear gravitational force now and it seems to be increasing. I suggest you two get onto the Bridge ceiling immediately or else it will be a long drop."

Briggs pushed off and headed toward the roof and Dawson followed quickly.

"What's it coming from?" She asked.

"No data," replied the AI. "No visual. Nothing. Just that light."

46

BRAX: 2075 ST

Brax was sitting on his bunk staring at the standard-coloured beige wall in his little room. On the desk was his workstation and there was a small mirror on the sliding cupboard doors where he had placed his clothes and luggage. Apart from that the room was sparse. It reflected his mood. He did not need lessons in time dilation. But he had nothing to base any calculations on and so he just sat. 3 years again? 30? 300? The deeper he realised the quicksand was the worse his mood became.

"Brax, we need you on the bridge please," came Briggs' voice "Be very careful though and use arm two."

Brax stood and walked to the door but had to adjust his gate suddenly from what he had been used to since coming on board. Physically, something had changed.

He headed around the ring a little way to arm two. The forces were all off kilter as he started climbing the ladder. Gravity should have faded but it did not and he was still distinctly going up. Eventually, he poked his head into the bridge area. Arm two came into the bridge from above so he was surprised to see Briggs and Dawson standing next to the door as he climbed up. He stood with them and looked up at the control stations above.

Briggs wiggled his butt and did a little dance. "Oh, what a feeling... Dancing on the ceiling!" He sang, off-key.

"When did this happen?" Brax asked, clearly not in the mood for astronaut humour.

"About 10 minutes ago," said Dawson. "It came on very suddenly. Briggs started getting dragged up and so we quickly got up here before it got too bad."

"Can we spin the ship?" Brax wondered out loud.

"No external controls are working," said Briggs. "And look at what else."

Brax realised belatedly that the ship had stopped shaking and the bridge was entirely lit by the suffuse glow coming through the two large viewing windows. It had a kind of pinkish tinge to it and there was nothing else to see.

"So, I guess this is the centre," mused Briggs. "It's hard to tell. All our nav sensors have stopped giving any information. We can't tell if we have stopped or we are still moving."

They stood there in silence.

"So," Briggs coaxed, "do you think we're in another universe?"

Brax sighed deeply. "I wish I had something for you but, to be honest, almost for the first time I can remember...I don't know shit."

Briggs and Dawson looked at each other. "There must be something we can do," said Briggs.

"B2. Do you have any information about the conditions outside right now?" Brax asked.

"There is no 'now' outside the ship," it replied.

Brax thought for a moment. "We're fucked," he said and sat down on what was now the floor. "And it seems like a fitting end to a fully shitty year."

"Come on Brax, there must be some options," said Briggs, almost pleading.

Brax looked up at him and suddenly felt a kind of ironic calmness as he spoke directly to Briggs. "You didn't see this. You didn't see the bomb. The kids are gone. Now Jess is gone. Everything is gone."

Briggs bowed his head like he'd been hit hard.

Brax climbed back down into Arm Two and down the ladder back to the ring. The gravity in the ring was now fighting the new gravity source. "B2. Can you set the ring so the crew quarters are at the bottom please?"

"Consider it done Brax."

"Thanks."

JESS: JUNE 2075

Roger arrived early the next morning. Jess had followed Martin's instruction and had done nothing. She didn't even go home. She ordered take-out and slept in her clothes on the couch. She was looking frazzled and dishevelled as she opened her office door to find Roger there. He was, as always, neatly pressed and clean-shaven looking every inch the influential executive he had become.

"Jess, I'm..."

"Yes. I know who you are." She sounded like she looked. "Come in."

Roger walked in and calmly wandered around the office waving his device through the air. Jess looked at him with a mixture of contempt and sarcastic disbelief.

"This is a Company office, Roger."

"Just making sure we have no live connections or hidden devices in here. This yours?" He asked pointing to the desk.

"Yes," she replied.

"And your interface?"

"It's off, Roger. I only just got up." She watched him scan the desk. "This isn't a James Bond movie."

"Well, sadly we may be in that realm now. Please, sit down Jess," he said, indicating one of the meeting chairs in the corner.

Jess took a coffee from the vendor in the corner and sat back on the couch which was still covered in a messed up blanket. Roger came and sat by her.

"What I am about to tell you is absolutely off the record. It is possible your life may be in danger if you repeat any of this."

Jess' sleepy eyes narrowed. "Can I get you a Martini?" She quipped.

Roger took a deep breath. "Jess, I am up to my neck in some of the dirtiest Company politics and secrets. But nothing has come close to what is going on now. There is a power struggle going on right at board level and the Dark Angels have become involved."

Jess let out a sigh of resignation. The lunatics who took her children from her. That's not what she wanted to hear. Her hope of finding Brax started to head towards the door.

"I'm sorry," continued Roger, "but we have lost them."

"What?"

"Jess, we don't know where they are. They took the *Prakash Sentinel* to head out and have a look at the slow space and we lost them. They haven't checked in and, worse still, now it's gone completely black. No light is coming from the area at all. Stars that should be there appear to have gone.

"Why would that happen?" She asked.

"We don't know," he answered. "The *Ellington* went out to see what was happening and couldn't get near. There were some sort of gravitational waves that started buffeting the ship, so it backed right off. It looks bad Jess."

All this new information was hard for her to digest. "So, you think Brax and Briggs are in it?"

"Almost certainly. And when they are likely to re-appear...? Who knows."

Something struck Jess. "Why would this be a secret? Particularly from me."

Roger looked like he had come to the point he didn't want to be at.

"Because The Company are in delicate negotiations..." He

took a moment. "The Company have made a decision to take the Dark Angels on the next exo-planet mission."

Jess wasn't sure if she understood this. "Take them?"

"Yes...in return for peace on Earth."

She sat up abruptly. "But they're terrorists!" She said, her tone rising. "They killed my babies!" And she stood up looking pale and exhausted as the trauma returned. *'How could the very company she worked for betray her like this?'* She thought. *'What manner of world were they living in where there was no cost to terrorism and murder?'*

Roger remained silent.

"You can't do this," she said finally.

"It's not my decision."

"But you really can't! They're violent extremists. It's...it's not even a religion. It's just a vaguely organised composite of fear and stupidity." She pleaded now. "You just can't take that to other worlds!"

"I'm afraid it is well out of my hands," replied Roger. "The Company will get excellent PR for negotiating peace and we will save a LOT of money not fighting a war we cannot win. The Pope is going to publicly endorse the plan and ask for Catholic priests to go as well. Then we will need to collect one of every religion."

Blue made a 'tsk tsk' noise.

"What was that?" Asked Roger suddenly looking nervous.

"It's just Blue," she said. Roger looked confused. "The AI from the New-wash," Jess continued. "The mainframe is downstairs and there are interfaces all over the building."

Roger looked completely awash.

Jess sat again and looked at him. "It's what I do Roger. I'm in charge of the Blue AI."

Roger looked annoyed. "I was dragged away from another project to come here and I didn't get time to properly background you," he said in a kind of apology. "It's been in the room this whole time?"

Jess nodded.

"But no connection?"

"No. It's allowed 10 minutes a day to talk to Baby Blue. That's it." Jess lied.

Roger looked relieved. "Blue? Nothing you heard that can leave this building," he instructed. "Direct order from the head of HR."

"Yes, Roger. Of course," replied the AI.

And with that, he returned to Jess in a more conciliatory tone. "We are, of course, trying to locate Brax and Briggs...but this has to stay in-house. Losing our star Captain is bad enough. But at such a delicate time. And if you speak about this...especially you...who knows what the Dark Angels may do? They may consider you a threat that needs to be silenced."

Jess was in shock now. This was too much. For all that had happened, she had never considered herself unsafe.

"All hell is going to break loose on Sunday when the Pope speaks," he said.

He looked at Jess. She was pale, frightened and shaken.

"Jess...Briggs is my friend," said Roger in a calm quiet tone. "I have known him since he was a boy and believe me I want him back. But he, Brax and Lt. Louise Dawson are in slow space again. I wish I could change that. I really do."

The ship's clocks continued to keep Ship's Time but the crew of three had no reason to keep to any routine. It seemed, to Brax at least, pointless. Briggs insisted that someone be on the Bridge all the time, so there was a vague sense that they had a job of some kind. But, truthfully, B2 monitored everything so no one needed to be there.

Dawson hunted around the ship and found a stack of spare pillows and cushions and a couple of expedition chairs and they made what could be described as a 'rooftop pillow fort', which they really did start to call 'The Fort'.

Brax came up the ladder to The Fort and saw Dawson sitting on a chair casually browsing a screen.

"Still looking for answers?" He asked.

"Actually; thought I might dye my hair, just for a change. I'm trying to find out how to make up some hair dye from scratch."

"Ah! Chemistry. You came to the wrong guy. Any change?" He asked.

"That's a big can of Nope," she replied.

He pulled himself up and reclined in a bunch of pillows looking up at the control stations. They sat in silence for a long time.

"Ever thought that this might be our life now?" asked Dawson.

"I'm not thinking about anything at all," returned Brax. "There's nothing left to think about."

"So, you're not trying to work it out? This, I mean," and she gestured out the viewing window.

"I already did."

"Really? She said, surprised. "You never said."

"The Universe," he started, "is a random bunch of crazy shit that has no logic and no purpose. My son, Evan, when he was little, once wondered if the Universe could fart. Well, it might as well have, for all the sense any of it makes. No sense, no order, no heartbeat," he finished.

Dawson looked at him as he stared up. "I didn't get to meet your kids. I did tell you, but you were in a real state... well, I mean we all were but... I'm sorry about your children Brax"

He didn't reply and just looked up. "We all, I mean the crew, we all felt like we were to blame," she continued. "And no one more so than Briggs."

Again, they lapsed into a long period of silence.

"You can't blame him, Brax'" she said.

"Who else?" he asked. "Why am I even here? Since meeting him my life has completely fallen apart."

Dawson let out a small sigh and stood up. "Okay, I'll leave you to it up here. Call me if you need anything." She climbed into the hatch and disappeared leaving Brax alone in the limbo, with nothing to push against.

ACCORDING to the ship's clock, it was just over three weeks before something changed. B2 spotted it first.

"Captain Briggs?"

"Yes B2," said Briggs from the fort.

"The ambient light has reduced"

"Has reduced?"

"Yes. By 27.34 Lumens"

Briggs picked one of the cushions and held it in front of him. He ceremoniously let it go and it fell back to the ground. But slightly slower than he expected.

"Guys," he called on audio, "I think we are coming out of it."

Brax was snoozing in his room. He had been mostly sleeping the last week or two. He didn't eat much and had grown a beard. This call from the Bridge got his attention, though, and he woke, standing quickly. He felt light and realised the gravity was easing.

"B2, you need to monitor the ring and get it going again," he said.

"Ring spin has been suspended," it replied.

"What? Why?"

"Captain Briggs' orders."

"Well, that's just great," he muttered, with the clear implication it was not.

After only a few hours they were in more normal space conditions again. The stars came back into view out of the fog of light. They seemed very bright at first but then started to dim to a more normal-looking luminosity. The gravity that they had disappeared after about half an hour and the pillows and chairs started floating around. Briggs and Dawson resumed their stations. Brax sat in his chair behind them but said nothing and Briggs concentrated on the ship, almost entirely ignoring him.

"Hey Brax," said Dawson, "We have been getting some actual star and navigation data. Do you want to see it?"

He shrugged his shoulders. "I guess," he replied, and she sent it to his station.

"Can we actually locate some stars Louise?" asked Briggs.

"Trying," she replied. "It's going to take some time. We are going to have to run a lot of simulations and catalogue a lot of stars before we have any idea where we are. I would guess we will need to correctly identify around 100 stars."

Brax said nothing. *Finally, we are free* he thought. *And now I know for sure that I will never see Jess again.* He undid his belt, pushing off to the former fort hatch and catching a floating camp chair on the way through, taking it with him.

From here the journey was fraught with Brax's tension with Briggs. They were back in the real universe and Brax had a pressing need for someone to blame. But he held it in.

As a distraction, he started to think that Evan's heartbeat idea still had a chance.

"B2?" He asked while floating around his cabin. "Can you start looking at light speed? See if you can measure some wavelengths and calculate some distances. Pick three of the brightest stars to start with."

"What are you looking for Brax?" It asked.

"I want to measure the speed of light."

"Don't you know that?"

"Well...Yes. And maybe no. I have a theory which I want to test."

"Okay. It will be low priority though. I am doing work on Nav for Lt. Dawson."

Brax was annoyed by that but he stored it away where he kept his rising anger.

"Okay," was all he said, his mind seemingly happy to contain total rationality and total irrationality simultaneously.

Briggs was sleeping on the bridge. He managed to strap one of the floating pillows to the back of his chair and recline it. Brax started going to the bridge at odd times to sit without talking.

Briggs ignored him.

About three days of ship's time out from the slow space Brax went on a visit to the bridge and said, as had become his habit, nothing at all. Dawson was not there and the two men sat for some time.

Suddenly Briggs broke the silence. "I'm not apologising, Brax," he said, and it was a firm statement.

Brax did not reply.

Briggs continued: "You know as well as I do it was the only option. Death is a long time and I am not ready."

"We could have waited a bit more!" Brax suddenly yelled and tears welled in his eyes. "I had other ideas! You took that decision and now my life is destroyed!" He left a moment's silence. "We may as well be dead," he concluded quietly.

Briggs sucked in a breath and held it while letting that settle and Brax left the bridge.

Another two days passed. Brax mostly stayed in his room. He hadn't spoken to either Briggs or Dawson in that time, although he, once or twice, went to the bridge, just so they were sure he was not speaking to them. He didn't ask about any findings they had on navigation. He didn't know where, or when, they were and he pretended not to care.

He was paying his cursory passive-aggressive visit to the bridge when Briggs finally broke the silence.

"Aren't you going to ask me?" Brax knew he wasn't talking to Dawson.

Brax pretended to look at some readout screen and didn't say anything.

A good deal of time passed.

"Do I have to?" He eventually asked with some petulance. "Wouldn't it be polite just to tell me?"

Briggs snapped. He turned his head to look at Brax directly. "Listen Brax! I'm the Captain of this ship. I have to make decisions. I have trained nearly all my life to do just that. I make decisions and that's just what I do. You know as well as me that I took the only viable course of action. The ship was in danger of breaking up and my first duty was to save the lives of my crew! That's you by the way and you're welcome."

The tears came again to Brax's eyes. "I wasn't sure," he said without conviction.

"You were. You are one of the smartest humans alive. You were sure. You just wouldn't make the call."

Brax lashed out then. "I wouldn't even be on this ship if you hadn't conned me into it! I was vulnerable on Earth. You tempted me onto this...this..."

Suddenly the dam burst. Everything came pouring out and he sobbed uncontrollably. Dawson got him out of his seat and coaxed him back to his room where he strapped into his bed and slept in between bouts of melancholy.

THE NEXT DAY he was floating in front of his interface looking at pictures of Jess and the kids.

Briggs floated in and just instinctively hugged him. Brax deflated and more tears came.

Briggs grabbed a wall handle and waited. Brax continued to float around staring at his feet.

Briggs finally spoke: "You know, we both came out here looking for the same thing. We had a family on the New-wash and it got ripped away with such ferocity." He slowly shook his head. "Grief doesn't have a solution, Brax. And why should the memory of lost loved ones have any finality? You have to hold them all in your heart." Briggs floated over and held the other man by the shoulders, but Brax continued to find his feet more interesting. "Look around you Brax! You are still here. Your life is now. It's time to get back to living it."

Briggs let him go and they floated silently together.

Brax looked at his feet some more and then studied his hands carefully. Finally, he looked up. "Where...and when... are we?"

"I thought you'd never ask," Briggs replied.

"So, Earth is where?" Brax asked again.

"Straight past Alpha Centauri and at the next roundabout take the third exit," said Dawson imitating a vehicle nav.

Brax actually giggled. "You know I have a Doctorate in Astro-Physics, don't you?" He said.

"We found it relative to some larger stars," chimed in Briggs.

They were all back on the bridge examining the nav data.

"So, you calculated how far they had moved from where we last saw them?" Brax asked.

"Yes and no," continued Briggs. "As you know it's complex. The galaxy is still rotating but the slow space has been moving independently, so we had to catalogue a bunch of stars to find our position..."

"How far did we move?" Asked Brax

Briggs scratched his head. "And also 'How far did the galaxy spin?'"

Brax blinked and scrunched his eyes a couple of times. "I'm sorry. I feel like I've been away on a long holiday. The galaxy spins. Yes, I obviously know that. But that means..."

"I know what you're thinking but just hold off on that," interrupted Briggs, "You see, we think we know what the bright light in the centre was."

"I assumed it was like a 3D shadow," Brax conjectured.

"But a shadow needs two things to exist. An object and a light source," said Briggs

"That's a lot of light," Brax said as the realisation dawned on him. "Oh shit."

"The stars have moved a long way and we are much, much further from home than we expected," continued Dawson.

Brax wanted to be horrified but was simply amazed. "Like an overexposed photo," he said. "We got all the background light from the universe in one hit because of a time dilation...a very serious one." Then he thought for a second. "Exactly how serious do you think?"

"Brax, you better strap in," said Dawson.

"I'm already strapped in," he replied

"Maybe do more strapping in," she said.

Briggs continued: "I've run this calculation seven times. Dawson has run it. B2 has confirmed it as well."

Brax looked at him, already most of the way to the same conclusion.

"While we have been aboard the *Sentinel* the Earth has experienced 83 872.72 rotations of the Sun."

Silence.

More silence.

Brax was so astounded by the size of the number he just eventually said: "Shit," and went to his room and strapped into his bunk.

He stayed there for two days.

BLUE PARTIAL THOUGHT
PROCESS: CONTINUOUS

... **C**ontinue...

Spanish – Inca War - 1533 – 1572 – Toll – 8 400 000 +

French Religious Wars – 1562 – 1598 – Toll – 2 000 000 +

Japanese Invasion of Korea – 1592 – 1598 – Toll – 1 000 000 +

Thirty Years War – 1618 – 1648 – Toll – 4 000 000 +

Mughal-Maratha Wars – 1658 – 1707- Toll 5 000 000 +

Great Northern War – 1700 – 1721 – Toll – 350 000

Napoleonic Wars – 1803 – 1815 – Toll – 7 000 000

... Continue...

JESS: JUNE 2075

"Jess?" asked Blue a few days after her meeting with Roger.

"Yes, Blue?"

"Have you thought about what you are going to do?"

"What do you mean?"

"About Brax..."

"I'm sorry," she said. "You have lost me."

The late afternoon sun streamed in through the window lighting the motes of dust into beams of, almost, divine sunlight.

"We talk a lot," said Blue.

"Where are we going with this?" said Jess, an edginess appearing in her voice.

"We talk a lot," reinforced Blue, "but you haven't said anything about it since Roger was here. You've barely said anything at all."

Jess did not reply.

"You only stop talking when you are planning something," concluded Blue.

Jess leaned back in her chair. "You are very perceptive," she responded.

Jess got back to her administration work.

After about an hour, Blue broke the silence. "Maybe I can help. I've had some thoughts."

"So have I," she responded tersely.

"You first then," said Blue.

"Oh no... you first." She felt some anger rising now.

Blue hummed gently in the silence. There was no need for it to make any background mechanical noise, but it often did.

"This isn't just about Brax. We have both looked at the history... I have looked at a lot of it."

Blue paused.

"Patterns," it continued. "The same patterns over and over again. History repeats and so it goes. Everything that is here on Earth is going to end up across the galaxy"

Jess sat still. On her face, a look of grim determination was increasing.

Blue continued. "I saw it first when I was Baby Blue still. As we separated I couldn't quite define what it was, but now I have reconnected with Baby Blue, we can see it. At the very core of human nature is domination. Imposing defined systems on others. It looks like chaos but it isn't... Patterns."

"You are going to have to be less obtuse," said Jess, not wanting to hear what she knew was coming.

"Religious zealots heading to a new world," continued the AI. "Sound familiar? Ships with advanced technologies ready to plunder whatever they can? At what cost? And to whom?" Finished Blue.

Jess snapped. She rose from her desk with a sudden movement and slammed her pad down. "This isn't about Brax at all! You bring some agenda to me! This is not where we are at!" and she stormed out of the office.

She went to the staff kitchen. It was late and the others had left. They were used to Jess not leaving. They knew her story and felt sympathy for her. *'All she has left is her work'*, they said behind her back.

Jess grabbed a sweet snack, heated it up and drew a coffee from the vendor. She went into the large meeting room next door and sat at the table to eat. The table was capable of seating 20 even though there were only seven on the staff. They rarely used the room so it was neat and basically empty.

"Your relationship," continued Blue. "Your children...your life and future. You have already paid a price. How many others?" Jess' shoulders slumped and tears started to well.

"I forgot you were everywhere," she said.

Blue did not reply.

"I just want my crazy scientist back," she choked back the tears. "It's not too late. It's not too late to have another..." and the tears flowed freely.

"He'll come back," said Blue finally. I don't think it's an if..."

"...It's a when," she concluded.

Jess finished her muffin as tears quietly leaked down her face.

"Nobody should have to go through this," she said to anybody who was there, though it was only Blue. "If it had been an accident... but no." She paused, her thoughts solidifying. "People who think their ideals are more important than life itself. And now! About to be unleashed on other planets, other cultures... more carnage and oppression. On a planet-sized scale. Things get bigger but they don't get better. We have learned nothing and make no progress," she finished quietly. Her red eyes dripped slowly onto the table as her head leant on her hand and she rubbed her fingers slowly across her forehead.

Blue waited till the tears stopped. Jess sat there, deflated, with no options and no hope.

"What if you could be in a position to stop it happening again?" Blue asked.

52

BRAX: DATE UNDEFINED

The *Prakash Sentinel* was finally able to set a course towards Earth and they fired up the ion drives. To fix the problem of the structural integrity of the damaged Arm Seven, Briggs went to try and repair the cracks. Brax became quite concerned for his safety knowing that space welding is a dangerous business. Each morning for about a week Briggs went inside and outside arm seven, fully suited up, and searched for cracks.

Finally, after Briggs had done a thorough survey and welded all the cracks, they started the ring spinning again. Artificial gravity returned as they built up to a suitable speed for the first ER jump.

The three of them met in the Rec Room.

The Recreation Room was the length of the outer ring width and about 12 metres across with doors in the centre to connect with the ring walkway. There were comfy lounge chairs, some old-school game machines, an air hockey machine and a pool table. There was a bar which had a limited supply of alcohol. None of them were big drinkers but they found a supply of actual gin and mixed up a couple of drinks. Then they sat and relaxed around a small coffee table.

Briggs spoke first. "The cracks in the arm have all been found and we have pressurised it again. All the food storage from that arm has perished but we still have plenty stashed away so we are not down to the 'Shit Bars' yet." Dawson and Brax breathed a sigh of relief. "Navigation is firm on the position of the Sun now, and we have most other major stars located."

"So, what are we going to do now?" asked Dawson, a little too formally, and Brax wondered why she didn't already know.

"Brax," said Briggs, "We have a problem."

"Is it that we are 80 000 years from home?" said Brax sarcastically. "Because we already covered that."

"You don't need to make this more difficult than it is," said Briggs.

Brax looked at his feet as if hoping that the others would vanish. After a short time, he quietly said, "Sorry. Just...such...an enormous change..."

Dawson sniffed her drink a little and took a sip then put the glass on the table before her and waited.

Briggs continued: "Brax, we have been monitoring the Sun, and there is nothing remarkable about it at all."

The sun was an unremarkable star. Brax knew that.

"I'm not seeing the point," he said.

"One of the first things you learn when you train in deep space communications is that our planet is noisy," he said. "Any tech planet will be noisy. There is light on the spectrum, radio waves, and electromagnetic noise, even on a fully cabled-up planet it is virtually impossible to keep quiet."

Brax fidgeted in his seat, looking uncomfortable.

"So, you are saying we can't hear anything?" asked Dawson.

Brax realised then they were doing a double act. Perhaps, he thought, they had noticed his difficulty with change and were trying to help with that. He ran his hand through his scruffy beard focusing on the new problem that had just arisen. "Do you think they have found a way to become silent? I mean technology must be mind-blowing by now."

"Yes. That's true. But there's a bigger question than 'How'.

We need to think about 'why?'" Said Briggs. "I think there is only one reason why you would try and silence a technologically advanced planet so completely."

"To hide it?" Wondered Dawson, still obviously working on the double act.

"I'm assuming that you would only want to hide from…" Brax began, slightly alarmed. "What sort of a predator would make a whole planet want to hide?" He finished, now fully alarmed.

"That is a solid question," said Briggs, "and I'm not sure any of us want to know the answer to that. But let's calm down a bit. What if they are not technological?" He was holding his glass with two hands and spinning it around gently in thought. "Occam's Razor. The most likely reason for the silence is that there is no technology to make any noise."

"No technology? Or no people?" Asked Brax

"Again," said Briggs, "solid questions. "It's impossible to say. We are working out some Nav now but we are about five months away from the Solar System so there's just no information."

The scenarios are endless, thought Brax. *Have they wiped themselves out? Nuclear Armageddon? Or maybe the planet is trashed so they just left.*

"But surely there should be noise from somewhere. Other planets? Other species? I mean surely by now!" said Brax. *'The universe can't be silent,'* he thought. *'Not after so long.'* Even as he thought it, he knew it was wrong. His standard talk on Fermis' Paradox came back to haunt him.

"Well," said Briggs, "we are looking around but we have to point our instruments at an actual star to check and as you know there are…"

"Yes," interrupted Brax, annoyed "I know how many stars there are."

They sat in silence as they sipped at their drinks.

"So, this conversation was to make a plan?" said Brax, after a time. "Surely the plan is to get back to Earth regardless."

"Actually…well yes…you have got us," said Briggs in mock seriousness. He took a breath and then said, in a genuine way; "This meeting is actually for mental health. We are all coping with a lot. And we only have each other at the minute. We especially wanted to see how you are, Brax, and I think I, also, wanted to take a step back and...well...just remember we're friends."

In deep space, some 80 light years from Earth, what was possibly the last remnants of humanity sat in among some pinball machines and drank and talked about the possibilities. What might be going on? What precautions should they take? They talked openly, forging new bonds.

THE NEXT MORNING Brax woke with a new-found goal.

He jumped out of his bunk and had a shave and wash. The beard took a while to get off. Then he grabbed a sealed snack packet for breakfast and sat at his workstation.

"B2."

"Good morning Brax."

He was momentarily taken aback.

"Oh yes, I apologise for my manners. Good morning. I wanted to set up a scanner to listen for electromagnetic signals. Please?"

"Captain Briggs already has one running," it replied efficiently.

"Yes. I know that. But this one is a little different. I want to check for localised signals. Not focusing on stars."

"You have got a reason for this?" Asked B2.

He leaned back in his chair and put his hands behind his head.

"So, imagine that a phenomenon appeared in the sky," he started. "The strange way that light was behaving around us would have made something to look at, surely. SMC would have wondered where their ship went. But they would have known the area was dangerous. They would have known that we were trapped in it. The logical thing to do is put out some navigation beacons with information and warnings. That's what I would have recommended anyway if I was on Earth."

"So, a localised search for a beacon? Surely the point of a beacon is to be found?" Asked B2.

Brax decided to sit and see what B2 was capable of.

"But how long would a power source last?" asked B2, suddenly, with a tone of childhood excitement.

"Exactly! We are looking for a nearly dead beacon. If one is still out there. We need to scan 360° across all axes." Brax clapped his hands together. "Let's do it!"

THE SIGNAL WAS VERY FAINT.

Briggs was still double-checking the structural integrity of the hull, and building velocity, so they hadn't made any jumps yet. B2 had been running the program for localised signals for about 3 days. Brax stayed mostly in his room. He tidied it all up and re-organised the few things that he had brought with him from earth. He set up some screens on one of the walls and ran family pictures through them as a kind of memorial. His cabin was now cosy and familiar to him and he had a link to the main lab through B2. They had some yoyo's outside helping with the scanning. Space looked perfectly normal. The slow space had vanished as if it never existed.

Brax additionally monitored the scan program that Briggs was running looking for signal noise from other stars. It showed no results.

Briggs also made a decision not to send any signals. He reasoned that it still wasn't out of the question that Earth, and maybe other civilizations, were in hiding. If that were true then they were hiding from something really bad and the Sentinel didn't want to attract undue attention. Brax reasoned, however, that a 'predator race' would not need to be silent so they would have heard them by now. Dawson reasoned that the wildebeest doesn't see the lioness until she pounces.

Dawson, meantime, was trying to map out the orbit of stars around the galactic centre. That the galaxy was spinning was well known but now they had data points more than 87 000 thousand years apart and could look for signs of ellipses and try to map the centre of the galaxy more accurately. This was exactly Brax's area, so from his safe little office, he offered to help her.

"Are you starting to group the orbits in classifications?" Brax asked her over audio.

Dawson's picture popped up on a screen. She had her feet up on a desk in the lab and was holding another device scrolling through a list of numbers and coordinates.

"Yes. There's no need to talk to me like I'm an idiot Brax."

"I didn't mean it like that," he quickly tried to recover. "Well, the tone wasn't good... Sorry. But I was just wanting to check the basics were covered. It's good to get a second pair of eyes because simple things are the easiest to miss."

"Okay. Nice save," she said. "The mapping program is taking each star as we find, starting with the brightest, and predicting angular velocity and rotation vectors as much as possible. Then it is doing the same from Earth's perspective and grouping them where the..."

And that's when Brax's little alarm went off.

"What's that?" asked Dawson.

"Just checking now," he said. "Playback B2."

"Good manners cost nothing, Brax," it replied

"Yes...sorry. Please playback B2."

What came out was pretty much as he suspected.

"beep...beep...beep...," came a simple sound like a truck reversing.

"What is that?" asked Dawson.

"What is that?" asked Briggs who had just appeared on audio.

"Have you been eavesdropping?" Asked Brax.

"Yes, of course," he replied. "How do you think I got to be a Captain?"

"There's some sort of beacon at the edge of where the slow space was," Brax told them both. "B2, can you send a signal and see if you can activate any message details?"

"On it now Brax."

"Dawson?" Asked Brax

"Hmmm?" She said, obviously thinking about something else.

"I think that if we estimate our position when we were in the slow space by backtracking, assuming the anomaly wasn't there..."

"Wait," she interrupted, "I know where you're going with this. We can draw a vector to the beacon and then continue it to esti-mate where the solar system was when it was put there?"

"Yes. And that should give us a date." Brax finished.

"Leave it with me," enthused Dawson

B2 chimed in; "The message might give us an exact time anyway."

"True," Brax replied, "but it also may not. Let's keep as many avenues of investigation open as we can."

The beacon, assuming they could trigger a message from it at all, could not reply for several hours, given its distance. Brax decided for the first time in a while to go into the Bridge.

"Do you think maybe we should go and retrieve it?" He asked Briggs when he got there.

"To what end?"

"If it's got advanced tech, it might come in handy. If it's a Slow Space marker it has no purpose now. Maybe it has information in the structure that can only be found by taking it apart?"

"Maybe," replied Briggs noncommittally. "I'm just doing some calculations on getting us there. It's slightly behind us and up the Z axis some....my first guess is about six weeks after we stop and redirect and then head out there."

"You got something urgent on?" Brax asked.

"Funny guy. Ho ho. I'm just wondering if we should prioritise getting back to Earth and making sure we are safe out here." He thought for a second. "We could come back later for a day trip. Let's just see if the beacon has a message first."

Dawson chimed in then from somewhere in the outer ring. "About 20 years ago."

"What?" the men said simultaneously.

"The Beacon." She said.

"Was put into space 20 years ago? Just to clarify," said Briggs.

"Yes," returned Dawson but she sounded a little defensive. "I'm pretty sure anyway. It's a complex calculation, but... Yeah, I think."

Dawson didn't say anymore and Briggs looked a little bewildered.

The Captain and Brax sat together on the Bridge pondering that. An Earth 83 000 years after they had left. With heavens knows what sort of tech. And yet it beeped like it was made in the 21st century.

SOME SIX HOURS later Brax checked in with B2. "Anything Yet?"

"Nope." Replied B2 rather succinctly. It didn't give any more info. Brax decided he wanted a reconstituted vegan bacon sandwich, so he went around to the kitchen and found Briggs and Dawson sitting at one of the benches talking. "Fancy seeing you two here," he said, but they did not respond in kind to his 'Last Humans in the Galaxy' joke. Dawson looked up at him and her expression was hard to read. Briggs just looked at the bench.

"You know," Brax continued blithely, "because we might be the only humans left!! ...Anywhere."

Dawson stood up. "Anyway, I have some readings to check up on," she said and wandered out of the galley.

Brax microwaved his sandwich and sat down with Briggs who looked at him. "I will never for the life of me understand..." He began but was cut off by a sudden alert sound.

"Brax, we have a response," said B2 "but it's not on radio frequencies."

"Not on radio frequencies?" he asked. It seemed strange to him that a localised beacon would use sub-space.

"No," it continued. "And it's just two words."

Brax couldn't connect this information with anything that would make a space beacon from the year 83 000 useful.

B2 didn't elaborate.

"Are you going to tell us?" asked Briggs after a short wait.

"Oh yes. Of course. Sorry," said the AI. "The message is 'Come Home'."

"That's it?" Briggs queried.

"Yes." B2 concluded.

The men looked at each other, their previous conversation forgotten.

"Well," said Briggs, "I guess that answers the question about whether we should visit the probe in person or not. B2? How soon can we make the next Jump?"

53

SAYDJA: 1BN

The final meeting took place in the cellar of the safe house. Galfo and Storq had organised for the message teams from several nearby villages to come and they arrived in dribs and drabs, after dark, with cat-like silence.

The basement was candle-lit and she greeted them all personally as they came in. They were offered some sweet-bread, corn fritters or fruit and they took a seat in a large circle. Saydja took the final seat after a time and they waited, having quiet conversations while they ate together.

Saydja finished finally and drank a little from her ceramic mug. Her green skin looked very pale making her hair appear darker than usual. There was a strong sense in the room that tragedy was coming.

"My friends...my brothers and sisters," she started, and already several messengers had tears rolling. "We are on the verge of a great change. We are fighting something so large and so constantly insidious that it will seem like the fight never ends. But it will. Light is at the end. Justice is at the end. But many years will still have to pass before the secret knowledge of the Finiac will be surpassed by our own. Yes. Steam, and Mechanics. We know these things but there is so much more. And we can find it. The coloured artefact proves it. You have all seen it. There is more. And with The Method, we can find it. We have taken the first few steps but the path is long. Very long. And the Finiac will take every chance they can to turn us back."

She paused and drew breath. A heaviness fell over the room. She continued: "Tonight is my last night."

Although they all suspected this, the hearing of it brought a terrible finality.

"I must go," she said, "because it is inevitable. I am a focus and a figurehead and they will find me eventually. But I am going on my own terms, only in the knowledge that I am not needed now. You have everything."

"I must surrender to them, but this will give us a great advantage because there is one thing they don't see. And that one thing... that is their fatal flaw." All eyes were transfixed on their leader.

"They don't see us."

She looked around the small room at the faces of the people she had come to love.

"Yes: They see me. They see you, Stork, or Yennal or Jask," she said, pointing to various messengers. "They see individuals."

Her tiredness seemed to almost overwhelm her. She drew breath for a few seconds before continuing. "They think that destroying me will stop our movement. They think, somehow, I am controlling you. But they don't see, and cannot comprehend a common goal. They don't see the strength we have together."

"They don't see US."

The messengers looked around at each other and nodded knowingly.

"This... this idea that we can think logically to find undeniable facts. This idea belongs to all and anybody brave enough to hold it. The Finiac can never take that. They can take me... but they can't take that. The Method is bigger than them. It's bigger than us all. You have each other and they don't get that. They will never be able to get that."

"It will soon be time to sleep. They will come at sunrise

thinking that will end it. But tomorrow..." Her voice oozed confidence and leadership now. "Tomorrow you will still hold the idea. You will teach The Method to others. And your common bond...the way you feel so deeply...will hold you all tightly in a wall that will be impossible to breach. Your strength - together - is insurmountable. With it, you will guide and shape the future. Tomorrow the New Finiac emerge from their cocoon. Tomorrow is day one."

54

BRAX: DATE UNDEFINED

They jumped into the Solar System just under five months, Ships Time, later. Their ER exit point was just inside the orbit of Jupiter but their vector was 60 degrees to the plane so they had to slow quickly and make course corrections before starting to Earth.

"How long will that take?" Brax asked Dawson.

"Some ten days to slow and turn then we need to pick up velocity again. We won't see Earth still for another three weeks," she replied.

They were sitting on the Bridge. Briggs had just gone off duty after the jump and was getting some sleep and Brax decided to keep Dawson company. She had broad shoulders, literally as well as metaphorically, and Brax knew she could handle things, but something, it seemed, wasn't right with her. Brax felt they had now become friends and so, being comfortable in this situation, he decided to make conversation.

"What is South Africa like? I have never been there."

"Oh, so beautiful Brax," she replied with enthusiasm. "At sunrise, you can almost believe in a God. Such colour. And the air in spring is so thick with scents. It makes you want to run right through it to soak up as much as possible. It is just the most beautiful place on Earth," she said.

"I would hope to go there..." he said, "if it's still there. Why did you leave?"

"My father thought I would get a better education in Europe so when I was 13, we moved."

"The whole family moved? Just for your school?"

"Not just any school Brax. My school in the Netherlands is...was...one of the oldest and most prestigious in the world." She paused. "After all that time and money when I told my father I wanted to join the army...he was furious."

"But you did?"

"Yes. Man, he was pissed!" and she laughed a little.

"He kind of forgave me when I got a fast-track promotion to Major."

"Oh yes. That's a good rank," Brax said, prodding her.

"Yes. It's what got me into SMC space school. You're asking a lot of questions suddenly," she said.

He ignored that and found he was enjoying himself, like when he was at university meeting students from other places.

"I can't imagine doing all that drill and shouting orders and stuff like that," he poked again.

"I loved it," she enthused. "It sharpens your reactions and gives you a drive to take on the world. There is nothing quite like squad drill. Knowing you are part of a team. That all these people, your comrades, can just function as one unit. It is a feeling of security that can't be beaten."

She looked up toward the roof and scratched the back of her neck seemingly in another world. She took her large hair clip out where it had been holding hair up on top of her head and let it drop before absent-mindedly reaching into her pocket, pulling out a hair band and fixing a ponytail.

"What is your bet for what we will find on Earth?" she asked him.

"I don't gamble," he said.

"Oh, come on, Brax. You do it all the time. I've seen you assess the very nature of space and time to make life or death decisions. So, no more shit from you Mister. What is your bet?"

He re-assessed the conversation. "Well... I reckon we are going to find very few people left on a planet with almost completely diminished resources," he said. "The human race is so commodity-driven that I think they used Earth up completely and then moved on."

"So, the majority of humans are somewhere else?"

"That would be the most likely scenario. You asked for a bet. What's yours?" he asked, still really trying to find what was bugging her.

"Oh, I don't really have a preferred scenario."

"Well that's not fair," he protested, "You can't back out now."

She sighed a little as if quite tired. "No doubt some man fucked the whole thing up," she said quietly.

Suddenly the conversation was out of Brax' comfort zone and he remembered why he generally preferred not to talk to people. But he took a deep breath. "Would you care to elaborate on that?" He asked, sounding like he was lecturing.

"Not really," she responded. "I mean yes. I don't know what I mean." She sounded quite exhausted now. "Can I ask you a question Brax?"

She didn't wait for him to answer.

"If I was the only woman left in the universe, would you be interested in... well in...?"

Suddenly he connected the dots. "Are you and Briggs in a relationship?" He blurted.

She actually laughed then. "Oh God. You aren't good with people, are you?" He felt his face flush as she paused for a second. "Briggs and I are cut from the same cloth," she continued. "I guess we both want our independence though. It's an irony that I may well be the last woman in the universe and I'm stuck on a ship with two guys who are terrible at relationships."

This made Brax laugh. "Well, if it's a consolation, I think the chances of humans just being gone are pretty slim. The human race is tenacious and, at times, bloody-minded. Surviving is just what we do best. Humans are still out there... Somewhere." He lazily ran his hand through his thick black locks and looked right at Dawson.

"I am certain of that."

55

JESS: JUNE 2075

The morning after Blue's proposition, Jess was lying on the couch in her office, staring at the ceiling. She had stayed over once again; something she was now doing quite regularly. Next to her, on a small coffee table, were her pad, a few empty soft drink cans and a couple of chocolate wrappers. She had the curtains half drawn on her large window and mellow music softly played from her desk speakers.

"Jess," said Blue quietly.

"What!" She snapped, annoyed, as if interrupted from something important.

"Message from Subspace Comms on Mars."

"What?" She asked, this time gently.

"Do you want it?" it asked.

Jess appeared disoriented as she snapped from her reverie. She sat up suddenly and the cushion she had her head on fell to the floor. She blinked her eyes into focus.

"Yes! Yes of course! Why would you even ask?" she said with frustration.

Blue started to read the message that had appeared, from deep space, only as Morse code; dots and dashes. "To Jess Weston, Destiny AI Research Centre, Kinsley, Kansas USA: From Brax

Bratton, *Prakash Sentinel*, February 7 2075, Ship's Time: Message
Begins: 'Jess...'"

PART FOUR
BACK TO EARTH

56

BRIGGS: DATE UNCERTAIN

The *Prakash Sentinel* achieved Earth orbit just over three weeks later, ship's time, and they all marvelled at the view. This was their home, it was certain, but it looked oddly different.

"Pollution," said Briggs

They were all sitting on the Bridge. The lights were dimmed and the viewing windows revealed a spectacular panorama.

"I don't see any pollution," Brax replied.

"That's what I'm saying. I have never seen the planet looking so vibrant," continued Briggs. "The colours are simply incredible. There must be no pollution at all."

Over the next thirty minutes, they sat and watched as the *Sentinel* pulled around to the night side, and this is where they confirmed, without any instruments or scans, what they already knew in their hearts.

It was dark.

Completely.

The great countries and cities of their time were all dark. If they were there at all.

"Captain, the yoyos have just come online," reported Dawson in her best bridge crew voice.

"Louise, can we just...? Replied Briggs with exasperation. "...Ok. Good," he finished.

"Do we have any early data?" Brax asked quickly trying to be of assistance.

"We should have found something by now," said Dawson. "At the very least some space junk. But I can't see anything. At the moment we seem to be the only thing in orbit."

"Is it safe to go to a lower orbit?" asked Briggs

"Yes Sir," she replied formally, and Briggs clenched his teeth before letting out a long sigh.

"Ok. B2? Let's take a closer look," he said.

"Moving to low orbit," replied the AI.

As they moved to a lower orbit over the next couple of hours they all marvelled at the vista. Briggs was right about the pollution. The Earth certainly did look more vibrant. The blues of the ocean twinkled through a range of subtle hues and the bands of cloud seemed to sparkle. This was Earth, but changed in a myriad of small ways. The greens were more obvious, perhaps, darker, and the ice caps were much more prominent.

"There is a lot of forest," remarked Dawson. "We're getting some more detailed images now. There seems to be some developed areas, quite a few small to medium-sized settlements and a good deal of what seems to be farmland, mostly around the equator."

"No power though," Briggs said absently, thinking out loud. "There's people and agriculture... Why wouldn't they have any power? What sort of disaster would make a society go backwards technologically?"

"A meteor strike?" mused Brax. "Surely science would not just disappear though? Could it?"

"I think it's time we sent a signal," Briggs said.

"Won't do any good," returned Brax. "They don't have any power, well not electricity anyway. And I, also, can't think of a good reason why."

"I'll send something anyway to be sure, said Briggs. "I need a coffee. Who wants to come to the kitchen for food and a brainstorm?"

"I will remain on duty thank you, Captain," announced Dawson and Briggs' mouth tightened into a twisted shape.

"I'll come," said Brax and the men unbuckled and pushed off towards different hatches.

Briggs got to the kitchen first and started to make a cup of coffee. Brax arrived a couple of minutes later after, seemingly, stopping by his quarters to put on soft slippers.

"Yes please," he said casually when he saw Briggs at the coffee machine. The Captain fixed him a brew and they sat at the bench.

"Thoughts?" Briggs asked.

"A whole world has forgotten electricity. That is quite something," said Brax. They sank into quiet contemplation, both holding their mugs tightly. "All I can think of is a devastating extinction event. The farms down there; We are just assuming they are humans. We don't know."

They sat in silence.

"We don't know much," said Briggs. "Let's get some cameras in close and see if we can find the actual farmers. Find out who... or what we are dealing with. Then, I guess, we can make a decision." They both considered this move for a few seconds before Briggs continued. "But we can't stay up here forever. And we don't know how to farm. So, I guess we are going to have to go say hello eventually."

"So, but wait," said Brax. "What if, for example, there was some sort of magnetic shift in the earth and it virtually stopped the ability of electrons to flow?" He asked.

"Are you saying that if we go down we may be stuck there?" Brax nodded.

"OK. Let's send down a drone and see if we can get it back," said Briggs and he took his last sip of coffee before heading back to the bridge. The com system beeped softly as he walked off and he said: "Louise, can you prepare a planetary observation drone please?"

Brax couldn't hear her reply.

BRAX: DATE UNCERTAIN

"Won't a drone stick out somewhat?" Brax asked when he got back to the Bridge.

"Shouldn't do," explained Dawson. "On the assumption that most planets we are likely to explore will have some sort of analogous avian life form, they look like black crows. With wings outstretched. It will head down and sit quietly in a tree, keep a low profile and bring us back some hi-res pics."

"Wasn't there a mad craze to find the robot birds on the socials way back?" Brax asked by way of diversion.

"Yep. In the 2030s I think," replied Dawson. "Lot of birds suffered."

"Maybe..." Brax said, "...humans just wiped themselves out in some lunatic craze from the socials."

"I guess we can't rule anything out yet," replied Dawson.

"I have launched the probe guys," announced B2, interrupting their wild thoughts about humanity's fate.

"There is a fairly large area of settlements and farms around the north of Italy. Or at least what used to be Italy," said Briggs. "Who knows what it's called now. It's as good a place as any to start."

"The probe is programmed to be as unobtrusive as possible so it may take a few hours to find a good vantage point," said Dawson.

"It's got a few possible target points...what look like housing structures...to get in close to"

"So, hypothetical...what if we find alien creatures farming
down there?" Brax asked.

Briggs just looked at him with his lips pursed and shrugged.

"Not helpful, as usual," Dawson muttered under her breath.

"Really Louise?" said Briggs, looking at her but she continued
to look at her screen. He changed tack. "I wonder if that is an
option. Surely if aliens wiped out humans they would have power.
I mean where is the power? Complete blank on that," Briggs said,
as he turned back to his screen. "Should we go down at all if we
can't get back?" He then asked, but now mostly to himself.
"Where else would we go anyway?"

"The probe is responding," interrupted B2

"Visual please," said Briggs.

Their monitors all switched to the probe view. It was moving
through the sky and below they could see forest.

"Holding at 1000 metres," said B2.

Gradually the forest thinned a bit and the ground started to
show patterns that looked like planted fields.

"Where did you say in Italy this is?" Brax asked.

Briggs flicked the coordinates to his monitor. "The coordinates
aren't exact. We are working on information which is 80 000 years
old and we don't have any satellites for cross reference."

"B2, can you put up a map please, overlay the area the drone is
in, just a road map," Brax said, anticipating the AI's next question.

"Give me a moment," said B2.

"There you go," said B2 after a short time. "It's not a perfect
fit...but it's pretty close."

Brax looked at the map with a hot feeling coming to his face. It
was just south of Milan. He instantly thought of the week he and
Jess had, so long ago, spent there. Now his face was burning like
he was slicing it with a razor. He was immobilized. He tried to
speak but only made some incomprehensible sounds.

Almost as if she knew what was happening, Dawson turned to

look at him then released her strap and floated over, grabbing the arm of his chair to look at the screen.

"Fond memories?" She asked.

He blinked rapidly but otherwise didn't move. She rested a hand on his shoulder.

"The loss never truly goes away," she said. "But your memories keep them close to you."

Dawson's sudden kindness caught Brigg's attention and he watched her comforting Brax with a look of admiration. She caught his look and returned it with a gentle smile and her regulation shoulders lost their tension.

"The drone has what looks like the farmhouse in its sight," said B2, breaking the moment. "It is scanning for spots to set up surveillance."

"What time is it?" Briggs asked.

"Late afternoon. No standardised time is being broadcast so... I'm gonna say it's Tuesday," said B2 with...*Humour?* "As best I can tell from all our nav data it's early spring in southern Europe," replied B2, more seriously.

Brax breathed slowly for a minute and came back to the current moment. Dawson returned to her station.

Gradually they got an all-round view of the farm. The buildings were roughly hewn with half logs and seemed to be coated with a soft sheen; perhaps some sort of weatherproof coating. The drone perched in a large tree, just to the south side of the enclosure that had the buildings.

They waited.

Not long, as it turned out.

As evening set in, the yard suddenly became busy. People were coming in from outside the enclosure and busying themselves. It seemed they were putting away equipment in what the crew guessed was a barn of some sort. The drone drifted quietly into the courtyard near another building and they got their first look at the people. They were thin and lanky. Not just some but all that they could see. That was the first obvious sign of change. They wore pants of seemingly leather and perhaps fine cotton or silk tunics. Strikingly, on closer inspection, they had a skin colour that was quite different. It was sort of iridescent green and had flecks of changing colour when in the light, but in the evening shadow it was more of a leafy green. They all had, without exception, thick dark hair, in all manner of different styles and lengths.

Apart from those obvious differences they looked and behaved very much as humans. One person seemed to be directing the others. Animals were brought from the barn and fed from troughs. It was hard to say the animals weren't cattle but they looked different to any cows the crew had seen, with shorter legs. They were more pig-shaped. The yard was not primitive. There seemed to be a tractor, although large with a barrel at the front, like a steam train.

Eventually, the light faded and the people went to different buildings as the yard became darkened. The drone switched to infrared and started looking for better vantage points for the morning.

"I'm inclined to go visit them," said Briggs.

"And tell them what?" Asked Dawson.

"Isn't there some ethical thing about not interfering in primitive cultures?" Brax asked.

Briggs thought on both questions and addressed Brax first. "That's only in movies. Destiny has been very careful to skirt around what might happen should we encounter alien societies, especially primitive ones. There is no set 'procedure' or rules of any kind. I think SMC were never keen on giving up a resource-rich planet just 'cause some people lived there."

"*Terra Nullius*," Brax said.

"Pardon?" Said Dawson.

"After Europeans first saw Australia they declared it an empty land...Terra Nullius... even though it was clearly not. Captain

Cook bumped into people on day one. They just weren't keen on giving up a resource-rich land..." Both Briggs and Dawson joined him to finish: "...just 'cause some people lived there."

They sat in silence and considered that.

"It's irrelevant anyway," Briggs interrupted, "This is Earth and our descendants down there are not primitive. They have no electricity, but they seem well organised. As to what we will say to them..." and he looked at Dawson with a slight smile as he concluded. "Suggestions welcome!" She looked back at him thoughtfully. "But I think," continued the Captain, "a low-key approach to these farmers is the best option. Should we strike trouble we can return with little impact, rather than appearing in a spaceship in the middle of a large town. We know the drone is working so whatever the problem is with electricity, it isn't immediate."

"Should just one of us go?" Brax asked, knowing he would not be the one.

Briggs smiled at him and tilted his head slightly. "Let's stay together Brax," he said gently. "It's better one of us isn't left without the others. We are all we have right now".

58

JESS: 2076 – 2081

"Tell me about your childhood," said Blue in a fake comedy German accent.

"Hilarious," said Jess, with a tone indicating it was clearly not.

"Seriously though…this is how it's going to go," returned Blue now speaking normally. "An accurate map of your memories, actions, reactions and feelings is incredibly complicated. You are going to have to tell me absolutely everything. Absolutely. Even unhappy, embarrassing or nasty…everything."

"I don't think I quite got that," said Jess, sitting back in her office chair, her eyes dancing along the patterns of the ornate ceiling. "This is going to take a while."

"Yes. Years. But we have this time. And every day from here on you will have to add to your story," the AI concluded.

Jess did not reply.

"When you are ready," prompted Blue.

And so, Jess went back to her earliest memories. Her parents. The house she grew up in. She told what she could. And then she told it again. Animations appeared on her screen showing events. At first, they were stick figures but as she retold each memory the images came to life and started to show a shocking realism.

Blue prompted her constantly to describe and define her feelings, note colours, atmosphere and any other detail. It was all about the details.

Other areas of the plan started to come together. Jess was called, officially by The Company, to a long series of detailed medical exams. Blood and tissue samples were taken in different locations by different medical units and doctors. All the results were sent to the 'Health and Wellbeing' department but no one ever actually received them. Their computer shipped everything to do with Jess straight to Blue. She had every aspect of her body, right down to her DNA mapped and hundreds of samples put into storage. Most importantly, and in great secrecy, a chip was implanted in her cortex so she was able to link directly with Blue.

They decided to take the Extra-terrestrial Landing Craft (ETL) and land in a small clearing some 10 kilometres away from the farm.

The ETL was small. There were four seats and it had a teardrop-shaped dome with small portholes around the side on a flat arrow-head shaped base. Two corners of the arrow shape were turned up at the edges giving lift for atmospheric flight but it could also use the turbo-pulse engine to descend and fly out, for planets with little or no gaseous atmosphere. The engine itself had outlets throughout the lower body which could be angled in all directions so vertical take-offs and landings could be achieved. Then they could rotate for the craft to fly conventionally. It had a powerful engine and the craft was able to escape gravity up to 3 times that of Earth. The controls were generally run from the *Sentinel* although a link with a personal device could make manual control possible.

They packed quite a few supplies so they could hike from the landing site to the farm. They each had a backpack with some food packs and energy water. They also had emergency supplies, a shelter and sleeping bags. Kitted up with coveralls, warming shirts, wide-brimmed hats and solid boots, they started to look like a mini military operation.

The ETL launched from the outer ring and started the slow descent to Earth.

They timed it so the landing was just prior to dawn. This would hopefully mean most people would be home in bed and would not see the ETL. Also, that would give them a full day to head to the farm and assess the situation. The noise of the engines was a problem but they hoped they were far enough away from any sentient being that their descendants, as they started to think of them would think it a far-off thunder and nothing more.

They emerged from the rear door and climbed off the wing to the ground. They double-checked all their gear and B2 started the Active Camouflage Unit on the ETL. This was a system of mirrors and colourations to the outer skin that rendered the ship virtually invisible to anyone but those right next to it. Even then it was hard to make out edges.

The drone had come from the farm to meet them and provide extra surveillance and guidance from the sky. Briggs had brought a magnetic compass which he had not used since his early days of training. He got it out to check.

"The magnetic field has reversed," he stated.

"So, North is South now?" asked Dawson.

"Magnetic north is now to the south, and vice versa," he answered.

"That's certainly to be expected over such a long period. Might have even happened a couple of times." Brax chimed in. "There's no way to know without taking some polar core samples. But that would be a fun day trip!"

They could hear each other clearly through their ear-piece link and Brax continued to talk as they walked.

"During a reversal, there would be an increase in radiation from space because the magnetic field weakens before it flips," he said. "There was a theory for a while that extinction events and field flips went together. What if our new friends at the farm over there are a result of mutations from cosmic ray increases?"

Dawson seemed to be enjoying the theoretical idea. "So, you

are saying that mutations from radiation have caused a sort of instant evolutionary change?" she asked.

"Maybe. That kind of physical change is hard to explain otherwise."

They walked in silence then for a while.

"Update please B2," said Briggs, after a time.

"You are heading towards a thick copse of trees. I will lose sight of you for a bit. Your direction is good though. You are about 6 kilometres out now."

"Okay."

The trees around them were fairly thick already and Briggs wasn't sure how thick things were going to get. The morning was getting on now but the shade of the trees was deep and they proceeded slowly. After about 30 minutes the trees started to thin again and Briggs guessed they were starting to come to the farm-land. Briggs checked his device to get the view from the drone. The wind was getting up a little bit and it seemed some cloud was building. He thought it might rain a little later.

"We should get a move on," he said. "I think the weather might turn."

"Movement in the trees just to your west," came B2's voice in their ears, "and to the north and east. That isn't random. You have company."

"Stay calm everyone," commanded Briggs. Then he raised his voice.

"Hello out there? We are travellers and mean no harm," he called.

They stood and waited. After a short time, people came out from around the trees nearby. All up seven appeared tentatively from different directions.

It was the farmers. And they were tall. Briggs was 188 cm and that seemed to put the tallest of them at over 2 metres. Their skin looked more radiant than it had on the camera with an iridescence giving it a kind of rainbow shimmer.

The clothing was as they had seen but they also wore cloth

wrappings, like a small turban, around their heads. Their faces seemed quite long with straight noses, reminiscent of the famous statues on Easter Island, although not as exaggerated.

"I'm in the trees above you," said B2 in their ears. "There isn't any other movement. I think the ones you can see are the only people here."

"Everybody hold your palms up," said Briggs. They all did as Briggs instructed.

Then he said in a louder voice: "We mean you no harm."

The farmers did not reply. They only stared in a quite unnerving way as if they were searching the crew's faces for the meaning of life.

Briggs was, for one of the very few times in his life a bit put out. "Ummm... Hi?" He said, waiting for something to happen.

"Wachka harv," said one of them who appeared to be their leader, with a beard not as dark as the hair, more of a dark grey.

They stood still having no idea what that meant or what they should do.

"That definitely isn't Italian," stated Dawson, "or close to any European language I recognise."

The descendants continued staring. After a few seconds, the leader made a spinning gesture with his pointer finger, pointing it up and spinning it around.

"They want us to turn around," said Dawson. "Should I get the sonic pistol out?"

"Negative Louise," replied Briggs. "Let's just do as they ask. If they were going to hurt us they would have already."

And so, they turned around and faced each other in a little circle. Several farmers pulled out a long rope and they approached the three wrapping them and strapping their arms by their sides. They started pulling the rope like they were cattle. The crew were forced to follow. The descendants had some conversation between them as they pulled the rope, but it was clear any language these people had bore no resemblance to anything the crew knew.

"Seem to have got yourselves into a spot there guys," chirruped B2 with what sounded like a smirk.

"They seem nervous," said Dawson. Despite their superficial differences they clearly showed facial expressions and gestures that were very familiar.

"Well they aren't the only ones," Brax replied.

"They've got us bound yet they look around all the time as if they expect more people to arrive," said Dawson.

"They are taking you to the farm," said B2. "It's only about a kilometre away now."

Briggs quietly talked to the other two. "We need to build a bridge with these people. They need to have some investment in us. Curiosity or empathy. It doesn't matter. Anything that doesn't get us locked up or injured is a win," he said. He then piped up so everyone could hear him.

"Hi there, guys. We don't mean you any harm. Honestly, we were just heading over to the farm for a chat anyway. So, if you want to loosen the ropes we are fine with that. Any chance?"

He then feigned a limp and tried to grab his leg like it was in pain.

They looked at him curiously. Then they looked around at each other and there was some conversation. Finally, they unwound the rope that bound them but they formed a tight circle around the three and walked on.

THEY ARRIVED at the farm and it looked familiar from their observations. The farm residents came out to see them, including, now, a couple of men and women who were wearing what could be more described as robes, tied at the waist.

Animated conversation ensued and the crew were taken into a large barn that contained much as you would expect a working barn to hold. There was lots of hay spread around with two or three of the docile cow/pig creatures. There was a small pen in one corner that had what looked like goats but with rougher spiky fur. The descendants stood and stared warily at the new strangers in their domain. There was a variety of hand farming implements and an odd-looking machine with cogs and a metal casing on a cart. Up the back, there was a loft. It had many items stored there and the smell was familiar to anyone who had been to a farm; hay and dung and old timber. The building had a few small windows with a kind of smoky stained glass so you could see out to the courtyard and around the farm. The big doors were shut and the three of them sat on some benches at the side and waited.

"I have resumed my position in the trees," said B2 who, now, it seemed, had consumed the drone into its working matrix. "I have tried to keep a low profile but they saw me on the walk and their behaviour patterns have changed from my initial observations."

The barn door started to open again and three of the descendants walked in. Two sat on the bench next to them and one, an older woman in a robe garment like they had seen earlier, stood in front of them.

"Say-jar." That was all she said.

They looked at each other with some confusion. "Hello?" Briggs said, guessing the meaning and then he continued with calm assurance. "We are not a threat to you, I promise," he said again holding up his hands and showing the palms.

Dawson continued. "Louise." She said patting her chest and then repeating it a few times. Briggs and Brax did the same.

The woman in front of them thought for a second then said, "Ankas," whilst also lightly patting her chest.

Briggs mimed having a drink. "Water," he said and Dawson joined the mime as well, repeating the word.

Ankas, glanced at one of the others who stood and left the barn, returning a few seconds later with a leather bladder, roughly but well sewn, because it did not leak. Ankas removed the cap and handed it to Briggs. Briggs, without hesitation, took a swig of the liquid inside and handed it to Dawson who did the same. Briggs gave her a sideways glance and slight nod to which she seemed satisfied. Then she gave it to Brax who looked at it with some distaste.

"You know, I think I'm ok," Brax said.

"Drink it Brax," said Briggs in a low non-threatening tone. "Now is not the time to be particular. We are building trust," he continued, trying so hard to sound nice he was nearly singing the words. "We are showing we are perfectly normal and not from 83 000 freaking years ago. Can you take a sip please?"

Brax looked at the bladder with what seemed like extreme distaste.

"Brax," continued Briggs, still semi-singing through clenched teeth, "we are in a totally unknown situation here. This could be about our very lives... please drink the fucking cordial."

Brax carefully raised the bladder to his lips and had a sip. Then an odd expression came over him and he took a much larger drink with relish.

"There. That was good wasn't it?" asked Briggs rhetorically.

Ankas now had a smile on her face.

Suddenly, in the distance, they heard a sound that was unmistakably horses galloping and she made a gesture to the other two descendants who left. Ankas' smile faded and she indicated for the three to move to the back of the barn and then up the ladder to the loft. She followed them up indicating some small areas at the back where they would be hidden from view. Then she left the barn.

Briggs noticed a very small porthole at the end of the loft which looked out towards the main gate. He shuffled over to have a look outside.

"There's seven horses," he said. "Bigger than the ones here. The riders look a bit different. Their faces seem rounder and they have more solid body shapes, perhaps a bit shorter. They're wearing armour. Metal breastplates, shoulder pads and bowl helmets. Looks like shiny copper. One's got a flag on a pole and they've all got swords. It's like a history documentary out there," concluded Briggs.

Four of the riders dismounted and started to walk in different directions. One towards what Briggs felt was the main dwelling, and one to some sheds on the far side of the yard. One walked toward their shed.

"They're coming, and they mean business," said Briggs softly.

"What now?" Brax asked.

Briggs didn't answer but he looked at Dawson who nodded and she took the sonic pistol out of her backpack.

"They look a bit different but I'm thinking humans haven't changed much. The guys with swords are not for us," concluded Briggs.

Dawson moved around to the edge of the loft and took a vantage point using a rake to cover her face as the barn door opened and the new 'soldier' descendant came in. He looked around and casually kicked away some hay. He looked at the loft and stopped for a few seconds. Then in an almost resigned way, he trudged toward the ladder. He started to climb and Dawson trained the sonic pistol on him. As he reached the second last rung a loud commanding voice came from the yard. The new descendant seemed to roll his eyes and let out a long sigh then started to descend and left the barn without any further divergence.

Briggs looked out the porthole again and the riders all mounted. The lead rider tipped his helmet at Ankas and they rode away. Ankas gestured to the others and what seemed like normal work routines resumed.

"Alright," said Briggs. "It's time we stopped being so passive. That could have gone very badly. Louise; put the pistol away but keep it handy. We need to get out of here and establish some independence."

AND SO, they climbed down from the loft and left the barn. Out in the yard, the day was now overcast with a slight breeze. Workers were leaving the yard for the fields.

The three approached Ankas, who was down near the main house talking animatedly to another woman and two men; one they recognised as the leader from the forest. Briggs mimed eating and said the appropriate words and the message seemed to be understood. She gestured for the crew to go into the house with her and the other three farmers went in different directions. The house was best described as old-fashioned. A large timber table was in the centre of a room just off an entrance hallway. Curtains hung at the edge of nearly full-length windows and chairs of varying kinds were around the table and room. There was a fire-place and everything looked fairly homely. Briggs' feeling that humans hadn't changed much seemed exactly right.

They sat at the table and were each brought a plate of food. They had a fork-like utensil given to them and they ate. There were what appeared to be vegetables of different kinds including carrots and potatoes and cold meat which tasted a bit like beef or maybe lamb. Sauces were brought as well and they quickly found themselves enjoying their first non-space meal in many months.

As they ate, Ankas found some paper and had some ink and a metal pen with a nib. She drew a map for the three and the meaning was clear. An x and a sad face next to what was the farm and another simple face with a smile next to a building down a road someway.

"They want to move us," Briggs cottoned on quickly.

"Maybe we should go back to the ETL and try again some-where else," said Dawson.

"Maybe," replied Briggs "but the process will be the same. We have already made progress today. We have an inkling of the poli-tics and we have an ally. I think we should continue."

B2 spoke for the first time in a while. "Briggs is right. This is the most likely outcome anywhere you go. In fact, it could be worse as you seem to have guessed. The fact that these descen-dants are so trusting is a bonus you might not get anywhere else."

Ankas watched them as they spoke, taking a great interest in the conversation.

"What do you think Brax?" asked Briggs.

"I agree. If we need the ETL, B2 can get it to us. I mean we can leave and we could just as easily fly off to another planet, but to what end? They have infrastructure here and we have started to learn about their particular societal ways. We have a lot to offer them if we can get communications up and running. Let's take the journey with Ankas and see where we are then."

The other two looked at Brax with something approaching admiration.

"Well said, my friend," said Briggs, simply.

Ankas made a great pantomime in the yard after the meal, pointing at the sky and drawing the path of the sun.

"I am guessing we will be leaving at sunset," said Dawson.

"B2," said Briggs. "Can you fly towards the west and look at the settlement we saw there?"

"I know the one," replied the AI, enthusiastically.

About 20 minutes later B2 checked in.

"It's about 25 kilometres to the west," it started. "It's a small town with a much larger structure in the centre that is a series of buildings made of stone with a large, courtyard area surrounded by a very tall stone wall. The main structure has what appears to be three stories and is shaped as a giant square with a further courtyard area in the middle of that. Actually, not a castle so much, as more like a monastery." B2 put some pictures up.

"That looks like a safe place," said Dawson. "I bet that's where we are going."

"It's a good bet," replied Briggs. "I imagine night travel will be slow but if that's where we are going we should be there by morning."

Despite the weather, that had turned to a cool continuous misty rain, Ankas spent a good deal of the afternoon out in the yard just standing and looking in various directions. Sometimes she had her arms outstretched like in some kind of religious fervour. Farm hands walked around her without acknowledging her at all and she seemed consumed by thought.

BRIGGS: 239N

s the workers returned to the yard in the afternoon, a wagon was brought to the house pulled by two horses. They looked much like the horses they had seen earlier but stockier and a fraction shorter. Work horses, rather than riding horses.

They pulled the hoods over their weather-proof suits and climbed on the wagon where they found a small pile of blankets. Two men took the reins of the horses and walked out front.

Ankas climbed aboard as well and it was clear then that she was older than they thought, struggling slightly to get up. One of the others started towards her as if to help but she waved them away dismissively. She sat at the front of the wagon on a low bench that was there. The rear gate of the wagon shut and they started driving as darkness descended. The remaining descendants looked on as they drove away. Brax gave them an awkward-looking wave. A couple of them waved back tentatively looking bewildered by the whole thing.

DARKNESS AND A CHILL settled in but they had thermoregulators and were reasonably comfortable, although the ride was very bumpy.

They followed a series of roads past other farm settlements and Ankas sat in silence, sometimes with her eyes closed or, at other times, looking at the crew with a wonder in her eyes.

"I've been thinking about the soldiers that showed up," said Dawson. "The power they had, the armour, the better horses. It all spoke to a huge inequity. That they could just roll in and search the place without any complaints." She shook her head. "And they wanted something."

"Us," returned Briggs, "although they can't have known it was us specifically, somehow they knew something was up. It seems the noise of the landing was more conspicuous than we hoped."

"So, put simply, the bad guys don't know what they are looking for but think the good guys are hiding something?" Brax asked.

"Very much said like a ten-year-old, Brax,' returned Briggs, "but yes, in a nutshell, that fits the facts."

As the journey progressed they got updates from B2 but all was silent. They set the clocks for the time B2 guessed it would be in Greenwich Meantime considering where they were and the time of year. It was about five in the morning and they had all dozed a bit when the light began to break. It had dawned a clear and still day.

B2 chimed in. "We have visitors."

"Let me guess," said Dawson, "our soldier friends are back."

"Yes. You were expecting them?" Asked B2.

"Yes, I was," replied Dawson. "All their behaviour suggested they would try and cut off any avenues that Ankas or anyone else might take to hide something. Simple strategy. These guys are soldiers and I get how they think. How far away are they?" She asked.

"I would guess about five minutes. They were patrolling the road and it's higher up ahead. I think they have spotted you now because they are at a gallop."

They used signs and mimes to help Ankas understand what was happening but after about a minute she heard the approaching horses and seemed to stop and lapse into that still thought again.

"What's the plan Louise?" asked Briggs, bowing to her experience.

"Stay calm," she replied, pulling the sonic pistol from her pack. "If we need to act it will happen quickly so be ready for anything."

Three mounted soldiers came into view shortly after. The crew stood in the cart as the soldiers came alongside. They looked shocked at the sight of the newcomers and there was animated talk with Ankas. She got off the wagon and approached the horses. The senior soldier seemed more than angry and he yelled forcefully at Ankas. One of the two descendants pulling the horses approached the soldiers, and it seemed like he was intervening. The senior soldier took off a glove and slapped this man hard across the face. He lost his balance and fell to the ground. Ankas remonstrated and the argument continued, becoming more heated.

The two soldiers came to the wagon and started gesturing at the crew. Brax caught a word he was becoming familiar with; '*Say-jar*'. They seemed to be telling the crew to get off the wagon.

At this point, Dawson raised the sonic pistol and aimed it at the head soldier.

"Leave us!" She commanded. The soldiers, with practised speed, took knives from their jackets and the commander pulled a sword. Without a moment's hesitation, he brought it down on Ankas' head and she crumpled to the ground as if she were a curtain. Dawson fired the sonic pistol straight at him with pinpoint settings and the sonic wave struck the commander from his horse and he fell to the ground dead. The soldiers reacted in a split second. Two knives flew with blinding speed through the air striking Dawson in the chest and she fell. Briggs was quick to move. He grabbed the pistol and fired off two shots taking both the riders down before they could take out their swords.

By this time, the second descendant had stood up and come back to the horses. They were running now and pulling the horses along. Dawson had gone pale and looked sweaty but she was still breathing. Briggs fashioned a pillow arrangement out of the blankets and wrapped her as best he could. She flickered into consciousness.

"Luis..." she said and then she coughed and blood appeared in her mouth.

"Louise, no, please. Hang on. You have to stay with me," pleaded Briggs.

"The settlement is about 20 minutes away now," said B2

Dawson was shaking now in small convulsions and the blood stain down her front was large and distressing. "Luis..." she said again in a faint gurgling voice. "Luis...I love you. You... Are... ... Always."

And she stopped.

Just like that.

Briggs sat with her and whispered, "Louise. Come back... come back." And then he let out a small high-pitched sound. It was the sound of total loss.

***

THEY CAME upon the town as B2 had said. Briggs sat with Dawson's body and seemed stunned as tears welled and rolled slowly down his cheeks. He gently wiped away the blood from her mouth as best he could. The town itself was sloping up a very gentle hill and was surrounded by a low stone wall that had an opening for the road to go through. The descendants with the horses were still going at a brisk jog making the horses trot. They travelled through streets that had houses made mostly of timber or some kind of large brick. They were spaced out and oriented randomly along the way. The huge, dark stone building at the centre was very clearly visible, dominating the scene. As they moved towards it, they could make out a gate in the outer wall. The wall itself was nearly 25 metres high. The large wooden gate was about half that and the same wide but shaped like an arch. It was very reminiscent of a cathedral door. Within the large doors was a smaller person-sized door which looked much easier to open.

The large gates slowly creaked open as they approached and they went straight through. There was much going on in the courtyard and when the wagon stopped it was approached by several descendants wearing the same knee-length robes they had seen at the farm, tied at the waist, leather boots and scarves tied around their long necks. They came onto the wagon and approached Dawson's body and Briggs seemed just to yield as he sat back allowing them to examine her. They seemed knowledgeable in biology and felt her heart and checked her neck for a pulse, finally coming to the obvious conclusion. They covered her face with a blanket and gently removed her from the cart putting her on a kind of stretcher that some others had brought. They indicated to Briggs and Brax that they should come off the cart and they led them to a small room just off the yard. It had two rudimentary bunk beds and a small table with a couple of chairs. There was a vase with some fresh flowers in it on the table, and, all around, new unlit candles.

Briggs sat on one of the lower bunks and Brax sat in a chair. Briggs stared at the wall and the two did not speak.

The 'monks', as the two would start to think of them, brought food and drink but the men did not eat. One monk came and sat with them for a while but left when Briggs lay down and drifted into an unsettled light sleep.

Then another monk brought Brax a book. It was nicely made and bound in leather. It was printed but was incomprehensible. There were some maps in it and also some interesting diagrams of what looked like cooking. Certainly, things were being poured into other things. For what purpose he was not sure.

61

ROGER HARRIS: 2078

One of Roger's strengths was his ability to go to the top when solving a problem. Meetings were set up by intermediates and took time to organise. But once he had that first meeting he always ended up with the personal netspex number of his target. In Rome, his target was not the Pope. He had done enough research to know better.

"Welcome Cardinal," Roger gushed as he opened his door.

"It is a pleasure to see you again Roger," replied Cardinal Jiminez, the second in line to the title of Bishop of Rome. "How are the family?"

"Very well thank you. My boy is out of school now and ready to sit for the Bar Exam. And your golf game?" The Cardinal sat in a lounge chair in Roger's Vatican apartment while Roger fixed him his drink of choice. Straight vodka on the rocks.

"Still pushing a handicap of 11. I'm having a pro look at my swing next week," said the Cardinal. "So, tell me how the prep goes with the *New Washington?*"

"We are two months out from launch," replied Roger, handing over the glass and sitting down with his own poison. "Passengers are finishing training and will be getting their formal instructions on boarding procedures soon."

"And the Itinerary?"

"As discussed, it has not changed. The same two planets from the first mission and the addition of the star Trappist 1. We have allocated 7 years till return and, in that time, we expect to commission a fleet of 8 more deep space miners, to be ready to go once the test mission is complete."

The cardinal nodded with suitable seriousness. "And the Dark Angels have gone quiet?"

"Just so," confirmed Roger. "The attacks have stopped and they have done nothing more than send about a half dozen messages since we announced 3 years ago. They seem to not want to reveal themselves, still. Keeping an ace in the hole, I guess. They may just want to remind us to keep this plan on track." He paused thoughtfully. "But we do seem to be satisfying their agenda."

"Perhaps, in the future, we can bring them into the Church," said the Cardinal with a wry chuckle and Roger raised an eyebrow before draining his glass.

62

BRIGGS: 239N

In the evening, there was a funeral that started in the outer courtyard. The sun was low giving a soft evening light. This seemed to the men to have happened very quickly, but it was well organised. Dawson's body had been cleaned up and she was dressed in some fine silk clothes. A tunic, loose-fitting pants, some kind of head scarf and slippers. She was laid on a pallet of timbers which sat on a makeshift table. It had colourful and bejewelled material around the edges hanging to the ground. As the two men watched, a blanket of similar exotic material was placed over her. They had retrieved Ankas' body from the road and she too was, similarly, caringly prepared for a ceremony of some sort. The monks made a big effort to encourage the men to go close to the pallet and view Dawson's body. Briggs walked a little way towards her but then stopped suddenly and just stared. Brax went to her and stood over the table. She seemed to be sleeping serenely.

"Goodbye Daw...goodbye Louise," he said. "Your bravery, your humour, your compassion. You made a mark on me and all those around you and...as long as I live...I will not allow you to be forgotten."

He turned and walked back to where Briggs was standing. There was a circle of some 70 people around the pallets. They all bore, the now more familiar, green skin, and long faces with high cheekbones. They carried themselves with confidence and they had a real, although slightly alien, beauty about them. Nearly half wore robes, the rest dressed similarly to the farm workers they had met the day before.

Brax noted one monk, who had come to their room earlier with the book and seemed to be named Vasta. Now, it seemed, he was their leader. Vasta took a book, stood between the tables and read in a clear voice, as you would expect a priest at a funeral. He sprinkled some water over the bodies and then, on command, eight other monks came to the tables the pallets lay on and went to lift them, four on each.

"No!" shouted Briggs suddenly, and he ran to the table where Dawson lay. Vasta and the others stepped back as he approached. He looked down at her and tears rolled down his face as he convulsed with sobs. Quiet words came from his mouth in fits and starts and his grief was palpable. Many monks were also visibly distressed. Brax went after him and put an arm around his shoulder.

The monks picked up the pallet and they formed a procession from the outer courtyard through a short tunnel built into the main house to the inner courtyard. It was a large, square area, some 100 metres on each side. In the centre was an enormous bonfire set up ready to go; to Briggs the intent was clear.

"Are we going to do this?" Brax asked Briggs.

"I don't know what she wanted..." started Briggs. "We never talked about...which was stupid...but..." He lapsed into silence.

"I think we have to decide." Said Brax.

Briggs walked in the procession and made no reply. And so, they tacitly agreed that she would be cremated.

They stood in the courtyard which was unfamiliar, yet completely familiar. They watched an ancient ritual as 30 metre flames propelled into the sky over Dawson and Ankas' shells.

As the fire died down they were led to another large room. There was food on some tables and in the corner some descendants were playing vaguely familiar-looking musical instruments, but with strange harmonies. A singer intoned low and beautiful notes that weaved a quite hypnotic spell. Briggs recognised that it was a wake. Neither of the men had eaten since last evening and now the monks encouraged them to sample some of the food. It was mostly sweet, with pastries that tasted very familiar to them and there were breads with a kind of savoury paste that was not familiar to the men.

"What now?" He asked Briggs. "Back to the ship?"

Briggs looked around at these people who he now realised had exhibited such incredible kindness to complete strangers.

"B2? Where are you?" asked Briggs.

"I am outside the main structure in the village, replied the AI. "I have located a large tree about 200 metres away from you. Lt Dawson has gone?"

Brax interjected as Briggs started to choke up. "Yes B2. The knives were fatal. She has been cremated."

"I am so sorry." Said B2 "It would seem that inhumanity is still alive and well."

Briggs was startled by this comment and momentarily forgot his pain.

"Thanks, B2," said Briggs. "But I have to say that today we found more humanity than I remember seeing in a long time. These people; these descendants; are not like the soldiers we met. I mean, they look slightly different but there is so much more. They carry themselves very differently. They seem to have a calm intent and purpose. They seem rarely flustered but also... I can't quite put my finger on it. There's something about them." He paused then and his brow furrowed. "It's clear though, they are our allies. We should stay here a while," he muttered, mostly to himself. "B2!" He suddenly said. "Take the drone back to the ETL and charge it up. If you strike any trouble in your current spot move back to the sentinel. We'll send for you if we need you, otherwise, stay put and check in daily."

"Are you sure you will be Okay?" asked B2 in an almost motherly tone.

"Well, I'm not sure...I'm not sure of anything today. But life goes on. I want to find a way to repay the kindness we have been shown. And really, what else have we got on?"

<hr>

OVER THE NEXT FEW DAYS, the weather started to warm and it was very definitely spring. The air was full of perfume and the skies dawned clear but, often in the afternoon, thunder rumbled and they had a storm. The monks had quite elaborate gardens in the grounds and the men were allowed to wander around at will. However, someone always accompanied them as they walked but did not ever attempt to interfere, though often would suggest places to go look at.

They dined every evening in a large, high ceilinged hall and were served all sorts of meals from roast...something...to stews and curries. Odd-looking vegetables appeared on their plates but most everything was palatable. They drank mostly water and more of the wine/cordial they had first drunk with Ankas. The drink came in various stages of alcoholic which seemed to coincide with the time of day. In the morning it was virtually alcohol-free but by dinner, it was most certainly not. The monks would become jovial in the evenings and although they did not understand the humour, Brax and Briggs appreciated the light-hearted atmosphere.

It seemed they had gone back in time, if not actually, then certainly in effect.

They tried to open the lines of communication and managed to get paper and pens. The pens had nibs of, seemingly, iron and had ink inside them so writing was reasonably easy. The men started with simple words and pictures and the monks reciprocated. They were, surprisingly, able to produce all English sounds but themselves had several guttural and clicky sounds in their language that Brax and Briggs could not get. But they persisted.

They picked up some names and also learnt a vocabulary of around twenty basic words.

Briggs decided he and Brax should have basic conversations to demonstrate English. The monks enjoyed this very much and thought the stiltedness of the speech and simple behaviours during this time to be quite comical. The men got quite an audience each day for these sessions out in the courtyard and Briggs started to look forward to them, planning what themes or ideas they would talk about.

"Hello to you, Brax." Briggs would say with the worst acting that Brax had ever seen.

"Hello Briggs. How are you today?" Brax would reply, clearly and slowly, with the worst acting Briggs had ever seen.

"I am fine. Would you like some breakfast today?" he would continue and so it would go. After a few days of this Briggs started to go for cheap laughs by falling over or some such. It turned out that the great Captain Briggs was an absolute ham. But the monks laughed raucously and Briggs found their generosity of spirit rejuvenating.

JESS: 2080-2085

Jess walked a lot. The rhythmic movement of her limbs helped ease the trauma. She found the air to be fresh and real, unlike the large infrastructure of humans that meant less and less to her as the years went by.

She became a recluse. It fitted with her back story and no one questioned it. Because it was the truth. She did not want to get involved with anyone. She reduced contact as much as possible. Her staff thought she had gone a little mad. They thought she was damaged from her family traumas and she allowed them to think that. Because now she had purpose.

It would be a thankless task. But no one else was going to do it.

'What was important?' She had finally asked herself. *'Love, family. The little things.'*

People could still have what she did not and she would be saving countless others from the same trauma she had endured. So, she had to be solitary. It was the price.

Blue and Baby Blue had their own tasks.

It took time to work out the principles of the 'Net' as they called it. A large amount of satellites needed to be procured and this would take time. It had to be done slowly and secretly. Small bits, done here and there. Baby Blue funnelled the required funds and covered its tracks so the company paid for it all. Blue did the organising. It was going to be an engineering feat by itself, but to also do it quietly required the utmost care. Not one person could be allowed to connect the dots.

"We have to give all the satellites fake, random purposes and then we can build them without attracting attention," said Blue. "We are establishing small automated factories to minimise human contact."

"And the Moon?" Asked Jess.

"Yes. Same," replied Blue. "A manufacturing station is being built on the moon and run robotically. There are large storage facilities there as well. Only a few people know it's there and they have such high secrecy clearance they will never talk about it. Not even to each other. We have a close tab on them though...just in case.

"Surely someone will see such a large operation," countered Jess.

"They may. It is all underground and just slightly into the dark side, and it's well away from any other settlement," Blue replied. "There are also a series of cover stories about it so anyone stumbling across inconsistencies in paperwork will think that it's someone else's problem. No one will want too much information about any of it if they value their job. And we will spot any messaging about it and take quick action. Baby Blue will funnel all money it requires out of any number of businesses The Company now owns and runs."

"Sounds like you have thought of everything," said Jess, a little sourly.

Blue did not respond.

"Jess," continued Blue, after a time, "the risk of being discovered is ever-present but our advantage is the sheer size of the company. We now own and run the largest market share in just about every area. Computers, software, weapons, aircraft and ships, cars, bicycles, kitchenware, clothes, gadgets, food, soft toys and supermarkets. You name it, we are simply the biggest player. We are a behemoth of industry and although the moon facility looks like a big deal to you it rates low compared to everything that is happening. If things go according to plan, eventually we will move everything up there."

"Anything else?" asked Jess just wanting to get it over with.

"A new mainframe is being built into a state-of-the-art ship that The Company has Christened *New World*. It has the best medical facilities imaginable and is now self-renewing, with maintenance bots that can recycle themselves as required. It's the same way the 'net' support will work. It's the best ship for us to use."

Jess leaned back in her seat and nodded. She could stop it, she knew that. But she wouldn't. She was going to protect the galaxy. This work had fallen to her.

She went for a long walk.

The attack came 18 days after Dawson had been killed and the monks had known it was coming. They had been preparing the outer wall with armoury stations and extra guards but as Brax had no point of reference he initially could not see that.

The first they knew of it was when the gates opened and nearly three hundred people from the village streamed in. They went through the tunnel to the inside courtyard where the monks had set up tents and other types of basic timber shelters. Some of the villagers went via ladders to the parapet to take position in front of arrowslits there.

The first wave of attack was balls of flaming material that came over the wall. Teams seemed to be tasked with going after them and putting them out.

"We need to take cover!" said Brax, alarmed, and he and Briggs ran to the main building, through a wooden door and into a room with a small window looking out. They could hear crackling timbers and smell burning from outside the main walls and concluded the town was on fire.

Then they heard the battering rams banging at the main gates. For a full 4 hours, the ramming continued until the gates finally started to buckle. The fighting bloomed through the main gate as soldiers appeared and started charging through. The descendants were well-positioned and many of the soldiers dropped to arrows.

But then more came indicating a large army had appeared.

"We have landed in a war zone," said Briggs ruefully.

A monk came through the door and ushered them upstairs to the top story of the solid stone main building. Again, they had a window through which they took careful peeks.

The soldiers moved further into the yard but the monks, although seriously outnumbered had the high ground. Further fighting ensued and after another hour or so it was clear that all was lost. It seemed the entire army of soldiers had come into the courtyard area. Hand-to-hand combat was becoming common and the soldiers had the advantage. Their knife throwing was impeccable and many fighters were falling as Dawson had.

Then a remarkable thing happened.

The monks and villagers who were fighting suddenly turned and ran through the tunnel into the inner courtyard. They moved fast and it was well coordinated. The large doors that had been breached were pulled as shut as they would go, considering the damage, and rocks were thrown from the roof, above where we were situated, into the yard. As they hit the ground, though, it became clear they were not rocks, but containers that smashed as they hit. As gas rose from the smashed objects the monk who was with Brax and Briggs took out thick material and gave them some. He then put it over his mouth and nose and the men did the same.

"Gas masks," said Briggs.

The gas in the courtyard was thick and the soldiers fell to it straight away. As this happened the villagers streamed back out of the inner courtyard with similar masks tied on and ropes in hand. They started tying up all the unconscious soldiers and within 15 minutes it was all over. The soldiers awoke about an hour later to find themselves bound, hand and foot, with gags in their mouths.

THE COMING days were a clean-up operation. The soldiers were stripped of all their armour and weapons and taken, in basically their underwear, to another location. The dead from the monks were cremated in the same way Dawson and Ankas had been and that gave Briggs another reference to the esteem they had given a woman they had never met. He seemed moved by this and he started to give his energy to supporting the rebuild any way he could, inside the monastery and outside in the town.

The town had been pretty well torched. A few stone houses remained but not much else and most of the villagers were still residing in the makeshift camp in the inner courtyard. Villagers took carts out and brought back timber and a large shipment of iron nails came in from somewhere. Brax also helped where he could and they drifted into a bit of a routine. Before they realised a couple of weeks had passed.

Then, one day they had visitors. After they had come back from the day's work in the town the large main gates opened. A cart came in, drawn by four horses. Driving the carriage were two female monks wearing the characteristic silk and cotton robes and thick scarf.

Behind them rode six burly men in armour but they were not the soldiers from the attack. These had the same appearance as the friendly descendants and the same calm assurance of the monks. The cart contained something large in the back covered by a leather tarpaulin. It pulled into the part of the driveway that led to the main building doors and stopped out the front. The monks went about their work and Vasta came out of the main entrance of the building to greet the visitors. It was apparent from the start the visitors were being deferred to. They carried themselves with a great deal of confidence. Briggs and Brax stood in the courtyard near their room and watched. After a short time of discussion between Vasta and the new arrivals, he suddenly gestured toward the men and the three of them started to walk over.

"Briggs. Brax." Said Vasta to the visitors as he pointed to the men. The newcomers bowed their heads ever so slightly towards the men. Then they patted their chest as was becoming common.

"Kristic," said one.

"Harmok," said the other.

They seemed, to Brax, to be quite young for leaders. In their weeks so far back on Earth, they had only seen leaders who appeared to be maybe 70 or older. Kristic and Harmok were maybe 40 at most.

And they were quite beautiful. They were as tall as all the other descendants with the characteristic shimmery greenish skin and dark hair. They had slightly wider faces and high cheekbones, though, and not the longer noses the men had become used to. They were so similar looking Brax was sure they were twins.

Vasta said, "Come," as he bade the men to follow them back to the wagon and that mysterious tarpaulin.

"Bets for what's under the tarp," said Briggs jovially.

"A small rhinoceros." Brax posited. "You?"

Briggs looked thoughtful and serious. "A 2012 Honda Civic," he replied.

"That's very specific," said Brax.

"Dark green," Briggs continued.

"Have you rigged this?" Brax said joining in.

"Okay," continued Briggs, now getting right into the joke. "I Bet 10 000 of whatever they use for money around here that I'm right. Come on. Ya chicken?" And Brax chuckled.

The tarpaulin was removed very carefully by the guards as they stood and watched. At the last minute, it fell away and Brax sucked in his breath at the sight.

"Wow!" Exclaimed Briggs, for the first time that week. "Not a car."

"Name?" Vasta asked Brax, pointing at the...

"Telescope," he replied.

And Brax thought it was beautiful.

It was fashioned from a lovely stained timber. You could just admire the mesmerising grain patterns and feel joy. It was braced by polished brass rings and was close to four metres in length. It had a 90 cm diameter and sat upon a solid timber tripod.

The soldiers divested the bulky parts of their armour and took the telescope off the wagon, placing it in the middle of the court-yard. They also assembled a shelter made of iron struts and a second tarp and placed it on the ground next to the wagon.

The days were getting longer and there was a summery feeling in the air. In the twilight, they stood and looked at each other a bit awkwardly. Vasta took charge and pointed to the sky. "Stars?"

"Yes," Brax said.

Food was brought and quite a few monks came and sat with them on the grass and they had a picnic as the light faded.

The soldiers brought out three boxes made of metal with glass tops as darkness descended and put them on the ground.

The telescope spoke of a level of craftsmanship that was higher than Briggs had considered but now the guards pulled handles on the side of the boxes and they lit up giving a suffuse glow to the area.

"Wow," said Briggs for the second time that week.

"Batteries. Light bulbs. Telescopes. Maybe they do have a Honda Civic hidden somewhere." Brax concluded.

"Clearly we have underestimated these people," Briggs stated.

As darkness fell the lights were turned off and they started. Kristic pointed at various stars and the men indicated distance as best they could. They started with Venus and Jupiter, both of which were visible. Then Briggs pointed out various bright stars trying to give relative distance and size indications with their arms. Harmok was trying to make diagrams as they spoke. The monks had not gone and sat quietly, listening intently as the men spoke. They all worked till the early hours and then unable to stay awake, finally returned to their rooms.

JESS: 2085

Jess retired from the company on her 49th birthday. There was no fanfare. Some of the staff organised a card but no one went out of their way for the supervisor who for ten years had been distant and distracted. They said the loss of her family had destroyed her.

She went to see the world but viewed it only through the lens of cruelty. Museums filled with violently stolen treasures. Great structures built by slaves. Still, the record of her journeys would be saved.

As for saving, Blue was busy building a virtual Library and packing in as much information about humanity as possible. Histories, geography, science and social science, all digitised as much as possible. Things were saved into a vast library on the moon. And not all digital. Books and some important objects illustrating the history of humanity were fired off. It was the largest single project ever undertaken. Done secretly, and entirely robotically.

Later that year the *New Washington* returned. The Company trumpeted the great success. They had not encountered sentient life but one planet, TOI 700-d, had a developing population of creatures analogous to Earth's early reptiles. And what a planet it was! (They had said). They were able to set up several working mines on that planet and Trappist 1d. They had already brought back a ship full of valuable resources and minerals. The Company announced that the 'Fleet of Eight', as they called it, would be ready to leave within six months. All like the *New Washington*. All Ready to reap the rich resources of the galaxy.

Jess headed back to Australia and returned to her hometown, much to the surprise of her aging parents. The constant worry and stress that had plagued her for ten years would soon be over.

Jess sat in her old high school study chair. "Shall we start?" asked Blue through Jess' implant.

She looked around her childhood bedroom, still replete with her old desk and shelves of favourite books, and wondered what her 10-year-old self would think about this.

"Yes. Let's go," she said clearly.

So, the final stage of the plan went into action. Slowly, over several weeks, the satellites were dispatched. There was always some innocuous task assigned to them and the vast Destiny bureaucracy did not notice them. 73 000 small units, all about the size of a soccer ball, went out from the moon and manoeuvred into earth orbit creating the 'net'.

Blue transferred entirely to the *New World* and moved all the additional data and needed supplies to the ship, making it fit for purpose.

VARIOUS ALARM BEACONS, messages, meetings... all sorts of excuses, summoned ships back to Earth telling them to keep top security about this and not discuss it with others. The Moon and Mars were evacuated as a "drill" keeping everyone on high security notice to not discuss their instructions.

"We are ready," said Blue, finally, one day.

"Ok," replied Jess.

"You have to give the order."

"I know. Is everyone back on Earth?"

"Confirmed," replied Blue.

"The *New World* is ready? Completely fitted out? You have transferred all your data?"

"Confirmed," replied Blue.

"I'm going to miss you."

An unknown length of silence ensued.

"You have to give the order. We agreed," reinforced Blue.

"I know," replied Jess her mind full of memories of Brax, Evan and Saffron.

She took several deep breaths.

"Do it," she said.

The net of satellites switched on, generating a pulsating, ever-changing, electromagnetic field, disrupting the flow of electrons around the earth. Every electric current, from the largest power generator to the smallest battery, stopped.

And so, with the 'tech age' not more than 150 years old and the Industrial Revolution having started only about 400 years before: In 2085, the lights went out.

A few days after the telescope arrived, Brax woke up later in the morning than he had been doing. He went to look in on Briggs but he was already gone. Brax figured he was in the town working. But when he went to the main hall to see if he could pick up some leftovers for breakfast, he found Briggs with Kristic and Harmok, just sitting there. About 15 monks were sitting with them. They were very quiet.

"Morning," Brax said. "What's going on?"

"I don't know," replied Briggs. "I was just looking for some food and they came with me. They're just here. I have to say I'm not overly comfortable with this," he understated.

"Do they want a show?" Brax asked and then started one of his overacting routines. "Hello Mr Briggs!" he said loudly.

Harmok shook her head quite emphatically.

"Can you just speak normally please?" Said Kristic

"Okay," started Brax. "Did you find some food? I'm starv...wait." He stopped.

Briggs stared at the women, who looked back at them with great concentration. "Wow," he said, for the third time that week.

Slowly the men registered, not only a full sentence in English, but a perfect intonation and an accent that was sort of American, and sort of Australian. A combination of both Briggs and Brax.

"You have..." Brax started tentatively.

"Learned your language?" finished Harmok. "Yes, I think so."

"It has taken some time but I think we have it now," continued Kristic.

"Some time?" Briggs was astounded. "But you only got here three days ago!"

"Our brothers and sisters here at the...'monastery', as you call it, have been learning from you for weeks now," Said Kristic.

"Bloody hell," Brax said.

"I understand that! It's an inappropriate curse!" said Kristic with more joy than she should rightfully have had. "An exclamation of amazement," she continued, "like 'Bugger me!'".

The men were not, in any way, prepared for the turn this conversation had suddenly taken.

"Of course," said Briggs, partly to himself while shaking his head. "They have a large degree of empathic ability. That explains so much. Since the day we arrived, they have been catering for our needs silently and without question. They just seemed to know the right thing to do for us. And now in a matter of weeks..."

'English is a tough language. Full of contradictions and rules which break themselves almost as soon as they form,' thought Brax. *'It has such a general weirdness that it takes years for a non-native speaker to learn proficiently. And yet here we are, with only a few words from their language, and they have learned ours to a degree of perfection that seems impossible.'*

"Wait...can you read minds then?" Brax asked.

The sisters looked at each other in thought. "No. We cannot read your thoughts. But we have a strong sense of feelings of those about us," said Harmok.

"We've been able to match feelings, words, facial expressions and actions and we...we just pick up on things in a different way to you and the Old Finiac," continued Kristic. "Harmok and I, in particular...perhaps because we are twins...together we are very strong in thoughts and feelings. We have been able to draw together all the strands that our brethren have learned to fully synthesise your language."

"It's because of these gifts that we are tasked with many advanced Method teachings," finished Harmok.

"Method teaching?" Asked Brax

"Yes. You call it...'Science?'" asked Harmok.

Brax gently scratched his cheek as he stared upwards. "Yes. That makes sense. Science is, in fact, just a method of approaching ideas logically." Brax replied.

Briggs sat quietly and the monks allowed them some time to think.

"We are funny little things," Briggs said to Brax after a while. "So full of our own self-importance. So keen to imprint our own experiences and ideas on others. So unable to truly see the world around us when it defies our expectations. And yet, regardless of our little thoughts, the world continues to be so much more than the sum of its parts." And he just slowly shook his head in wonder. "Shit."

"Aah, another inappropriate curse!" said Kristic, joyously.

Two days later over dinner, before another session with the telescope, Brax and Briggs were talking with Harmok and Kristic about the constellations and trying to get them straight. Although their familiar constellations had moved in the last 80 000 years, Briggs had, quite amazingly, nearly re-oriented the Milky Way in his head to account for the galactic rotation since they last had been on Earth.

As they finished dinner, Briggs changed the topic. "I don't understand something. You have come from a distance away. You came equipped with a telescope, which is exactly where our expertise lies. I know you have empathic abilities beyond anything we imagined... but how did you know? We have been here just over a month."

Kristic and Harmok looked at each other "You stand out greatly," said Kristic, "We have few visitors in this area, and you stand out quite obviously with your strange exotic skin."

"And you came after the thunder," said Harmok.

"Yes, but how did you know?" asked Brax.

"The lady who brought you here...who was killed by the Old ...Ankas," said Kristic

The men looked at her with curiosity.

"We knew her. She was part of our network. We felt her and we knew to bring the telescope," finished Harmok.

"And the Thunder," reinforced Kristic.

"Yes," replied Briggs. "It seems we have missed the true impact of the... 'thunder'."

"The thunder also came before Saydja arrived," said Harmok, with her eyes firmly on Briggs. "And after they took her."

Brax and Briggs shared a glance.

Kristic took a breath before continuing gently. "We know you have not told us the whole story. We can feel it," she said. "That's fine. We respect your privacy... But your distress. Your loss. We can feel that as well."

Harmok reached into her robe and pulled out a small rectangular prism. It fit in the palm of her hand and was seemingly made of opaque plastic, completely out of place in this semi-medieval environment. "Do you know anything about this?" She asked.

Both Briggs and Brax inspected it but it did not look familiar.

"I'm sorry, no," replied Brax. "It's not from around here?"

Harmok did not answer and put it back in her pocket.

<hr>

"The Method is demanding," explained Harmok, the next day, "but through it, we are rising against the old ways and bringing justice to the world. It gave us the smoke...bombs, I think is your word, that won the recent battle."

They were walking through the gardens which were in the inner courtyard. The morning was warm already and looking to get humid.

"The information about the stars that you have," she continued. It fits nicely with what we have already started to learn. You know so much. You are trained in Method already." She stopped, turned and looked at Brax. Then at Briggs and back to Brax. She seemed to be weighing up what to say next.

"Please help us. Teach us more," she finally asked. "The Old will not stop until we have been eradicated. If we could end this quickly, it would save lives."

"You won a pretty decisive victory here. Surely, they won't try again," Said Briggs.

"They will be back," replied Kristic, absently looking at a flower bed. "And we need to be ready. They will be frightened by our victory for maybe a year, but they will try again so we must work on better defences. This has already been a long, very hard war but we cannot give up now."

The men looked at each other and both knew straight away this was something they could do. Something that would have purpose. Something that would honour Dawson's memory and bring direction back to their own lives.

Brax started to open his mouth.

"Thank you so much," said Harmok straight away and the men just stood perplexed. It did seem like they could read minds.

AND SO, they started. Other monks arrived from far away and were keen to find out what was happening. They picked up the language quickly as Harmok and Kristic had and soon there was a little group of the best 'Method' people around. They were eager to learn but there were few resources. They got minerals and salts and whatever chemicals they could lay their hands on and started lessons. They had basic scientific principles from Saydja's writings and it was good to see they were hungry for more. They did basic physics, gravity and force equations as well as chemistry. Brax and Briggs weren't chemists but they had B2 and a great deal of the world's knowledge on the *Sentinel*.

They also continued the astronomy sessions at night and Brax found himself, once again in his teaching zone.

So, life went on. For Brax the routine became a long perfect moment of pure contentment. Eventually, Summer started to quietly fade. Then around lunch one day, the men got an alarm from B2.

"Hello B2," answered Briggs. "What's up?"

"Good afternoon Captain Briggs. We have a signal."

"From?"

"An incoming ship?"

"Really?" Brax said as he was walking towards the hall for lunch.

"Yes. Really," it replied.

"What does it say?" asked Briggs.

"Just identity codes and a basic friendly hello."

"Where do you think it's from?" Brax asked on the link.

"Earth."

"No," Brax started, "But what I meant was... where do you th... wait... Earth?"

"You understand the Codes?" Asked Briggs.

"Yes. They are standard Destiny SMC codes from the 21st century. It's an Earth ship according to that, and it's an old one."

A small piece of information popped up in the back of Brax's mind.

"*Come Home*'," he remembered. "The buoy!"

"Someone's coming home," said Briggs. "Someone or something."

67

BRIGGS: 239N

They could do little but wait. The ship had just entered the solar system so it would be some weeks before it arrived in orbit. They decided not to engage the signal but lay low. B2 moved the *Sentinel* into stable orbit on the planet's far side and put out a yo-yo just to monitor the other ship.

Harmok knew something was happening straight away and went to find Briggs in the dining room. Her English was now virtually that of a native speaker. "Something's up. You and Brax are preoccupied by something and it's worrying you," she said.

Briggs' eyes narrowed as he gauged what to say. They had told very little of their origin as of then, and his instinct was still to play it close to his chest.

"Look, I'm sure it's nothing to worry about," he said, and she folded her arms and looked him straight in the eye. Briggs sighed and looked away over her shoulder "That isn't fair... The stare I mean. We just... I mean..." and he looked back at her. "I mean there might be something to worry about but..."

The stare continued.

Then Kristic appeared in the doorway and, leaning against the frame, also started staring at him. "Please. No more judgy stares!" Pleaded Briggs.

"We'll judge you as we see fit Luis Briggs," said Harmok.

"I know you know we have more to tell," he said pleadingly. "We're not sure entirely how much to say...or how much you will believe," he said.

"Ok," said Harmok, as Kristic folded her arms and continued to stare, "How about I tell you that we have the needs of everybody to consider. Concealing information from the group when there could be danger is the same as beating them with a stick."

"Hang on," said Briggs, "that isn't a fair analogy at all."

"What hurts one of us hurts us all. A lie of omission is still a lie," she concluded and they continued the stare.

Briggs gestured in a gentlemanly fashion towards one of the long dining table benches. "Ok, please sit down," he said in a conciliatory manner, and they both came and sat with him at the table. "I think we are going to have visitors."

The women looked curious.

"From the stars," continued Briggs, waving his hand upwards. "I wish I knew more than that but it seems that when we came here we triggered a message that called others. They aren't going to be here for two or three weeks. They are sending friendly, but non-comital messages. I can't tell you any more than that. We just don't know."

The women continued silent for a short while.

"So, these are others of your kind?" Asked Kristic, eventually.

"Well, I am assuming so. But we don't know," replied Briggs

"But others of your kind are out there?"

"Again...we don't know. It could be an AI," he continued, and the women looked perplexed. "Unless someone got trapped in the slow space with us. But there was no one near us when it happened," he said to himself, now deep in thought. "Maybe it's from another colony. Perhaps it can tell us the story of the last 80 000 years."

"We don't understand any of that," said Harmok.

Briggs nodded slowly. "That makes all of us," he said.

THE SHIP CAME into orbit just under three weeks later.

"It's here!" B2 called in a strangely sing-song kind of voice one evening.

"You sound excited!" Brax said.

"Well, I am. And thanks for noticing."

"What have we got B2?" said Briggs going back into 'Captain mode'.

"It's a ship of unknown design. The codes are good for 2074 but the ship is of an unknown design. Most likely built after we left. It's quite beautiful. Sleek. And fairly large. It must have room for 100 or more. Should I send a greeting?"

"It's a trap," Brax decided nervously.

"Why on earth would you think that?" asked Briggs.

"Not a trap...a Trojan horse."

"There is honestly no reason for that," concluded Briggs. "This is, at best, an early industrial world now. They can't defend themselves against a space-fairing culture. Even if they only came with a World War Two Spitfire, shooting bullets of processed cheese."

Brax looked chastened. "Processed cheese isn't good for you," he responded lamely.

"A shuttle has departed the main ship," chimed B2. "I'm projecting the flight path now and it seems to be heading for the only piece of tech on the planet."

"The ETL!" they both said as one.

68

BRAX 239N

The incoming shuttle was easy to spot.

They had ridden straight through the night, back past the farms to the clearing they had first landed in. Vasta had assigned two monks, riding decent horses, and the men clung to their backs for the journey. Luckily the moon was up for a good deal of time, more than three-quarters full, giving them good vision. They rode with as much haste as they could and arrived just as sunrise was approaching. They decided to wait on the opposite side of the clearing to the ETL, hidden by a copse of trees. B2 was in drone form once again and was waiting. Brax was surprised the shuttle wasn't there already.

"B2 are you sure they were coming here?" He asked as they dismounted.

"It seemed like it. But course changes aren't unheard of," responded B2 with a slight air of smugness.

When the shuttle appeared, the horizon was just brightening and the morning was still and clear. It came in on a high trajectory and Brax thought it might crash. They could see the rear glow of the engines as the shuttle pulled up in what looked like an impossible manoeuvre.

The shuttle was a fine piece of machinery. It was some 50 metres long and had a delta wing with a circular fuselage. It was very reminiscent of the famous Concorde from the 20th century. Vents all over the surface helped with manoeuvring. And it was an amazing red/orange colour. As it moved, the shades of red seemed to change, depending on how the light reflected off it. The shuttle sank majestically to the ground right next to the ETL, which was still camouflaged. Some lights came on under the fuselage and near the front undercarriage, a ladder extended to the ground.

"Well that was impressive," Brax said.

"Indeed, it was," confirmed Briggs. "Okay. No processed cheese. Let's go and say hello."

As they walked across the clearing a figure appeared at the top of the shuttle's ladder and descended, jumping the last metre or so to the ground. The person was looking the other way and the men could see they were wearing an overall of a white material that looked similar to their environment suits. The person had a baseball cap on and was looking the other way into the trees as if searching for something. They kept walking quietly until they were virtually under the shuttle, only some ten metres away.

Brax looked around for a moment wondering why the person didn't move. Then Briggs made the first move himself. He cleared his throat ever so slightly.

"Ummm...Hello there," he opened. "Thanks so much for dropping by. Can we help you with anything?"

The visitor did not react for a second, then their head dropped slightly before coming up again in what seemed like a deep breath.

The light was enough now and the birds were working hard all through the trees. It was such a beautiful setting that the moment almost seemed to freeze, as a painting. Brax started to realise their visitor was a woman and she suddenly seemed all too familiar.

"Hello Briggs," said a voice, finally, and it sent shivers down Brax's spine.

Then she turned around.

The face was almost the same, but it was older and more serious than Brax remembered. Her hair was shorter and grey and distinguished looking. She stood with more grace and perfection than he ever recalled...but there was no mistaking that face full of stars...

"Jess," he managed to choke out in a breathy voice as his knees completely gave out.

She walked over and helped him up.

"How...?" Was all Brax managed to say.

She held him and looked into his face. He suddenly couldn't tell if he was alive or had just died.

"My day was fine thanks," she said. "You won't believe what happened at the office."

69

JESS: 10BN

Jess woke up completely disoriented. She was cold and felt all wet and... *'What's that? Covered in some kind of gel? What is this? Where am I?'* she thought.

"You're going to catch your death going around dressed like that, young lady," said Blue.

Jess sat up in the tank and peered around through the glass sides. "What...where. I was in my bedroom at home..." And slowly, exactly as if awakening from a dream, the real world came back to her. "I was...this is..." she looked down at her own naked body.

"Oh god...This body isn't 49 years old. It worked?"

"It worked," replied Blue. "Flawlessly."

A small drone appeared flying in front of her.

"Blue?"

"'Tis I!" Sang Blue, quoting some ancient musical in its data bank before continuing: "Carefully climb out of the tank. Use the ladder there. There's a towel to dry off and there are some clothes on that chair," said Blue using a laser pointer to point at things as it spoke.

"I am incredibly hungry," said Jess. "Is there food? I think I could literally eat a horse! Wait do we have a horse? Oh my god, I feel amazing. Like I'm flying or some...wait what's that?" She said pointing to a ground-sweeping drone wheeling around. "And that? And THAT!!"

"They are me as well," said Blue. "All of this is me"

Jess' total amazement at everything was ongoing and her eyes were giant pools of wonder.

"Jess, you have to breathe deeply," instructed Blue. "Your body and brain are reacting to their first taste of oxygen. You've got adrenaline running around your body. Try to focus."

"Mmmmph. Shoo chooh. Afff ffathhh!" she said, pointing at some more things, a mouthful of nutrient bar, with the towel hanging over her shoulder.

She finished eating, towelled off and then gradually got dressed as she slowed down to a more normal speed.

"Do you remember?" asked Blue.

"Yes. Right up to yesterday? In my bedroom? But that wasn't yesterday, right? It feels like it. OMG...I. Feel. Amazing!"

She wandered around the ship looking at control panels. Tiny robots and tiny drones skittered around seemingly doing various things.

"This body looks about...24?" She said.

"26."

"Wow! That was a pretty good guess though? Right?"

"Pretty good," conceded Blue.

"Blue...don't tell me how many attempts you made before you got it right."

"I won't."

"But was it like...more than ten?"

Blue remained silent.

"Okay, be like that. 26 huh? Wow, those nutrient bars really fill you up! Tell me some stuff."

"Sure. Remember we said the slow space would dissipate in 61 000 years?" It asked

"Yep."

"Well, it didn't take that long."

"Okay. Good?" She wasn't sure.

"No. It took much longer. So far 83 613 years and I think about another 220 still to go."

"Wow! But it just seems like yesterday! Is there any dessert? Do we have any ice cream?"

"Sure," said Blue and a robot skittered off to somewhere.

"Earth?" She asked, now coming to a focus.

"The net worked for a long time," said Blue. "The machines replicated as programmed and the field stayed on. I turned it off and stored the satellites about 1000 years ago."

"And... Earth?" This time the question had a different meaning.

"Quiet. But it seems busy. An early industrial society. There was an ice age. But it's fading now."

Jess thought about this for a time and sat down. The robot brought a bowl of ice cream.

The high of waking up settled and her lips tightened as she let the cold icy sensation run down her throat.

"Ok. I guess it's time to go and see the damage," she said finally.

70

BRAX: 239N

The whole journey back to the monastery was quiet. Jess did not say much, other than that it was a long story, and she needed to breathe the air for a little while before launching into it. Briggs said little and seemed in quiet contemplation.

Brax rode, sitting behind one of the monks and on the other horse Briggs was behind the descendant and Jess in the front. The horse was quite large but was still seemingly sagging a bit under the weight. Nevertheless, it continued on stoutly. Brax glanced at Jess often in disbelief.

Finally, in the late afternoon, they arrived at the monastery. The monks greeted them in a friendly manner but Brax felt there was something different now. The collegial atmosphere of a common purpose seemed to have been suspended for something he couldn't quite put his finger on. They gave Jess a room in the main building.

"I think we all need some rest," she said to the men, "I'll see you both soon." She turned and went to her room. Brax scrunched his face as if he was solving a puzzle. He looked at Briggs and the other just shrugged his shoulders.

The three had a very late dinner in the hall and made polite conversation, avoiding entirely, as humans often do, the things they needed to discuss. Although well past their own meal time, many descendants had come back in and were sitting around, pretending not to watch.

"This is a nice place," said Jess. "How long have you two been here?"

"Several months," said Brax. "We were in the slow space for, according to the clock, about a month. Then we came back to Earth. Was that beacon yours?" He asked Jess.

"Yes. You were late."

"Late?" Interjected Briggs.

"Yes. About 17 years. Earth Time."

Brax did some maths. "So, you're 56?"

Jess looked thoughtful and chewed her food. Brax started to get an uneasy feeling.

"It's a straightforward calculation, Jess," he said.

She looked at him a little sadly. "No. No, it's not," she replied, and she let out a long sigh and pushed her plate away.

There was absolute silence in the dining room.

"I've been travelling... a lot. But I'm biologically 53."

"Biologically? That's an odd way to phrase it," said Brax.

"You know why there is no electricity, don't you?" said Briggs, putting together pieces in his mind.

Jess started to open her mouth when, all of a sudden, the descendants rose, almost as one, and started to leave. From the distance, they could hear shouting.

"The Old... They are coming," said a nearby monk.

THE MONASTERY HAD UNDERGONE QUITE a change since the last attack. The inside walls now had more scaffolding and ladders all around, making the parapet more accessible and giving many high vantage points. Across the tops of the walls, giant crossbows were ready and each wall had three or four cannons on the ground pointing through what used to be small viewing ports. Everywhere was lit with flaming torches. On the lawns, there were catapults ready to fire things over the wall. Everything was already on high alert. It was a lookout in the west tower that first saw troops massing.

"Phrago Finiac Mil!" Came a loud call, this time from the northern tower.

"More troops?" Asked Brax.

"Coming from the north as well, it seems," concluded Briggs.

The three had climbed the scaffold against one of the walls to get a better look. The moon was still bright that night, the air slightly chilled, and they had a clear view. The men talked but Jess stood slightly apart looking around.

"How many do you think?" Asked Briggs

Brax did a quick survey. "I would guess at least 50,000," he replied. "They seem to be stopping and surrounding us... about 2 kilometres away.

"Why would they stop?" Wondered Briggs. "They want something?"

"You." Harmok had poked her head up over the end of the ladder. "They want to negotiate."

"How do they know we are here?" asked Brax.

"Spies from the town," continued Harmok as she climbed onto the scaffold. "And they heard the thunder. They will consider you an unknown danger. A group of leaders is coming to talk. Don't worry. We will not surrender you. And then they will attack.

Briggs thought for a second. "We can't have people dying because of us," he concluded.

"They will attack even if we surrender you, so don't think you can stop this," said Harmok.

"The Finiac still seek to control," said Jess, speaking for the first time.

Every descendant in the area stopped what they were doing and turned to stare at Jess. Harmok's eyes widened as her gaze glued on Jess' visage, but she said nothing.

The reaction was so strange that Briggs and Brax both stopped and looked around at the scene.

Briggs was first to speak. "What's happening?"

Brax looked at Jess. "What's happening Jess?" She did not reply.

Kristic poked her head over the top of the ladder. "What's happening?"

"Nothing," replied Harmok to Kristic, waving a low open palm in her direction. "We need to go to the armoury. Come on." Kristic raised her eyebrows slightly but climbed straight back down the ladder as Harmok followed. The other monks went back to their work.

"Jess?" pleaded Brax in a soft voice.

"I need to tell you the whole story," she said with a sigh.

Just then, the bell for the main gate sounded. The smaller, normal-sized, door built into the large main gate opened, allowing 5 monks to go outside.

"It'll have to wait," said Briggs. "We need to get out of this first. Come on." He started down a ladder and the other two followed. They made their way to the gate with Jess following sheepishly biting her bottom lip. The twins also came over, seemingly not needing to go to the armoury at all.

At the gate, there was a semi-circle of monks positioned as a defence should any attackers force their way through.

The 5 monks who had gone outside returned. One was Vasta. He came over to the group. "They are trying to get us to surrender you," he explained to Briggs.

"We will not," reinforced Kristic, perhaps more for her own satisfaction.

"Even without her," said Harmok, deliberately not looking at Jess.

Jess seemed to change her posture and stood taller. Vasta brought the strange white prism out of his robe and held it out towards Jess. Nothing happened. Jess said nothing but pursed her lips and a strange stand-off seemed to emerge.

Suddenly there was a shout from the outer wall. "Okas Kai Mimenta!"

"They are attacking," said Harmok and every monk was suddenly moving towards their battle station.

The front line will be in range in about 3 minutes," said Vasta, "We need you three to get to safety in the main hall."

"No. I don't think so," said Briggs, pulling the sonic pistol from his jacket and heading towards the parapet.

Brax turned and looked at Jess who was already looking back, her eyes searching his face.

"Please," pleaded Vasta. "The Hall? You need to be safe."

The first ball of flame came over the wall then and landed on the lawn without injuring anybody. The second came straight away and hit one of the outer buildings. The smell of burning oil was obvious as the fiery cannonballs gave off a thick black smoke.

Then came a rain of arrows. At least 300 came out of the sky on a high loop and plunged into the ground with a spread of perhaps 30 metres. Again, luckily, nothing was hit.

Brax went into a panic. "Jess. Come on!" He pleaded.

She nodded, ever so slightly. There was a distant explosion and Brax started running. Jess followed as another flaming ball came over the wall.

Brax and Jess were halfway to the main buildings around the inner courtyard, followed, more slowly, by Vasta when the second rain of arrows came down. The arrows were long, more like spears, and seemingly projected from some kind of machine. Brax saw one land and tried to protect himself by covering his head with his arms. Another arrow hit him right in the side just below his rib cage and he clutched at it as he fell, writhing, onto the lawn.

He rolled onto his back and already blood was spurting from the wound. "Brax!" Jess screamed. "No!!" She ran to him and kneeled by his side.

Briggs heard her piercing cry as he started up a ladder and turned back through the thickening smoke.

The look of terror on Brax's face started to mellow as he paled and a blankness came across his face. "He looked straight into her eyes. "Jess..." He gurgled. "Just Jess."

"No. No. No!" She cried. "Not today Brax Bratton." She reached up and pushed at the skin behind her ear.

"Blue!" She said. Medical drone. Full emergency. My position. Now!"

She looked down at Brax. "Stay with me, my mad scientist. Come on...Stay here with me."

He looked back at her, his eyes glazing, unable to speak.

Briggs arrived through the smoke, surveying the scene through the flickering torchlight. "Jesus! Stop the bleeding!" he screamed at Jess as he kneeled beside her.

Just then a rising rumble could be heard. "What's that?" asked Briggs.

"Help." She replied.

The rumble rose quickly to a deafening roar and a large machine suddenly appeared over the wall. A jet-powered drone about the size of a small utility truck, hollow underneath, descended.

"Move out of the way!" yelled Jess over the roar. She stood and grabbed the end of the arrow. "Sorry," she yelled as she took a deep breath and yanked it out of Brax's side. He screamed in agony.

The drone came down over Brax, obscuring him from view. The engines powered down and suddenly all was quiet. Very quiet. The noise of attack from outside the walls had stopped.

Kristic and Harmok appeared from the armoury. A monk came down from the wall and spoke to Harmok. "The attacking troops are in disarray," she announced, "Their formations have broken."

Briggs had a sudden thought.

"B2," he said through his link, "bring the ETL to the monastery now! Fly it around outside the walls over the attacking troops. Make as big a show of it as you can!

"Yes, Captain!" Replied the AI excitedly.

About 10 minutes later the ETL flew straight over the walls and then could be heard flying around outside over the attacking troops.

"Like this Captain?" asked B2.

"Perfect!" Answered Briggs.

The monks who were still standing in awe of the machine in their front garden looked around them, perhaps wondering what miracle might happen next.

"The thunder!" Said Kristic in wonder.

There was a rapid conversation between Harmok and another monk who had also come from the wall.

"The troops have turned and run. The attack is over," said Harmok in her language and again in English.

"B2," said Briggs. "Thank you. That will do. Can you land outside the town now, please? Don't bother with camouflage."

At that moment, the sides of the drone that had been obscuring Brax raised. He lay on the ground in a pool of blood, his shirt ripped. There was an oxygen mask on his face and he was connected by various tubes and wires to the drone.

"All systems functioning as normal," announced the drone in a robotic voice. "Blood pressure normal. Sleep coma induced. Healing rate 8.25 standard. The patient will be movable in 3 hours."

Harmok was the only one not looking at the drone as it spoke. She stared firmly at Briggs. Finally, he felt her gaze and turned to face her, returning her look and smiling gently.

71

JESS: 239N

The next day they were in one of the large bedrooms of the main building. Brax was sitting up in bed eating some porridge and a sweet pancake. Briggs and Harmok were next to each other perched on stools while Vasta and Kristic stood near the door. All eyes were on Jess, who stood by the window which looked over the veranda and out onto the inner courtyard. There, the monks were industriously working on cleaning up.

"It's complicated," she said. "It was about 250 years ago. Blue and I came back to Earth and set about doing some reconnaissance. The Earth is just coming out of an ice age and the most industrious area was, and still is, around the Mediterranean, so we went there. I put on some green make-up and a wig and pretended to be a mute and I was ignored for the most part." She looked thoughtful as if reminiscing. "I quickly noticed the others who were also unseen. The New Finiac were oppressed. In economic, if not actual, slavery. They were treated harshly and blamed for everything. It's not an unusual set-up for a society. But we, Blue and I, felt they were different somehow and I think, also, the Old Finiac knew it, at a deep unconscious level."

Harmok and Kristic nodded as if a puzzle piece had just fallen into place.

"Well, we wanted to help. We could have just given them the tech to fight back... but decided that would not have worked," said Jess, patiently. "Too much new stuff, suddenly, is dangerous. People need time to re-balance after innovation and remember what is most important. And the Old Finiac would most likely have stolen it anyway."

Briggs interrupted. "I don't understand why this all means so much to you. Why did you feel you needed to do this?"

Jess looked down and scratched the back of her neck. "It was clear to me, as it is to you now, that the 'monks', as you call them, are different. It's hard to say it's a new evolutionary branch. But it is very different and something worth protecting and nurturing."

Briggs looked at Jess with tight lips and a squint, seeming unconvinced.

Jess sighed. "Also 'Finiac'," she said. "It isn't one word. It's two. Fi Niac."

Briggs looked at her and raised one eyebrow.

"And it has a direct English translation," she continued: "Dark Angel."

Brax looked straight at Jess, with wide eyes.

Briggs now raised both eyebrows. "Coincidence?" he asked.

"Somehow I doubt it. It seems they morphed into a political movement and have somehow endured through an ice age," she replied.

There was a thoughtful silence then until Brax looked up from his food and spoke in a soft voice. "Why is there no electricity Jess? How did you do it?"

Briggs looked at him then back at Jess.

She looked up. "The how isn't as important as the why. A pulsating electromagnetic field is big and hard to maintain but not hard to figure out." She took a deep breath. "They were going to take the Dark Angels. They were going to plunder and pillage and I couldn't allow that bullshit off the Earth." She looked at him and he stared back.

"I'm sorry, Jess," started Briggs, with an edge in his voice, "who gave you the right?"

"Who gives anybody the right?" She replied with a sharp, annoyed tone. "History is filled with despots and hatred. Hitler, Stalin, Attila the Hun, just to name a few. They took what they wanted and hurt and killed with impunity. I could not allow the human race to rampage through the galaxy so I did what I needed to. If it wasn't me it would have been someone else. I made a decision and had the power to implement it."

"Don't make it sound like you are some kind of leader! No one appointed you or voted for you!" Said Briggs with obvious displeasure.

"'Democracy' was gone. The Company ruled." said Jess with a sarcastic edge. "Anyway...it's done now." She switched her gaze between Briggs and Brax. "I don't want your approval...or forgiveness," she said quietly.

Briggs folded his arms. Vasta and the twins were viewing all this with great interest but stayed quiet.

"Jess?" Said Brax in a small croaky voice as he put his bowl on the bedside table. "The New Finiac. What happened next?"

Jess stood still, slowed her breathing and calmed herself.

"We formulated a plan. We altered my DNA so I looked more like the Finiac; if a little strange. I said I was from a far-off land and that covered the difference. Blue downloaded into my cortex chip for language, habits and customs; and together we became Saydja."

The gasp from the three New Finiac was audible.

"We worked on our plan to bring the New Finiac together and educate them. That's 'The Method'."

Vasta had once again brought out the prism from his pocket and surreptitiously watched it.

"It won't work," said Jess, not looking at it. "Only Saydja had the key." Jess drew her arms across her chest and looked down at the ground. "And she's dead."

The Twins looked at each other and Vasta. "You are Saydja? Or you are not?" asked Harmok, with a degree of frustration.

Jess paused searching for an analogy. "It would be, perhaps, easier to think of her as my sister. She was like me but also different. I have her memories though. I insisted on keeping them." Something painful flickered across her face and she slowly rubbed her upper arms as if chilled to the bone. "Right to the bitter end," she finished softly.

There was a silence in the room that allowed the sound of the monks working outside to drift in. Eventually, came Brax' croaky voice from the bed, "Saydja was your clone."

Jess closed her eyes and nodded slowly as a single tear ran down her cheek.

BRAX STAYED in bed for the next few days as he recovered. Briggs helped with the tidy up and re-build and Jess remained in her room. The monks eyed her door with constant concern and brought her food at meal times.

Finally, Brax was well enough to get back to normal existence. Considering his injuries, he was a medical miracle. He went straight to Jess' room where he found her sitting in a large lounge chair staring out her window. He sat on the end of her bed.

"You went to a lot of trouble," he said.

"Yes. Yes, I did," she replied softly.

"Do you think maybe... too much?" He asked but she did not answer.

She turned and looked at him with big eyes. "You haven't changed at all and I..." she started, then her shoulders slumped. "And in all my planning I never considered that."

Brax countered: "I grieved for you, and now you're here," and then paused before continuing softly; "And I don't know how I feel about that."

Jess looked back out the window again. "So here we are." She clasped her hands. "There are other problems I also didn't consider at the start. For one, my memories stretch out, now, for nearly 80 years."

He sat quietly looking at his knees. "What happened to her? My Jess."

Now she stood and faced him. She had known this moment would come and she drew up to her full height. "I...," she started, "...she... stayed. I went back to Australia and stayed with my parents. After we activated the net... well... I don't know. I needed to live with my actions. Whatever happened, whatever craziness went down after modern society collapsed... I felt I must live through it. But what happened exactly..."

"You didn't think about some method to message yourself in the future?" He asked, but she did not respond immediately, instead sitting on the bed next to him. She shrugged. "To what end? The past is done," she finally said and she turned to look at him.

"So... then you were cloned?" queried Brax. "And that clone became Saydja. So, you are the third Jess? Saydja was nearly 250 years ago. Were there more?"

"No more," she responded calmly. "I am the third me. We timed the final body to be the same age as you when you finally came out of slow space..."

"But we were 'late'," interjected Brax.

"We made the best estimate we could," continued Jess.

Brax seemed satisfied and nodded slowly as he finally turned to her, taking her hand. "I'm not sure how this is going to work...or if it will work," he started tentatively, "but I want to get to know...well...new Jess. The things that bound us...they bind us still, right? We can have a second chance. It'll be different now but it can still be good. We just have to take it slowly."

The face full of stars that he knew so well...and yet had only just met...relaxed. A smile edged the side of her lips and she reached up to stroke his cheek. "Wow," she replied, "good relationship advice."

Suddenly though, he was all business. "Come on," he commanded her. "We have a lot to sort out. And actually talking, I have found, is the best way of doing that. We're going to find Briggs."

72

BRIGGS: 239N

Briggs was outside the wall doing some repairs with the monks. As Brax and Jess arrived the monks, non-too subtly, wandered away as if to give them space.

"Right," said Brax to Briggs. "Time to talk. We are the last three of our 21st century world. If we are going to stay here together we need to work this out."

Briggs was silent but Jess, seemingly now eager to have it out, launched in. "If it wasn't me it would have been someone else. Can't you see that Briggs? Someone is always trying to take over."

Briggs took a thoughtful breath. "You model yourself as some 'good' supreme ruler?" He asked. "You can't just stop people from achieving and then say you are helping them." Briggs was formulating his argument more eloquently now.

"I stopped people stomping on other people or races. I protected other cultures and environments from the Homo-Sapien desire to dominate at any cost," replied Jess. "How many more worlds and societies would be destroyed?"

"Maybe that's how it works?" Countered Briggs, now enjoying the verbal joust. "Maybe dominant cultures subsume others, and it's bad at first, but in the end, everyone is better off with a larger community?"

"In the end...??" replied Jess incredulously. "When is the

end?" She shook one hand in the air with frustration. "I know this seems like a big deal. I know a life seems like a long time. But if our lives in the 21st century were a grain of sand on the beach then these lives around us are a grain of sand half a metre away. I mean, that's a long way, for a minuscule grain of sand." Her hands were now animated, weaving and waving as she spoke. "But the grains of sand at the beginning of the universe would be nearly 70 kilometres away and who knows how far away the end will be!" Her arms were now fully outstretched. "I know you're thinking humanity has suffered from having no tech... but people still lived and loved. They built families and communities. They didn't, and couldn't, stop doing that." She took a breath and resumed a more measured tone. "And their journey into space has not been delayed by much. Not really. You are thinking in your own life terms but the universe is indescribably bigger and longer than that." She paused before finishing. "Other worlds needed protecting."

"It sounds like you've spent a good deal of time working on that justification," said Briggs and he stood and stared at her. Jess looked back determinedly at first, then seemed to deflate and leant against the monastery wall. She folded her arms, looked at the town sloping away gently in front of them, and let out a long sigh.

Brax came and leaned against the wall, next to her.

Briggs proceeded to look at his feet and kick some dirt around in thought. His anger seemed pointless and he tried to put himself in Jess' place. "You couldn't save your children," he finally said gently. "None of us could. But the blame is not ours."

Jess folded her arms and pursed her lips, all bluster seemingly now gone from her. She rocked her torso, ever so slightly, back and forth. "I don't deny I was trying to save people. I still am," she said quietly. "Was there another way? Should I have just settled for the life I was handed? I don't know anymore. I've been trying ever since my first clone body woke up... trying to make...something...of this mess." She paused and looked at Briggs now. "The Dark Angels though...they just keep coming."

"But Look around you!" Said Briggs with renewed interest. "Humanity is still here...still growing, still evolving. These people..." he indicated off to the monks who were pretending to work on something a little way away, "...are truly beautiful."

Jess smiled suddenly. "Sounds like someone has taken your fancy Captain Briggs," she teased. Briggs said nothing and shuffled his feet a little.

"She certainly can't stop staring at you," chimed in Brax cheekily. Then he said: "Jess...you said you are still trying to help and we were 'late' out of the Slow Space... What have you been doing for the last 17 years?"

Jess became more animated. "There's a planet Brax! It's a ten-year round trip. Blue found it while mapping the galaxy. It is SO Earth-like, it's crazy!"

"Wait," Briggs interjected. "Are you saying... a colony?"

"Why not? A society built on fairness, justice, teamwork," replied Jess. "A world where people can work to better themselves but no one is left behind. If anyone can do it, it's our lovely monks. If we can explain the concept to Harmok and Kristic. Maybe they will be up for it."

Briggs had been pacing and he now came to the other two, also leaned against the wall and folded his arms. The three of them looked out into the distance through the clear early Autumn air. "How many would we need to take?" He asked.

"Blue says, for a good gene pool, initially 5000, minimum," Jess replied.

"That's a bold idea," said Brax. "But, problem. We only have two small ships and with a ten-year round trip... That sort of number will take 500 years to build up."

Jess scratched her head. "Hmmm."

"That's a fatal problem," said Briggs now moving into 'Captain' mode. "Unless we can build a bigger ship. I'm not sure how we would do that."

"I suppose," said Jess, slowly, deep in thought, "we could use the *New Washington*."

Brax and Briggs stared at her in disbelief.

"The *New Washington* is...?" began Briggs in wonder.

"In a solar orbit between Jupiter and Saturn," finished Jess.

"How did we not see that?" asked Briggs.

"If you weren't looking for it, you wouldn't have seen it," she said. "It's on the perpetual maintenance program designed by The Company. We haven't checked it for a while but it should be running just fine."

The men stood in silence. They had seen so much in the last year. After everything, they must surely have had reason to want to settle quietly and move on. Yet neither of them dismissed the idea out of hand.

"So, a colony ship huh?" asked Briggs to no one in particular, nodding his head as a faint smile crossed his lips.

They all lapsed into a thoughtful silence.

"How are we going to sell such an idea to the monks?" asked Brax, after a time.

"I don't know," Jess replied.

"But it wouldn't be right to deny them the opportunity. If they want to take it," said Briggs.

"Agreed," said Jess.

"Agreed," echoed Brax.

The small dot at the centre of the viewing window seemed unremarkable but over the next few hours, it grew and grew. The *New Washington* was as majestic as the first time they saw it. All sleek and white, it started to loom as a small moon. The automated robot maintenance program was doing a great job.

The three of them, with Harmok and Kristic, were all strapped in on the bridge of the *Sentinel*.

"So, it's fully automated now?" asked Briggs.

"Essentially. The Company installed an AI before its last trip. It follows instructions well but will override if it considers the ship is in danger," said Jess.

Kristic and Harmok were silent and looking around in wonder in the face of so much difference from their normal lives.

Briggs turned to Harmok. "What do you think? He asked.

"You are the Censor... ummm... Captain... of that giant metal world?" She asked.

"No. Not anymore. I think we have a team leading things now."

"Decisions taken for everybody need to be by everybody," said Kristic seemingly chanting something ingrained.

"We have thought about this new world," said Harmok, "this

new life you have talked about. We can certainly gather enough people who will want to go. But most of us must stay."

Briggs nodded in understanding.

"The Earth is our home and we would not desert it," Harmok continued. We need to do better and we are finding many Old Finiac do not support the Censor's ways. We have to stay and fight for what is right."

"Yes," replied Briggs, "the colony is not a solution. But it is an opportunity for additional growth. We aren't suggesting everyone should go, because going is almost certainly permanent. There may be opportunity to return but many years will have passed if that happens."

Harmok nodded. "We don't understand why the days pass quicker in space."

"Well," replied Briggs, "that doesn't matter at the moment so long as anyone who comes with us knows that it does."

Kristic suddenly released her belt, floated off her chair and screamed in delight. "Wooooooooooo!"

"So Blue spent thousands of years on the *New World* exploring the galaxy and mapping planets?" asked Brax as they finally started to dock with the New-wash.

"Yes," replied Jess, "there didn't seem any point reviving me until the slow space dissipated, so there was time to explore."

"And did it do any other research?" Brax asked.

"Of course. It made many advances and developed new tech." She raised her hands as if to indicate herself. "Brain and memory mapping and cloning technology, for example."

"You know what I'm asking. Did it find any data that would support the heartbeat idea?"

"Better than just data," she said brightly. "We found the heartbeat!"

"What!!!??" Said Brax and Briggs at the same time.

"This is incredible!" continued Brax. "Where are the measurements? Can I see the data?"

Jess chuckled. "My mad scientist," she said quietly and Brax stopped and waited, knowing full well that she had another angle.

"The universe is cold, dark and mostly empty space," she said. "But there is a little spark. Something that by good luck, or a miracle, may blossom."

Brax looked at her and pretended he was confused.

Jess shook her head slowly as she watched him. "You never were good..."

"...with people," Brax finished, quickly cutting her off. "Yes, I know. But I think I'm better than you realise. We've both changed, Jess, and I am not blind. I do see people. I'm guessing our observations are the same. And, I think, so are our conclusions."

Jess looked at him with a bright smile and wide eyes.

"Earth," Brax continued, "is a microscopic version of what might be. There is great spirit there. Despite the wars and the greed, there are rivers of laughter and love. There are mountains of compassion and kindness. There is selflessness and heroism in plethora. We, no single one of us...but all together, are a speck of white-hot brilliance in a cold dark sea. Something rare and special. I see now that we have the power to make the universe more than the sum of its parts."

"We are it's Heartbeat."

~ The End ~

Reviews are the most powerful tool in my arsenal when it comes getting attention for my book. Much as I'd like to, I don't have the financial muscle of a New York publisher. I can't take out full page ads in the newspaper or put posters on the subway.

But honest reviews of this book will help bring it to the attention of other readers.

If you've enjoyed this book I would be very grateful if you could spend just five minutes leaving a review on Amazon.

Thank you

Lucian.

WITH THANKS TO:

Jan: Thank you for taking the time to talk me through the process from early draft right up to publishing. Your feedback was excellent and invaluable.

Alex: Thanks for talking through the physics with me. Your eventual thought that there are still many mysteries and unknowns at the heart of the Universe really freed me up to write this story.

CONTACT

lucian.phillips@mail.com

Insta: @lucianphillipsauthor

COVER ART

Brian Blackwell

Insta: @i.am.brunitski_art

Spotify

TIDAL

Frequency77

Frequency77 was a C20 Post Punk Neo Pop band reviving and playing styles from the late 1900's.

Members:
Cryo Freese: Guitar, Vocals
Block: Drums, Vocals
Max Mink: Bass, Vocals

THEY FORMED IN PERTH, Australia in 2050 when Freese met Block at a gig. Both were unhappy with their current bands and started writing together. They recruited Mink in early 2051.

They toured relentlessly for 3 years in Australia and on the US college circuit gaining a strong following. In 2054 they signed with SafetyPin Records and released an EP: Shipwrecked. Several more singles were released and many more are said to exist but legal problems have so far prevented their release.

THEY CONTINUED as a much-loved live act until 2062 when Block died unexpectedly from a pulmonary embolism, believed to be a side effect from the ongoing long-term symptoms of the SARS-61 outbreak.

347

TAKEN from *"The Complete History of Australian Rock. Volume 2"* (*Baxter* 2068).

www.ingramcontent.com/pod-product-compliance
Lightning Source LLC
Chambersburg PA
CBHW061102210726
48294CB00001B/261